URBAN FICTION

Loving You Is Killing Me

Loving You Is Killing Me

Kinshasha Serbin

www.urbanbooks.net

Urban Books, LLC
97 N 18th Street
Wyandanch, NY 11798

Loving You Is Killing Me

ISBN 13: 978-1-62286-795-0
ISBN 10: 1-62286-795-5

First Mass Market Printing November 2016
Printed in the United States of America

10 9 8 7 6 5 4 3 2 1

Distributed by Kensington Publishing Corp.
Submit Orders to:
Customer Service
400 Hahn Road
Westminster, MD 21157-4627
Phone: 1-800-733-3000
Fax: 1-800-659-2436

I would like to dedicate this novel
to my mother, Ramona Boyd, in heaven;
and my sister, Keishanna Turner,
in heaven. Love you always.

Acknowledgments

First and foremost, I would like to thank God above because without Him I would not have the talent to express my creativity through writing.

I would also like to thank my family and friends for always supporting and believing in me. Special thanks to my father, William Boyd, for helping me put my dream into action.

Last, but definitely not least, thank you to all of my readers. It is your continued support that will help me write books that are relatable and will leave you entertained.

Chapter 1

Sixteen-year-old Shaniyah sat in the darkness, afraid to make a sound. She struggled to sleep while her mom and the latest stranger were drinking and cursing loudly in the next room. As often as this would happen, Shaniyah never got used to it. She never knew who her mom would bring home or how long they would be staying. Shaniyah's mom was on drugs and would mess with just about anyone to get a fix. Every night it was the same thing. Her mother would leave for hours, come back home drunk, and end up in bed or fighting with some stranger with a wallet.

Her mother had been on drugs for as long as Shaniyah could remember. It wasn't as bad for Shaniyah when she was little because her grandma Lee-La always made sure she was taken care of. As far as Shaniyah was concerned, her grandmother was the woman who had raised her and taught her everything she knew. Growing up, Shaniyah would go days, sometimes weeks, without seeing her mother.

But it didn't make a difference whether she saw her because her Lee-La was always there. Shaniyah got a harsh reality check five years ago when her grandmother became sick.

She remembered the day her grandmother sat her down one morning to have a conversation that would forever change her life. Shaniyah had noticed Lee-La had slowed down a lot over the past few months. They used to go to church on Wednesday nights for Bible Study and they never missed a Sunday. But it had been weeks since they had gone to church. Lately, Lee-La spent most of the day in bed and would struggle to get up just to use the bathroom. It seemed Lee-La was feeling better today because Shaniyah had woken up to the smell of bacon and eggs assaulting her nostrils. When she walked into the kitchen, her grandmother was humming and singing along to an Aretha Franklin song. Shaniyah set the table while Lee-La took some pancakes off the griddle.

"Nia, baby, I didn't want to have this conversation with you being so young." Lee-La took a deep breath. "But it seems the good Lord has plans for me and I need to get ready to go."

"Where we going, Grandma?" Shaniyah asked innocently, not fully realizing what Lee-La meant.

"You can't go where I'm going, baby. At least not for a long time," Lee-La responded. "I need you to know that I love you and I will be with you everywhere you go. You not gonna be able to see me, but you'll feel me right here." Lee-La reached over and placed her hand over Shaniyah's heart.

Shaniyah grabbed her grandmother's hand and held on to it. "Okay," was all she said. She could feel the tears welling up because now she understood what Lee-La was talking about.

"Nia, you're gonna have to be strong. Your mother has some demons she needs to fight, but she's not ready to fight them yet. So in the meantime, I need you to be a good girl and make sure you're going to school and doing what you supposed to be doing. I done taught you how to cook some things and do groceries so I expect you to take care of yourself. Now I know you only eleven years old, but I know you're a smart young lady and you gon' be just fine. Make sure you get to school every day and you keep your grades up. Don't do like your momma and get caught up in things you got no business in. You understand me, child?"

"Yes, Lee-La," Shaniyah said as the tears rolled down her cheeks.

"Don't cry, baby," Lee-La said as she wiped her granddaughter's tears. "Let's finish our breakfast before it gets cold."

Lee-La passed three weeks after that conversation. Shaniyah came home to find two female deacons from the church and the reverend standing in the living room. She could see sadness and pity in their eyes.

"She's gone isn't she?" she asked before they even said anything to her. They all looked at each other then back at her and they nodded their heads. Shaniyah fell to the floor crying, unable to control herself. The two ladies fell on their knees beside her and tried to console her. She knew the day was coming, but what she hadn't known was how much it would hurt.

That entire week felt like a dream. Her mother came home a day after Lee-La passed, too high and drunk for Shaniyah to even deliver the news to her. Shaniyah soon learned that her grandmother had made all the arrangements for her funeral with the reverend. On the day of the funeral, her mother showed up looking a hot mess. It looked like she had tried putting makeup on but it was smeared all over her face. She made a big scene crying and wailing at the pulpit where Lee-La's casket was. Her act didn't fool anyone though.

In the weeks after the burial, different deacons and church members were stopping by the house to check in on Shaniyah. They would bring her food, groceries, and would sometimes stay and talk. One lady in particular would ask Shaniyah what she planned on doing. As if an eleven-year-old really had that many options. She suggested that maybe Shaniyah go live with her dad. But Shaniyah never knew her dad and doubted if her mom even knew who he was. Shaniyah really had no place else to go. Being that her grandmother had left them the house, she figured the best thing for her to do was exactly what her grandmother asked her to: go to school, get good grades, and make something of herself. She decided that one day she would get away from it all.

She tried going to church on her own for a little bit, but every time she went, members would stare at her and whisper among themselves. She knew they were talking about her situation and it made her feel uncomfortable so eventually she stopped going to church and eventually members stopped coming by the house to check on her. She became used to being on her own. Years went by and her mother never changed. The only thing that changed was the men she brought home.

Tonight, Shaniyah sat on her bed, thinking about her grandmother, crying and praying to God to help her make it out. She dreamed of finishing high school, going to college, and becoming a paralegal.

The next morning, Shaniyah woke up only to find her mother and the visitor passed out on the couch. She quickly got dressed, and headed out in search of her best friend. As soon as Shaniyah opened the door, there he was, standing outside on the sidewalk. "What's up, Samir? I was just about to go to your house."

"Oh, hey, Niyah. You up mighty early. I'm 'bout to head to the park. Do you want to come?" Samir asked. She always found it funny that from the first day they met Samir started calling her by the same nickname her grandmother used to call her. Now, everyone in the neighborhood called her that too.

"Sure, I don't have nothing else to do," Shaniyah answered happily. She was just glad to be out of the house.

Samir had moved to North Carolina from New York a few years back. They met when Shaniyah saw him and his brother moving in next door. She went over and introduced herself. After that, she and Samir were inseparable.

Samir was only eighteen, but he had to grow up fast. His twenty-six-year-old brother, Sedrick, used to be a big-time drug dealer in New York but made enough money to get him and Samir out of the Bronx borough. Sedrick saved enough money to move him and his little brother out here to North Carolina. He didn't fully quit drug dealing, but he did slow down a bit once down here. Now with Sedrick working a part-time job as a cover and going to school, they were doing pretty well.

Samir was good to Shaniyah and made sure to protect her. Though his brother wanted him away from the drug game, Samir still had a street mentality and became a small-town dealer alongside his brother. He also knew Shaniyah's situation well and wanted to get her out of the messed-up environment she suffered in so much.

Shaniyah and Samir headed to the park. Shaniyah sat on the swings while Samir mingled with a few of his partners. Shaniyah knew what he did and she always distanced herself from it.

Shaniyah was minding her own business when a guy named Anthony from her school approached her. "What do you want, Anthony?"

"You, Miss Niyah. And I know you feelin' me too."

"Boy, please. I ain't studyin' you."

"Whateva, bitch. I wasn't feelin' you anyway."

"Who da fuck you callin' a bitch?" Samir stepped in.

"Man, I know you ain't gon' trip over this ho," Anthony barked, sticking out his chest.

Before Anthony could say anything else Samir hit him so hard that he knocked his front tooth clean out of his mouth. Samir was really getting the best of him, as Shaniyah stood there scared to death.

"Samir, that's enough," Shaniyah yelled shakily.

"I betta not catch yo' ass around her again, homie," Samir warned him.

Anthony got up and headed down the street. He walked to the end of the block, turned around, and began to yell. "Man, I'm tired of you New York niggas comin' down here thinking y'all run shit."

"I don't know 'bout the rest of the NY niggas round here," Samir stated, "but I do run shit, mothafucka, now try me."

"Shaniyah, you straight?" Samir asked.

"Yeah, I'm good. Thanks a lot."

"You know I gotchu, kid. You hungry?"

"Yep."

"Well, let's walk back down to the house, so we can ride out."

"Okay," Shaniyah said. "Oh, you betta not forget what tomorrow is."

"Chick, you know I ain't gon' forget your birthday."

When they had reached the house, they jumped in Samir's Cadillac sitting on twenty-six-inch rims. Selling drugs gave Samir a pretty good living, but Shaniyah wished he would do something else with his life. At least he promised to stay in school since it was his last year, and that made Shaniyah proud.

She liked having someone around who really cared about her. If it weren't for Samir she would be dressed like a bum, but he kept her in designer clothes and when he was icy so was she. The one thing that bothered Shaniyah most was that she wanted Samir to look at her as his lady. But, she believed he saw her as a little sister. He never brought another female around her so she didn't know what to think. All she knew was that she had a crush on him.

Samir was very sexy. He resembled a cuter version of Morris Chestnut. He was brown skinned, with thick jet-black waves. He was about five foot nine inches. He was definitely muscular and had never lost a fight. He especially favored Morris Chestnut when he smiled, showing off his pretty white teeth. She would often tease him about his resemblance, which made Samir mad.

When they pulled into Pizza Palace, it was super packed. It was the hangout spot for all the youngsters and she made sure to cling to Samir to let all the females know he was taken.

"What it do, Samir?" Reginald said giving Samir a handshake. "What it do, Niyah?" he said smiling at Shaniyah.

"Hey, Reginald," she said.

Reginald was one of Samir's buddies. After speaking to Reginald it seemed like all of Samir's homies popped up everywhere. Shaniyah, Samir, Reginald, De'Mario aka D-Money, Kelvin aka Kels, his girlfriend LaTia, JonJon, Darian, and a bunch more crowded one whole side of Pizza Palace. But his real partner in crime, the one he would ride or die for, was D-Money. D-Money was from New York too, but he came to visit his family in North Carolina every chance he could get. Of course, Shaniyah made sure she had a seat next to Samir. LaTia and Kels sat across from them.

After eating, Shaniyah and LaTia headed outside so LaTia could smoke a cigarette, while Samir and the fellas sat and hashed it up.

"So, Samir, when you and Shaniyah gon' hook up?" Kels asked jokingly.

"Man, please, it ain't like that. We just best friends."

"Nigga, you crazy. I would have been locked that up, fine as she is," D-Money added.

Samir looked at them and laughed. "Man, y'all wildin'."

"Naw, man, we serious. You know you want her so stop playin' yo'self before another nigga snatch that up. Hell you already buy her shit. Besides, I can tell she feelin' you. She would probably shit on herself if you got with somebody else," D-Money said.

"First of all, if it happens, it'll happen. Second, Shaniyah know the deal. She ain't gon' let no other nigga in. She know how I am when it comes to her."

"Yeah, that's true and she would probably kill a chick over you, too," Kels said.

Just then Shaniyah and LaTia walked back in. *My boys are right,* Samir thought. Shaniyah was beyond beautiful. She had long, curly black hair, gray slanted eyes, a light complexion, and a body to die for. She wore denim cuffed booty shorts and a halter top and, boy, had she developed. In his eyes Shaniyah already belonged to him, but he wanted her to have the title. *But what if she doesn't think of me in the same way?*

Shaniyah took notice of the way Samir was sizing her up. The thought of it all made Shaniyah's panties kind of wet. She was still a virgin but sometimes when she was around Samir, she would get hot down there and her lady parts would throb. *Samir keeps staring at me. He looks like he could just get up and eat me.*

"What are y'all talking about?" she asked, sitting down next to Samir.

"Oh, nothing," Kels said, laughing.

"It better be nothing," LaTia warned, looking serious.

"So, Shaniyah, you ready to be out? I got to go handle some business. This nigga Jamel been calling my cell for the past twenty minutes."

"No, but okay."

"A'ight, New York," Kels said, shaking Samir's hand. New York was a little nickname his boys had branded him with since he was from New York and he stayed representing.

"I'll catch y'all on the next trip," Samir said.

"See y'all later," Shaniyah said before heading back to her house.

Chapter 2

Shaniyah would rather be anywhere else than at her house, but she had no choice. Samir dropped her off and waited until she unlocked the door and went inside. Then he headed next door to his house. Shaniyah was relieved when she came into what she believed was an empty house. *Finally some peace and quiet.* She headed upstairs to her room, but was stopped dead in her tracks when she saw a strange man coming out of her mother's room.

"What are you doing here? Where is my mother?" she asked, trying to sound in control.

"Yo' mother is out making my paper and she late," he said with a cheesy smile.

"Well, you don't have any business in this house without her here, so get out before I call the police."

"I ain't going nowhere and you ain't gonna call nobody. I know your mother's broke ass ain't got no phone in this house," the gold-toothed stranger responded.

Shaniyah quickly turned and tried to run back down the steps, but her aggressor caught her by her hair and she landed flat on her back. Panic took over as she struggled to get away. She was furious that her mom would let a strange man stay in the house when she wasn't there.

"Please let me go," she begged. "I won't tell the police. Just go," Shaniyah begged.

"It's too late now, bitch. You wanna act like a woman, you can take this like a woman, too. You gon' get this."

He dragged her by her arms all the way to her room down the hall while she kicked and screamed, but he ignored Shaniyah's pleadings. Once he pulled her into the bedroom, he threw her to the floor, and closed the door behind him. Shaniyah tried to stand to her feet so she could get to her window, but he pushed her back down and climbed on top of her. Then he tried to rip off her pants.

"Y'all young bitches always act like you don't like this, but I know you do," he said as he tore her shorts off.

Shaniyah continued to fight, but her blows were nothing to him. She almost blacked out when he hit her with a blow to the face. She cried out in pain, then closed her eyes and prayed to God to save her from what was about to happen.

She tried everything she could to keep her legs closed, but he pried them open. She felt his thick fingers graze up and down her privates. She felt sick to her stomach as she could smell his sweat mixed with a stale cigarette stench. She felt his fingers ram up her insides and it burned like hell. She tried to yell out for help in hopes that maybe Sedrick was home next door and would hear her screams but the man placed a heavy hand over her mouth.

"Try screaming again, and I'll kill you, you little bitch," he said with his face against hers. He licked and slobbered on her neck while he kept shoving his fingers in and out of her. Shaniyah just lay there silently, too scared to scream and unable to move with the man's weight on top of her. Just when she thought things couldn't get any worse, he pulled his fingers out of her, unzipped his pants, and shoved himself inside her.

The pain took her breath away. She couldn't believe this was happening to her. She'd always dreamed of giving herself to the one who she loved, Samir. Yet it was being stolen by some nasty man she didn't know. A part of her felt so dirty. She could hear him grunting and groaning as he thrust himself in and out of her. After two minutes, he got up off her, and put his pants back on.

Shaniyah lay there hurt, disgusted, and bleeding from between her thighs, in shock from what just happened to her.

"Tell yo' mom I'll come for my money later, bitch."

As soon as she heard her rapist close the door, she made her way down the steps and locked the door. Her body ached everywhere. She felt like she'd been hit by a truck. But being hit by a truck might not have been as bad as what she had just gone through. She went back upstairs to take a shower. She sat on the floor of the shower and cried. She thought that washing away the filth would help, but it didn't. She had to get out of this house or who knew what would happen next.

When she got out of the shower she threw on a pair of pajamas and slippers, and was gone. She ran next door despite how bad her body was hurting, crying as she banged on the door waiting for Samir to open it.

"What's wrong now? What happened this time?"

Samir knew about Shaniyah's situation at home. This wasn't the first time Shaniyah had come over crying about something that had happened with her and her mother. But one look at Shaniyah and he knew whatever had happened must've been really bad this time. Her eyes were bloodshot and her face looked puffy and swollen as if she had been slapped up. She was so shaken up she could barely talk.

"Shaniyah, stop crying and come inside," Samir said comfortingly.

They headed to Samir's room quietly, so they wouldn't wake his brother. Samir closed the door. Shaniyah sat on his bed crying uncontrollably. Samir leaned against the door, patiently waiting for her to explain what was wrong.

"Samir, I gotta run away. I can't go back in that house," she said still crying.

"What happened, Shaniyah?"

"I like you too much, more than you know, and if you ever felt the same way about me, you probably won't now."

"Shaniyah, I love you. You already know that. Nothing can change that. I would die for you. You can tell me anything. Please know that."

"I was raped, Samir!" she screamed, not caring who she would wake.

"What? How? I just dropped you off a little while ago." Samir stared at Shaniyah in a state of shock. Anger was plastered across Samir's face as he waited for Shaniyah to explain. She had finally stopped crying, but now she stared off in space as if replaying the events in her mind.

"Shaniyah, tell me what happened and I promise I'll handle it for you!"

Shaniyah didn't respond. She just continued to stare in space.

"Shaniyah! Do you hear me?" Samir asked nervously. He didn't know what to do. Shaniyah was starting to scare him. He raced over to her, and gently began to shake her. Shaniyah finally snapped back to reality.

"Shaniyah, please tell me what happened. I can't fix it if you won't tell me what happened."

Shaniyah looked at Samir. The hurt and pain she just endured was written all over her face. She shook her head no as her face became a waterfall of her tears. She felt too ashamed and she wished she had not come here so upset. The love they had for one another overpowered her, but the events still played over and over in her mind. The more she thought about how that despicable man forced himself on her, the more embarrassed and disgusted she became with herself.

"Shaniyah, please trust me! I am here for you, but I have to know what he did to you," Samir pleaded. "You have to know that I will never look at you any different. You mean the world to me and I would do anything for you. You can't handle this one on your own."

Shaniyah continued to look into Samir's eyes and at that moment she realized Samir would always be there. No matter how disgusted she felt about what had just happened to her, she knew Samir truly cared. He would never look at her as used goods.

She parted her lips and slowly answered. "Yes, I trust you," she said through trembling lips.

"Please tell me what happened and we will get through this together."

Shaniyah lowered her head as she began telling Samir what happened to her that night. "When I got in the house my mom wasn't there. I was heading to my room and he was just standing there." She paused as tears rolled down her eyes. She shook her head in anger and hurt.

"It's okay, baby girl," Samir said through anger and clenched teeth. He tried to remain calm, but knowing that another man had taken advantage of his baby girl had him boiling on the inside. He knew he had not officially made Shaniyah his girl, but in his heart she was already his and it hurt him to his core to know someone had done this to her.

"Just tell me what happened. I got you. I promise," Samir said as he covered Shaniyah's shaking hands with his own and held her close to him.

She continued to tell him her painful story. "He dragged me to my room and forced my clothes off. He climbed on top of me and he raped me. I feel so dirty. I hate myself. He took my virginity. He took everything. I'm never going back there." Shaniyah could see the images of the abuse playing over in her mind as she sobbed uncontrollably.

Samir wrapped his arms around Shaniyah and held her closely as she poured out all of her emotions right there on him. Tears of anger and hurt poured down his face. He tried to remain tough, but he felt guilty for not getting Shaniyah out of that house sooner.

"Don't worry, baby girl. I will get him. I promise you that. You ain't going back to that house either. You can stay right here with me. I'm gon' talk to my brother in the morning. Just relax. Come lie down with me and let's watch some TV for a while," Samir suggested, trying to get Shaniyah's mind off her situation.

Shaniyah woke up in Samir's arms the next morning. She lay there and watched him sleep. He was sleeping so peacefully. Just then Sedrick burst in the door. She hoped he wouldn't be mad.

"Hey, Miss Lady, how are you?"

"I'm good, I guess."

"Yo, bro, wake up, man! I'm 'bout to head to school; then I got to go to work."

"Well, what you waking me up for? Go do you."

Sedrick looked at Samir wanting to run over and smack him.

"Whatever. Man, call me when you get a break. Shit I'm tired," Samir responded sleepily.

"A'ight, man. See ya later, Niyah."

"See ya later, Sed."

Samir sat up looking over at Shaniyah. "Good morning, beautiful. Did you sleep okay?"

"Yeah. I slept pretty well. I was with you."

"Good, 'cause now I need to find the nigga who did this."

"Listen, Samir, I know what that man did was wrong, but he looked like some kind of pimp and I don't want you getting involved in my mess. Can you please let this slide, at least for now?" Shaniyah continued, "Without trouble?"

"I'll think about it, but I know for sure you ain't going back to that house. And we are going to get your stuff right now, so come on."

"You haven't even talked to your brother."

"He's cool. He don't mind. I was just gon' let him know that you're moving in."

With that, Samir and Shaniyah got up and headed to the place that used to be home. As was usually the case, no one was there. *Why couldn't anyone be here yesterday?* They made a beeline to her room and packed as much stuff as they could carry. They packed a few bags full of clothes, shoes, and her feminine products and left the house. The only reason she had some things to take was because Samir was always buying her clothes and stuff. Shaniyah didn't bother to leave a note for her mother. God knows how long it'd take for her mom to even notice Shaniyah wasn't living there anymore.

When they finally had a chance to sit down, Shaniyah worried that Samir had forgotten about her birthday, but it didn't hurt her feelings because every day was like a birthday with Samir. The only thing was that, despite his obvious love for her, she still didn't quite understand if she was just his friend or his girl.

They stayed in the house almost all day watching scary movies and eating popcorn. She really enjoyed being around Samir. He never brought his street business to his house, so after the fourth movie ended, he told her he had to leave to make some drops. He handed her the remote and told her to chill until he got back.

She channel surfed for a little bit but couldn't find anything she wanted to watch. She began to wonder if her mother remembered that today was her birthday. Her mother was probably out whoring in the streets trying to make some money so she could get high. She most likely didn't even know what day it was let alone the date. *She's never remembered before, why would today be any different?*

Shaniyah's thoughts were interrupted when she heard a dog barking outside. She looked outside and noticed it was getting dark. Shaniyah's nervousness started to kick in. She started thinking about all that happened to her the night before and it gave her the creeps all over again. She tried to hide everything that happened in the back of her mind, but the visions of that monster on top of her kept coming back. Just when her imagination began to get the best of her, she heard someone at the door. Samir said he'd call when he was on his, way but she hadn't heard from him so she had no idea who was at the door. Shaniyah balled up in the bed scared to death. She heard the door open up slowly and she listened to the footsteps as they came closer to Samir's room. A figure burst through the door. Shaniyah screamed and covered her face with the covers so quickly that she didn't notice it was Samir.

In the midst of Shaniyah's fright, he screamed, "Surprise! Damn, girl, I didn't mean to scare you."

"I'm sorry, Samir. I'm really trippin'. It's just that I've been kind of shaken up since you left." Suddenly Shaniyah's concern was replaced with a big ol' smile. "Oh, God, Samir, you know you didn't have to do this," she replied happily.

Samir hadn't forgotten her birthday. He had balloons, a few outfits, a diamond bracelet with earrings, and a big teddy bear. Shaniyah was overwhelmingly happy with Samir's gifts, but finding out if she had his heart would determine if she could stay there in his house. She just had to know where she stood in his heart.

"Samir, I need to talk to you," Shaniyah announced.

"Oh, boy. What now?" he said smiling.

"Last night, after I told you everything that happened, you said that you loved me. Did you mean that?"

"Of course I meant that, Shaniyah. What did you think? I have always loved you. Don't you know that? Please tell me you know that."

Shaniyah shook her head no and asked, "Well, why haven't you made me your girl?"

"Why haven't you made me your man?" Samir said, blushing.

"Well, Samir, will you be my man?" Shaniyah asked, following her heart.

"Damn straight I will. I was yo' man anyways."

Samir walked over to the bed and kissed Shaniyah softly on the lips. The moment she had dreamed of had finally come, but then flashbacks of the night before kicked in. "Wait, Samir, I can't do this."

"Why not? What's wrong?"

"I feel so dirty and—"

"Shaniyah, I would never do anything to hurt you and you know that. I've always been here for you, and I always will. If you say you not ready then I understand, but know that I love you no matter what and I will make sure no one ever hurts you again."

She believed Samir and she also loved him. The love they had for each other grew even more as they looked for certainty in each other's eyes. In that moment, Shaniyah approached him with a kiss. Then she began to slowly, and with shaking hands, unbutton his shirt. She needed to show him that she was more than ready to share it all with him. She needed their love to replace the horrible thoughts. She needed him to fill that emptiness with his love.

Samir gently eased her down onto the bed and peeled off all of her clothes, piece by piece.

He took his time. He wanted her to feel relaxed and safe with him. He sucked on her breasts, one at a time, causing her to moan. He waited to make sure she was comfortable. He wanted this experience to be so good that it would replace her sad thoughts. With each touch, he wanted to rid her of her pain. He wanted her to enjoy a new start with him.

Samir made his way down Shaniyah's chest, continuing to leave his tongue's trail on every inch of her body. He finally reached her thighs. He couldn't wait to taste her sweetness. He plunged his tongue into her wetness, sending her body into overdrive. Shaniyah tried to contain herself, but she could not control the ecstasy she was feeling. The way Samir worked his tongue in between her thighs had her body shaking as she moaned, enjoying every minute of the feeling she had never felt before.

After giving her countless orgasms, Samir climbed on top of Shaniyah and made his way inside her. He wanted to see her face while he made love to her slowly. Shaniyah felt pressure and she was still sore from what had happened to her the night before, but this felt much different than that. This felt right. Shaniyah was a little embarrassed with Samir staring into her face. Thoughts of her rapist came back, but

Samir's calming voice pulled her back into the moment as he continued to move slowly on top of her. He could tell she was trying to hold back, so he increased his speed and penetrated her deeper, hitting her spot until she was unable to control herself. The sounds of satisfaction escaped from her lips as he continued at a steady pace. Samir couldn't hold out any longer. They both climaxed.

"Aaah shit! I forgot to pull out," Samir said sounding worried.

"Uh-oh," was all that Shaniyah could say.

"Looks like Li'l Samir might be coming to town," Samir said jokingly.

"That's not funny. If I end up pregnant you better not leave me," Shaniyah countered.

"Baby, I promise I ain't never gonna leave you no matter what happens. Plus, I have always wanted a li'l man, so I can prove to be a better parent than mine ever were. Let me see what I'ma name my li'l man."

"Boy, you don't even know if I will get pregnant yet. And how you figure it's gon' be a boy?"

"I know you will be pregnant, and I also know it's gon' be a boy. And, his name gonna be Samir Rasheed Hicks, Jr."

"Yep, and if he look like you his nickname gon' be Morris. You know, since you look like Morris Chestnut," she said jokingly.

"Hell naw, his nickname will be Junior, but not no damn Morris. First things first, we got to get our own place. I have been saving up some money. I just got to get a job to make it look legit. I graduate in two months. So we'll be straight."

Chapter 3

As time passed everything was going well in Shaniyah and Samir's relationship. She didn't get pregnant that first night, but Shaniyah and Samir wanted a baby boy more than anything, so they continued to try. Her mother never came looking for her. She would see her mom coming in and out of the house, but she never tried to talk to her. When she was living at home, Samir would help her keep up with the house. They would do yard work together and keep the house looking fresh. Now the house was looking run-down. Walking past it, it almost looked abandoned. Shaniyah felt sadness to think the house her grandmother worked so hard on was in such bad shape now.

Time went by quick and Shaniyah had just graduated from high school. Samir had graduated last year, so now they were both high school grads. She started working part time as a braid tech in a barbershop and she registered to attend the local community college for paralegal studies. It was Saturday and she was at her best friend Ky's house waiting for Samir. They planned to stay at Ky's for a couples weekend.

"Ky, I don't know where that boy is at. He ain't even answering his phone. That's strange."

"Chile, don't stress it. He probably still at Carlos's house. If he still there I'm sure Carlos is getting him drunk. You know how males are," Ky offered to help Shaniyah feel better.

"Well, Samir has never done this before and I'm getting worried," Shaniyah said. Shaniyah and Samir had been together for about two years. They had their share of arguments, but he never disrespected her or gave her reason to believe he was doing anything wrong. She also knew that Samir wasn't a big drinker, but when he did get drunk he could barely hold his liquor. Shaniyah knew Carlos's house was the last place he should be. "Well, I'm about to go over there and see if he is okay. I'll be back."

"Okay, girl. If you see Carlos tell him to call me."

"Okay. I will," she said before leaving.

Shaniyah headed to Carlos's house with a bad feeling in the pit of her stomach. Words couldn't describe how nervous she was. She also felt bad for not trusting Samir, but a girl had to do what a girl had to do.

When she got to Carlos's house she saw Samir's car parked in the driveway. The door was open so Shaniyah went inside. It seemed empty until she heard voices in the back room. Shaniyah tiptoed toward the back and listened. She could hear a female voice, but she couldn't make out what she was saying. That's when she heard Samir say, "I can't do this, man. I love my girl."

"If you love her so much why did you let me go that far?" answered the female.

"'Cause I'm drunk and stupid. I'm out."

"So what? You just gon' let me get on top of you and get all hot then dip on me?"

"Bitch, please, you ain't doin' shit no way. I'm out."

Just then Samir opened the door and saw Shaniyah standing right in front of him in tears. He looked at her with guilt in his eyes. She ran off, got into her car, and headed home. She was crying, hurt, and in shock that the one she loved and claimed would never hurt her had done just that. Shaniyah couldn't believe Samir had even gone that far. She felt betrayed.

Samir called Shaniyah's phone until she powered it down. For two whole days she stayed in a hotel room crying in bed. She was glad that she had been saving money and didn't have to go

back to Samir's place. She had the DO NOT DIS-
TURB sign hanging on the doorknob and didn't
answer any knocks at the door. She didn't even
show up for work at the shop. She felt as if her
whole world had been turned upside down.

Before, being with Samir made her feel like
all of her troubles and nightmares were gone.
He knew everything about her, even the rape.
Nobody knew about that. Now, all of her nightmares and negative thoughts were back on her
mind.

Shaniyah felt so sick of life and everything
in it, but after a few days, she finally pulled
herself together. She showered and threw on a
pair of old jeans and a T-shirt she had found in
the trunk of her car. She got her keys, unsure of
where she was going. She decided to go to the
house and grab some of her things. She got in
the car and turned on her cell phone for the
first time in days. Shaniyah had over twenty
messages from Ky, and even more from Samir,
but she still didn't feel like talking to anyone.

Shaniyah put her Camry in gear and just as
she was ready to pull out to the street, Samir
popped up in his Cadillac with the music blasting. He pulled right beside her car. She had no
idea how he knew where she'd be, but she wasn't
ready to talk to him. She backed right into the

street refusing to pay Samir any attention, when another car came out of nowhere.

"Shaniyah!" was the last thing she heard.

Shaniyah woke up in a hospital room and could barely speak. Her mouth was dry and her head was pounding. She looked up and saw Samir asleep in a nearby chair. All of her anger was gone. Now, she was more nervous and confused.

Samir woke up and rushed right over to her bed. He looked as if he hadn't slept in weeks. Shaniyah continued to look around the room frantically.

"Samir, what am I doing here?"

"You were in an accident and you been in the hospital for a few days. They thought you weren't going to make it, but you pulled through."

"Where is everybody else, and why are you even here?"

"They left already, but I've been up here every day with you. I'm here because I love you. I felt what it was like to live without you and I won't do it. I can't be without you, Shaniyah. I feel like all of this is my fault. I missed you so much and I need you. That's the only reason I came over that day. I never meant for you to get hurt but, baby girl, I promise on everything and everyone I love that it will never happen again."

"And how do I know that?"

"You don't. All I can say is give me a chance to prove that I am the one for you. Please," Samir begged.

"I can't imagine life without you either. I can forgive you, but forgetting is a different story. I don't want to lose you over one mistake, but it's your ass if it ever happens again."

"Baby, I promise it won't. This situation has completely opened my eyes to my feelings for you. Believe me, I have learned from my mistake. I love you and I will never do anything else to jeopardize this relationship."

"Yeah, Yeah, Yeah. I love you too, but I'm ready to go home."

Shaniyah stayed in the hospital another week before she was released. Apparently, when she pulled out, she pulled right in front a van and she was hit on the passenger's side. In her rush to get away from Samir, she didn't put her seat belt on so the entire left side of her body hit against the door of her car and she had a broken rib, arm, and wrist. Thank God her insurance covered everything or else she would've been in serious trouble.

***

Things with the couple were back to normal, but Shaniyah just couldn't get Samir's possible indiscretion out of her head, no matter what he did to prove he loved only her. She tried to keep the frustration to herself, but every time they had a disagreement she would bring it up. She knew it was hurting their relationship, but she couldn't help it. She loved Samir with all of her heart, but it was hard to trust him when he was out of her sight. Every time he went somewhere, she had questions about him being around other women.

It was a struggle, but she tried to keep all of her pain inside. The only time she felt any relief was when she was at school. After two years of classes at the community college, Shaniyah was finally done. Graduation day was so exciting. Samir had started attending a college in Raleigh, North Carolina, to study entrepreneurship. He wanted to own his own business and he also looked into buying a spot in the local area. Shaniyah was glad he gave up his dope boy dreams; if he hadn't gotten out of the game, she would have had to walk away. She had even threatened to end their relationship. She loved Samir with all of her heart, but she'd seen what the game could do to people. She couldn't lose Samir to the streets. It would kill her. He had to know that selling drugs was too much of a risk for the both of them.

Graduation day was a proud day for Shaniyah. She stuck to her guns and received her associate's degree as a paralegal. After graduation, Samir took her out to celebrate. She was surprised after dinner when he blindfolded her and led her to the car.

It was hard for Shaniyah to be blindfolded. It made her feel way too vulnerable and afraid. But she let him do as he wanted and let him guide her.

When they finally reached their destination Samir helped her out of the car and removed the blindfold. When Shaniyah opened her eyes, she stood, stunned at what she saw. Samir had bought them a new house and had invited everybody over. She was in tears. She showed her appreciation by jumping into his arms with excitement. She hugged and kissed him.

"You didn't have to do this. Boy, you are a mess."

"I would do anything for you. Baby, you deserve this. You worked so hard. Now I just want to make you happy. I told you that," Samir said.

"I love you so much," she said still in awe.

"I love you more, big head."

Shaniyah hugged all of their friends and promised to get them for not telling her. She was happier than ever, and she could tell Samir was happy just to see that she was happy.

The inside of their home was beautiful. He had everything already decorated to her taste. She knew their friends LaTia and Ky helped. Everybody was partying and having a great time. Shaniyah hugged Ky for what seemed like forever because they hadn't talked since the accident.

"Can I get everyone's attention?" Samir said as he pulled Shaniyah to the middle of the floor. "Shaniyah, you know I love you more than anything in this world and that I would never do anything to hurt you."

She just shook her head and tears fell from her eyes. She knew the words that were coming next.

"We have been through almost anything we can imagine together and, after these few years, I still feel the way I felt the first time I laid eyes on you. You are my everything, and I can't imagine life without you. I promise to be here for you no matter what. There's just one condition." Samir got down on one knee and gently lifted her left hand. "Will you marry me, Shaniyah?"

Shaniyah was in total shock. She felt as if her knees would give out. She yelled out, "Yes!" Everybody clapped for them, and she knew everything would be okay.

Samir and Shaniyah were doing well. More importantly, Samir's brother was glad to get rid of them. Sedrick was looking forward to finally having a house all to himself. Shaniyah loved their new house. The only thing that she hated about it was being alone in it so often. Samir was always coming and going, but he stayed away for the most part. He always claimed he had some business to take care of. Something wasn't right about the whole situation. Certain things just didn't make sense. Shaniyah knew Samir had a great job, but it wasn't enough to afford all the expensive clothes, gifts, and trips. The numbers just didn't add up.

This particular night, Shaniyah was at home alone and Samir was away visiting family in New York. She didn't want to go because she had too much work. She was working at a law firm in Raleigh as a paralegal. She enjoyed her work and she didn't want to put her job on the line. She hadn't heard from Samir all day. During that time, Shaniyah hardly noticed though. She was so busy typing up papers for Attorney Richard Boyd that she lost track of time. She was getting worried. It was getting so late, so she decided to call Samir's cell phone. It went straight to voice mail and, of course, she was pissed.

Their wedding was two weeks away and she was starting to have suspicions about how Samir was getting his money. Just then, her phone rang.

"Hello," she answered with an attitude, thinking it was Samir. She hadn't bothered to look at the call ID.

"Yo, Shaniyah, this D-Money. I got some bad news for you."

"What is it?" she asked annoyed.

"Me and Samir was 'bout to make a drop and we got set up. Samir shot at three cops, but I got away."

"Hold the hell up. What kind of drop you talking about?"

"Samir didn't want you involved, but now you have to know. He was selling drugs in New York. He had his own business and everything. We got to come up with a way to get him out of jail."

"I can't believe this shit. We're supposed to be getting married and he keeping shit like this from me? This is too much. I guess this is the reason he kept pushing our wedding date back."

"Shaniyah, I'm sorry, maybe ol' boy lied and all, but you can't leave him hanging like that. He 'bout to get some serious time and he gonna need us behind him, two hundred percent."

"I see I didn't know him as well as I thought I did. Is there anything else I need to know? Who set y'all up?"

"Man, I think it was some New York chick who was obsessed with him. She ran into him in New York. That's where she from. She threatened to get him caught up because he didn't want to have anything to do with her. She must have been following him and spying on us."

"Well, you tell Samir that I am done with his ghetto bullshit. He put our life on the line so I'm out. I'm glad I found this out before I made the biggest mistake of my life," she said crying and slamming down her phone.

Shaniyah stayed in her and Samir's house long enough to get herself financially situated. She had a decent amount of money saved up because Samir always paid for everything, but she wanted to one more month's worth of saving before leaving to be on her own. Ky tried talking her into staying and following up with D-Money on how Samir was doing but Shaniyah refused. She didn't want anything to do with Samir. He had lied to her about what he was doing and, from what D-Money had told her, he had been messing with some New York chick so she was done.

When she had everything situated and figured out, she moved to Greensboro, North Carolina. She found a job at another law firm and was doing well for herself. Her heart was still broken from all that Samir's mess had caused. She distanced herself from everyone and focused on a new life without her best friend.

The pain of Samir's lies and betrayal made her so angry. It wasn't just the fact that he was dealing drugs, but more so that he lied. And if there was one thing Shaniyah couldn't stand it was a liar. Five months had passed since Samir got caught out in New York. It had been a hard adjustment but she gotten herself together. She had a nice apartment and she liked the new law firm she was working at.

Things seemed to be looking up, except for the fact that almost every morning she would wake up feeling sick as a dog. For months she'd been sick and she had gained lots of weight. It was strange because she didn't eat that much. Her menstrual cycle hadn't come either, but she thought it was because she was stressed out. She'd been wanting to go to the doctor, but her health insurance benefits hadn't kicked in with her new job. She was told she couldn't get insurance until she'd been at the firm for ninety days. When her ninety days hit, she wasted no time making a doctor's appointment. Luckily, they had an appointment as early as the next day.

That morning she was sitting in the doctor's office waiting for the doctor to return with her pregnancy test results.

"Well, Ms. Alston, you are six months pregnant. Congratulations!"

"What do you mean, congratulations?" she asked with tears in her eyes. "I can't believe this."

Shaniyah went home devastated. She was in a state of shock. She considered getting an abortion, but she knew she couldn't live with herself if she did. She realized what she had to do, with or without Samir. *Plenty of women do it, so I know I can too.*

Two and a half years went by in the blink of an eye. Shaniyah was just getting out of the office and headed to the sitter's to pick up Li'l Samir. She had just made it to her car when her boss, Attorney Paul Reid, called her to come back into the office. She had been working for him since the move and she was doing great with supporting her and her son. She'd heard around the way that Samir had been sentenced and was going to be locked up for a long time. She missed him and wished things could've been different, but at the same time, she felt angry and bitter toward him because it was his fault things hadn't gone the way she'd hoped. Because of his lies, she was now a single mom and her son was growing up without his father.

"Ms. Alston, you have been doing great work and you have helped this firm grow so much. I'd like to tell you first that I'm selling the firm and moving to a firm in New York. David is going to hire his own people and I don't want you out of a job. Would you consider being my head paralegal in New York?"

"I don't know what to say. I mean, I don't know anything about New York."

"Look up some housing in Manhattan. I'll help you get settled. I know you have a little one. I'll help look out for you. It will be more money and I am sure with all you have been through that you could use a new beginning. Hopefully, being in New York won't be a conflict of interest."

"No way. I'll do it. When do we leave?"

Chapter 4

Sixteen years later
Manhattan, New York

Samir Rasheed Hicks, Jr. had grown up to be a fine young man. He was the spitting image of his father, except he had long, silky braids. Li'l Samir was six feet one inch and was very muscular. He looked to be much older than eighteen.

"Yo, Ma, is that you?"

"Yeah, boy. Who else gonna be walking in the house?"

"How was work?" Li'l Samir asked.

"It was fine. I'm just tired. I'm so glad to know I kill myself working long hours at the law office so you can sit around and do nothing, while I make all the money," Shaniyah said jokingly.

"Before long, Ma, you won't have to work. I'm finally done with high school. I'm ready to venture out and make big money. "

"Nah, you're either going to college or going to get a job. I don't want you getting caught up in the streets like your no-good dad and ending up in prison too. You know you look just like him."

"Whateva. I don't have no dad. And as far as I'm concerned, he is dead to me."

"Samir, what have I told you about your mouth? How you gonna disrespect me by talking like that?"

"Sorry, Ma," Li'l Samir said walking to his room.

Shaniyah didn't know what she was going to do with Li'l Samir. He was a good kid in school, but at home he was so bad tempered. Li'l Samir stayed out until all hours of the night, and the constant female calls were ridiculous. He was his father's child and she couldn't do anything about that.

Li'l Samir got dressed in his baggy designer jeans and big white tee, with his braids hanging down his back, and he headed for the door.

"Boy, where are you going?" Shaniyah asked.

"Out, why?"

"One, I'm your mother and I have a right to know where you're going. Two, so I will know where you are and won't be worried."

"I'm going to the block to meet Tray. I won't be too late," Li'l Samir said walking out the door.

Li'l Samir walked down the block to meet his partner in crime, Tray. He lived in Manhattan, but he wished he was living near his friend Tray in Brooklyn. Tray got off the subway and headed to the block.

"What up, man?" Li'l Samir said giving Tray some dap.

"Nothing much. Yo' momma still looking good as hell?"

"Man, shut up. I see you all iced out and shit. How you afford all that ice, son?"

"Why? That's grown-man business."

"What you mean, why? I'm tryin'a get where you at if not betta, my nigga."

"I don't know if you gon' be down with what I do," Tray said, sitting on the stoop of an empty house as he rolled a blunt.

"Man, you know me betta than that. If it's about money, I'm down."

"A'ight, if you say so. I'll ask my cousin D-Money to hook you up."

Just then, Tray noticed a fine-ass red bone getting out of the car with her mom. Li'l Samir looked in the same direction.

"Damn, she fine as hell," Tray said.

"Son, you ain't neva lied. When they move over there? I got to have her," Li'l Samir vowed.

"I bet I hit that before you do," Tray said.

"Nigga, please, you know me betta than that. Now pass that shit. Damn you hogging the whole blunt."

"Ha-ha, my bad nigga." Tray laughed with his eyes bloodshot.

"Yo, man, who dat pullin' up in that black Mercedes? That shit chromed out."

"Oh, shit. That's my cousin D-Money."

Tray motioned for his cousin to come over. As D-Money got closer to Tray and his friend, he could see the familiarity in Li'l Samir's face.

"What up, Tray? Who ya friend?"

"What up, D? This Samir. He wanted me to talk to you about puttin' him on."

As soon as Tray said Li'l Samir's name, D-Money's expression changed. *This kid look just like Big Samir. But, nah, he can't be,* D-Money thought. D-Money was puzzled. But, he knew somehow this kid had to be Big Samir's son. He couldn't stop staring at Li'l Samir. He looked just like his father.

"Oh, is that right? Son, you do know this is grown-man business. Do you know what you'd be getting into?"

"Yeah, nigga, I know. I ain't no dummy. I'm just tryin'a get this paper. Eitha ya want me down or you don't. It ain't hard, bruh."

"Ha, you got a lot of heart, li'l man." D-Money laughed. "Just like your father Big Samir."

D-Money decided he'd be straight up and mention Big Samir to see how Li'l Samir would react. He was curious to know if Big Samir was indeed Li'l Samir's father. It was definitely no coincidence.

Li'l Samir stood, ready to blow. "How you know my dad?"

Wow! Big Samir is definitely his dad. "Everybody in New York know yo' daddy. He was a big-time dealer until he got busted. The streets say he should be gettin' out soon though."

"Man, that's my father, but far as I'm concerned he ain't shit to me. Enough about that; what about this paper?"

"I see you all about business, li'l man. Look, I'ma put you down, but I don't want no disappointments or else. How you end up here anyway?" D-Money continued to quiz him.

"Man, I grew up here in New York. Me and my moms moved up here when I was two."

"Your mom?"

"Yeah, my mom, Shaniyah. She grew up in North Carolina though."

"Oh. Okay. I have family in North Carolina, so I travel back and forth from time to time. Anyway, I need you meet me right here tomorrow and I'll give you a job. Like I said, I don't want no disappointments. Come on, Tray. We got to go re-up."

"A'ight, man, I'll holla," Tray said. "We out."

***

The next day Li'l Samir went to the spot to meet D-Money. He was sitting on the stoop when the li'l red bone from the day before came out of the house across the street. She was walking down the block. Li'l Samir wanted her, so he went after her.

"Wassup, ma? Where you headed?"

"To the corner store. Why?"

"'Cause you don't need to be walking these streets alone. Do you mind if I walk with you?"

"Yes, I do mind."

Li'l Samir didn't pay her attitude any attention. He kept following her anyway. "So you new here, huh?"

"Yes. And?"

"Why you got to be so mean? I'm just tryin'a get to know you," Li'l Samir said. "What's your name?"

She smiled and said, "I'm Kiyah, and you are?"

"I'm Li'l Samir." They went into the corner store and Kiyah got a bunch of junk food. "Damn, girl, you pregnant or something?" Li'l Samir asked.

"No. I just have a sweet tooth." Kiyah laughed.

Li'l Samir walked Kiyah all the way home and noticed D-Money and Tray standing on the stoop talking.

"Well, I'll see you around. I got some business to take care of," Li'l Samir told Kiyah.

With that, Li'l Samir rushed across the street to the stoop. "Sorry I'm late, man."

"You good. I see you was tryin'a getcha li'l' mack on, but don't let it happen again," D said. "I don't wait on nobody."

"Samir, you think you slick. That's my chick," Tray said laughing.

"You too late, my nigga. I already claimed that."

D-Money, Tray, and Li'l Samir walked to an alley to handle their business transaction. That was the start of Li'l Samir's hustling gig. Before long Li'l Samir was iced out and rocking new gear, which was nothing new to him since his mom always kept his gear tight. Li'l Samir felt proud to be able to buy his own stuff and not have to ask his mom for money. He even kept Kiyah laced. They'd been talking every day since that first time he walked her to the store and he made sure she was always fresh. Li'l Samir thought he was doing it. He was clubbing all the time and spending crazy money on his girl.

Li'l Samir was in the club, at the bar smoking weed with Tray when a dude came in, looking just like him.

"Tray, you know D talking about letting me take over some blocks soon."

"Yeah, I always thought I was gon' be the one taking them over. I been in this game longer than you. That nigga shol' played me."

"Don't worry, my nigga. We 'bout to start this come up together," Li'l Samir said.

"That's what's up. Ah yo, who that nigga who just walked in? He look just like you," Tray yelled as he pointed across the room.

Li'l Samir looked at the man and couldn't believe his eyes. "Yo, that nigga don't look shit like me," he said trying to brush it off.

"If that's the case, why you look like you saw a ghost when I showed him to you?"

"Man, fuck you," Li'l Samir said.

Just then D-Money walked in and headed over to Li'l Samir and Tray. "What's up, li'l niggas?"

"Ay, D man, who dat nigga on the other side of the club?" Li'l Samir asked nervously.

"Ha, oh, shit, I think that's Big Samir. That's ya pops. You don't need to fuck wit' him though. He mad at me and everybody else 'cause I took over his turf."

"Man, fuck that nigga. He ain't my pops."

"Y'all follow me," D said as he headed to the other side of the club to get closer to Big Samir.

"What up, nigga? When you get out?" D-Money asked to Big Samir.

"None of yo' fucking business. After all that time I served you ain't got shit else to say to me."

"Damn, dude, you ain't got to be so harsh," D-Money said laughing. "Come see me. I might have a job for you. You know yo' ol' girl living up here with her son now."

Li'l Samir just looked and played along.

"Man, fuck you. I don't need a job. I own my own company. I don't do weed. I'm in it for the big bills, partna. You thought you put me out of the game, but I found my new connects in jail. As for that ol' girl, fuck that bitch. She left me hanging."

"Who you calling a bitch, mothafucker?" Li'l Samir jumped on Big Samir before anybody could stop him and he started punching him in the face. Tray watched for a few seconds, but then he finally pulled Li'l Samir off of the old head. Big Samir immediately saw the resemblance in the kid who had just jumped on him, but he was so full of anger that a kid had jumped on him he didn't give it another thought. Big Samir was just getting out and he had to maintain his street credit.

Big Samir pulled out his gun and started blasting. Two bullets hit D-Money as Tray, Li'l Samir, and everybody else ran out of the club. Tray ran to get on the subway and Li'l Samir ran to his crib.

Li'l Samir rushed through the door, startling Shaniyah as she lay on the couch watching TV.

"Boy, where have you been and why is there blood on your shirt?"

"Not now, Ma."

"What you mean not now? You betta start talking before I go upside your head!"

"I was with Tray, ran into yo' ol' dude, and he shot at me and hit another guy."

"What you mean my ol' dude? What are you talking about?"

"My fucking dad! He out. I don't even think he knew who I was. The bitch tried to shoot at me. His own fucking son. He got mad 'cause I whooped his ass for saying something slick about you. I swear I'ma kill that nigga!"

"Samir, calm down, baby. I am so sorry. Please don't do anything stupid. This is all my fault. I'm getting you out of here."

"No! I ain't runnin' from no nigga. You happy now. You got a good job and we ain't going nowhere. You keep being happy and don't worry 'bout nothing," Li'l Samir said going in his room and slamming the door.

All Shaniyah could do was cry. She realized that her son was now eighteen and he had to make his own decisions. She just prayed he didn't do anything stupid.

***

The next day, Li'l Samir stayed at home with his girlfriend, Kiyah. He couldn't believe that he was actually shot at by his own dad. Something inside of Li'l Samir wanted answers to why his dad wasn't there for him, or why his dad didn't care about him. He didn't learn about his father being locked up until he was almost thirteen. Every time he asked his mother about him, she never seemed to want to talk about it. He never received any letters or phone calls while his dad was locked up. Now that he was out Li'l Samir was curious to get answers to a lot of his questions. Was his father really that bad? Yeah, his father had shot at him, but that was after he picked a fight with the old man. *Does he even know that I exist?*

"Samir, are you listening to me?" Kiyah asked agitated.

"Oh, what did you say, bae? My bad."

"I asked what is so heavy on your mind?"

"Oh, nothing really." Li'l Samir didn't feel comfortable talking to anyone about his dad. "I was just wondering. If you know that we have been together for a while now, why you ain't givin' it up? I mean damn, a nigga tired of waiting."

"Well, Li'l Samir, you know I ain't ready to go there with you yet. If you love me, you will wait. Right?"

"Man, whateva." Li'l Samir was beginning to feel like Kiyah wasn't the one for him. She was too childish as far as he was concerned. He always dealt with older females because he didn't have to deal with none of the bullshit. Kiyah was a nice girl, but she could get a nigga in trouble quick with her teasing ways and Li'l Samir wanted a wifey, not immature, spoiled chicks.

Li'l Samir's phone rang startling him. "Hello," Li'l Samir said into the phone.

"What up, nigga? Where you at?"

"What up, Tray? I'm at the crib. Man, what's poppin' tonight?"

"Man, D-Money got hurt bad, but he gon' pull through. He still in the hospital. You know we still got to put in that work. We gon' get payback on that nigga fa real."

"Have you heard anything about Big Samir?" Li'l Samir asked.

"Nah, man, he cleared out the club like everybody else."

"I need to talk to him the first chance I get. I need answers."

"I feel ya, dawg, but D-Money ain't gon' like that."

"Oh, well. I'm beginning to wonder if D-Money is all he's made out to be. If everything Big Samir said back at the club is true, then we can't trust D-Money."

"The fuck you talking about, nigga?" Tray said with an attitude.

"Big Samir said D-Money left him hanging back in the day," Li'l Samir replied. "If that's true, how we know he won't do us the same way? Plus, Big Samir talking about making real dough, and I like the sound of that."

Tray didn't like the sound of Li'l Samir going against his cousin's wishes. He promised to keep that in mind once D-Money got well. For now, he would just play it cool. "Anyway, man, there's a house party in Brooklyn tonight. You need to hop on the subway and roll wit' me."

"A'ight, man. Give me a few minutes and I'll be there."

Li'l Samir closed his phone and ran to throw on his gear. He came out in some designer jeans, a fresh white tee, white Uptowns, and a fresh white fitted cap. His diamonds were shining like ice. He even had some iced-out fronts in his mouth. Sexy wasn't even the word to describe how fine Li'l Samir was. He was his dad's twin. He wore his hair in a curly ponytail with his hat tilted to the side.

"Ooh, where we going?" Kiyah said getting excited.

"You going home. Get up and let's roll. I'm going out."

"What? I know you ain't still mad at me for not giving you none."

"Girl, please. Let's go. You know you can't roll with me when I take care of business."

"Whatever. That's why I'm talking to someone else," Kiyah mumbled under her breath.

"Excuse me? What the fuck did you say?"

"I'm tired of you getting mad every time I refuse to have sex with you. I'm tired of you always running the streets with Tray."

"First of all, you ain't no fucking virgin so hell yeah, I get mad when you hold out on me. You know damn well I am a man and I have needs. And second of all why the hell you complaining about me running with Tray? You ain't complaining when I'm buying your spoiled ass stuff to keep you up to par. But, fuck all that. I asked you a question."

"You heard me. I am tired of your shit and that's why I am talking to someone else."

Li'l Samir let out a deep breath. He could feel the rage building up inside of him. He quickly calmed down. It was time to let Kiyah go. He already had his doubts. She had just proven what he already suspected.

"Kiyah, get up and get your shit. I'll walk you home, but after that we are done. I know now that you were never the woman for me. I'm cool with that though. Let's go!"

"Really? Instead of changing for me you gon' break up with me? Unbelievable."

"You must be on some shit if you think I'm changing for you. You should have talked to me if you had an issue. Instead you were too busy being a ho, screwing the next nigga behind my back. I don't want to hear anything else you got to say. Just get your shit so I can take you home."

Li'l Samir walked Kiyah home and made sure she got in the house safely. Then he jumped on the subway and headed to Tray's crib.

"What up, Tray? Man, you ready to roll?" Li'l Samir asked as Tray opened his apartment door.

"Yeah, man. It took you long enough. What was you doing? 'Cause I know Kiyah ain't give you none," Tray said laughing.

"Forget you, man. It's all good 'cause me and Kiyah are done."

"Word? Y'all broke up already?"

"Hell yeah. She was tryin' to play me, but it's all good. I'm on to the next one. You know how it go. And, we both know you can't pull no good-looking female. The only thing you pulling tonight is strays."

"Ha-ha, very funny, nigga."

Tray and Li'l Samir finally made it to the party without knocking each other out. The party was packed and you could smell blunts being passed around outside. Li'l Samir and Tray made their way through the crowd as they grabbed somebody's blunt on the way through. Tray made his way to the dance floor to dance with some ugly chick as usual. *The nigga ain't got no taste,* Li'l Samir thought.

Li'l Samir helped himself to a beer and sat on the couch. After a few beers and a blunt Li'l Samir was feeling just right. He noticed a very attractive light-skinned chick looking at him. The girl was drop-dead gorgeous. She had long, curly hair and smooth skin. She had curves in all the right places, and resembled Lauren London. Li'l Samir just played it cool and, just like he thought, she made her way across the room to holla at him.

"Wassup?"

"Nothing much, chillin'. What's up wit' you?" she replied very nonchalantly.

Li'l Samir remained cool putting the new girl to the test. "How come I ain't never seen you around before?"

"Maybe you have and you just don't remember," she said with a sly grin.

"Nah, I'd remember a seeing a beauty like you before," Li'l Samir responded with the quickness. He had game and he knew it. It was true that the girl was very beautiful, but the last thing he needed was another loudmouth immature chick following him. Truth be told, he was looking for something real. Kiyah wasn't the girl he had hoped for. He needed a rider he could trust.

"So what is a fine young lady like yourself doing in a place like this?" Li'l Samir asked.

She smiled, showing off her pretty dimples. "Well, it definitely wasn't my idea to come here. I am staying with a friend for the weekend. She talked me into coming out with her. Honestly the whole party scene is not for me. But, I'm here now so I may as well make the best of it."

"So you one of the good girls, huh? I like that. By the way, what is your name?"

"I'm Asia and I know you are Samir, right?"

"Yeah, that's right. The one and only."

"So you want to dance?" Asia asked.

Not really. He really just wanted to get to know her more. But he agreed anyway.

Tray was in the corner on the other side of the room, tonguing down some ugly broad. Li'l Samir just looked at him and laughed as he made his way to the dance floor. The song "No Love" by August Alsina came on. Asia started grinding to the music slowly on Li'l Samir. He tried to act like it didn't even faze him. When Asia dropped down to the floor, he grabbed her by her curly hair, pulling her up, and he started singing the song in her ear. Li'l Samir knew he was turning her on as he killed his dance moves on the floor. Everybody stopped and stared as he busted his moves all over Asia. She was stunned.

When the song was over, he asked if she wanted to roll with him. She was very hesitant at first, but Li'l Samir promised to be the perfect gentleman. Finally she agreed to go.

Asia waited for Li'l Samir outside as he motioned for Tray to come over. "I'm out dawg," Li'l Samir said.

"Damn, man, already?" Tray said mad.

"Hell yeah, man. It ain't poppin' in here like I thought. Plus, I'm trying to get to know this new cutie. I'll hit you up later."

Tray smiled and said, "Oh, that's what's up. Do yo' thang, homie. I'ma hang around here for a while."

"A'ight, dawg. Peace!"

Chapter 5

After the breakup between Kiyah and Li'l Samir, he started hitting it off with Asia. So far, she seemed to be the type of female he needed in his life. In his eyes Asia was very innocent and sweet. And, to top it off, she was loyal. The more time he spent with her the closer they became. Being with her made him want to be a better man.

As usual, Shaniyah was working over at the firm. She was always too busy to keep up with her son's love life. She hadn't been introduced to anyone as of yet. She had told her son awhile back she didn't want to meet any female of his unless he thought it was serious.

One Friday night Li'l Samir invited Asia over to chill with him at home. His mother called to let him know she was working late. They put in a DVD and relaxed on the couch. *Love Jones* played through the television. Li'l Samir felt just like Larenz Tate in the movie. He had fallen head over heels for Asia. And there would be no turning back. It was evident that his player card would definitely be revoked, but she was worth it.

Li'l Samir looked down and stared Asia deeply into her eyes.

"Why are you staring at me like that?" Asia asked.

"I don't know. I've never been the mushy type. But, it's something about you that makes me want to be a better me."

"Wow! That means a lot to me. I'm glad I have that effect on you. I see so much in you that you don't even see in yourself. I am falling for you too. And, I'll ride with you until the end."

"That's why I love you." Li'l Samir realized what he said. Before, he could never imagine speaking the words "I love you" to any woman other than his mom.

Without a second thought Asia replied, "I love you too, Samir."

Briefly, Li'l Samir froze in a panic. As if reading his mind, Asia smiled and planted a passionate kiss on his lips. Instantly she calmed him. He'd never realized how much he really wanted his ride or die until he met Asia. With her, he didn't mind waiting on the sex. He actually enjoyed just spending time together without them having to take things to the next level. With her, things just felt right.

Everything about her from her beautiful angelic face to her glowing, smooth skin tempted him to take things further. He leaned on to her gently. The heated kissing continued. She succumbed to his embrace. Li'l Samir took the green light to take things to the next level.

Li'l Samir continued to kiss Asia while lying in between her legs. He slid his hands underneath her skirt and down her thighs. Asia's body stiffened. She grabbed his arm before he could reach her warm, wet center. Her reaction confused him.

"Baby, What's wrong?"

"Ah, I'm sorry," she replied nervously.

"You can trust me."

"I know. It's just that I have never done this before."

Li'l Samir was shocked. He knew that Asia was a good girl, but he didn't know she was a virgin.

"Oh. Damn." The thought of her purity hit him like a ton of bricks. "Well, listen, you don't have to do this. We can wait until you are comfortable." Li'l Samir was rock hard. He couldn't believe his response, but he truly loved Asia and respected her wishes.

"No, I don't want to wait. I'm just nervous."

"Are you sure?"

"Yes. I am sure."

Li'l Samir could tell by the look in Asia's eyes that she was terrified.

"Maybe this is not a good idea right now," Li'l Samir suggested. He then removed himself from the compromising position on top of her.

Asia pulled him back to her. "I said I'm sure. Just promise to be gentle."

Li'l Samir wrestled with the thought of whether he should continue. He then responded, "I promise."

Gently, as Asia requested, Li'l Samir removed her pink lace panties and continued undressing her. Then, he removed his designer jeans and boxers. He placed himself on top of her and picked up where he left off, planting little kisses all over. He licked her neck creating a flow of wetness between her legs. Her nipples hardened underneath his chest reminding him that they needed attention as well. Li'l Samir licked his way down to her breasts flicking his tongue over each of her diamond-shaped nipples. A soft moan escaped her lips as he watched the look of pleasure on her face. Her eyes were shut tight. She bit down on her bottom lip and arched her back. Her chest rose up giving Li'l Samir more access to her perfectly round breasts.

Pre-cum seeped from the head of Li'l Samir's thick nine-inch dick. He couldn't wait a second longer. In a flash he reached to the floor for his jeans and wiggled his way into his pockets to retrieve a Trojan condom. Magnum to be exact. He slid the condom on to his erect penis. Asia watched in admiration of her man's skills. Slowly, he guided his dick into her warm, wet opening. He tried to push his way through, but even with her juices flowing she was super tight. He could feel her pussy muscles tightening. A look of pain showed on her face. Li'l Samir wanted to take away her pain and replace it with pleasure. The couch was uncomfortable. And, he needed more space to handle his business.

"I'll be right back," he said. He ran to his room to retrieve some blankets. Before Asia could blink he was back in the living room neatly spreading the blankets across the floor. After the layout was to Li'l Samir's satisfaction he made his way over to Asia and lifted her from the couch.

Laughing she replied, "I am a big girl. I don't need to be carried."

"I know you are, but I gotchu, baby." He placed her on the floor. Once he had her down, he opened her legs and with thirst he leaned down in an attempt to taste her juices. Asia realized what Li'l Samir was about to do. Abruptly she slid back and sat up.

"What are you doing?" she asked timidly.

"I'm trying to make you feel good. What's the problem?"

"I want to do this. But, that is nasty!"

Li'l Samir couldn't keep from laughing. "Just trust me. You will like it. I promise."

"Humph. I am not letting you do that."

"Well, this is a first. Most girls would go crazy for a man to go down on them."

"Yeah, and most girls are nasty."

"Baby, come here. I told you I gotchu. Now, I don't offer tongue to just anybody."

"No!"

Li'l Samir continued to laugh. With any other girl the constant debate would have made Li'l Samir furious; however, Asia's inexperience made him want her more. Ignoring her debate, he reached and grabbed her legs, pulling her to him. She gently fell back onto the floor. Like a pro, he quickly dived into her sweetness. She didn't have time to protest any further.

He devoured her juices. From that moment on he knew she would always be hooked.

"Umm . . . Ssss . . . Ahh!" she moaned in delight. Within a minute she came all over his mouth.

Li'l Samir looked up at her with a smirk on his face. "I told you, you would like it."

Asia was in such a stupor she was unable to speak. The look on her face said she wanted more. He gladly pulled her legs up to his waist. Then he slid his dick into her warm, snug walls. The thought of him being her first excited Li'l Samir more. Once again, a pained look crossed her face, but Samir refused to stop.

"Baby, look at me. It's okay. Just relax," he reassured her. "Kiss me."

She did just that. He moved in a slow rhythm until she felt secure. A look of satisfaction appeared on Li'l Samir's face as Asia worked her hips, meeting him with each stroke. Asia wrapped her legs around Li'l Samir's waist and dug her nails into his back. Her reactions drove him insane. She tilted her head back. Li'l Samir drove into her deeply while sucking on her neck. Her moans turned into screams exploding cum onto his dick. "Ah ssss shit!" Li'l Samir groaned as his semen spilled into the condom. He pulled out and collapsed onto the blanket beside her. The moment they caught their breath Shaniyah walked through the front door.

"Oh, shit!" Li'l Samir screamed. Asia rushed to put on her clothes. Samir threw the blanket over him.

"Samir, what the hell!" Shaniyah yelled. She turned her head, embarrassed at the sight of catching her son buck-naked on the floor.

"Ma, I thought you weren't coming home until later."

"It's nine o'damn clock. Get the hell up and put your clothes on! You have lost your damn mind!" Shaniyah continued to fuss as she made her way to the kitchen still in shock.

After Samir and Asia dressed and put away the blankets, they stepped into the kitchen where Li'l Samir's mother had just finished warming dinner.

"Mom, I am so sorry. Please don't be mad. I didn't know you were coming home so soon."

"Samir, just drop it. Let me at least get my nerves together."

Li'l Samir stood in the kitchen with a dumbfounded look on his face. Asia continued to shamefully stare down at the floor.

"Y'all go ahead and eat. I know y'all hungry, after what y'all just did," Shaniyah mumbled. "We will definitely be having a talk about this later, son." Li'l Samir and Asia took their plates and sat at the kitchen table.

"Mom, by the way this is Asia. Asia, this is my mother."

"Hi," Asia said, shyly.

"Asia? So she is the reason you have been walking around looking like you are on cloud nine. I thought it was because you were with Kiyah. Please fill me in because I am lost."

"Ma, me and Kiyah broke up months ago. I met Asia and we have been dating for about three months now. I'm sorry y'all have to meet under these circumstances, but she means a lot to me. She is the one I want to be with."

"Son, if you really care about her then you need to make better decisions. Sleeping with her here in my house especially since I hadn't met her is not a good look. I know I taught you better than this."

"You are right. And, I apologize for that. We got caught up in the moment. But, I have to admit I don't regret it," he said. He glanced over at Asia with love in his eyes. "Next time, I'll make sure I don't disrespect you or put her in a compromising situation, but I mean it when I say I love her. I will respect her in every way just like you taught me."

"Well, I beg you, Samir, please don't be like your father. Don't use and abuse women, and break their hearts. Love them if you love them, and don't bother if you don't. And, Asia, sweetie, I can tell by the glow in my son's eyes that he is serious about you, but if you have any problems feel free to call me."

"I sure will." Asia smiled feeling a little more at ease. "And, ma'am, please forgive me for what you saw. I am not that kind of girl, but as Samir stated I really trust him. I love him as well. And, I don't want what you saw to be your first impression of me."

"Oh, girl, please drop it. I don't want to even think about what I walked into. That was completely horrifying." They all laughed.

"Oh, and, Mom, do you mind if Asia stay here just for tonight?"

"Well, since you are grown I will allow it this time since it is late. But be respectable. Now I am going to bed. I am tired and it has been one hell of a long day. And night might I add. It was nice meeting you, Asia. I look forward to learning more about you."

"Nice meeting you too," Asia said.

Li'l Samir cleaned his plate and Asia's. Then, he and Asia headed to his room to lie down for the night. They spent the whole night talking. The young couple knew that they loved being with each other, but in that night they told each other things that they had never shared with anyone else before. They were both goal-oriented and loyal. Asia was a daddy's girl and got whatever she wanted. She made it clear to Samir that she didn't need his money. She just wanted him to be there for her.

Li'l Samir admitted he wished he had a father to look up to, but he couldn't wait to be a fa-ther to give his son all the love he didn't have from his father. Asia also opened up about how her mother walked out on her and her father's life chasing crack. Her father remarried and his wife adopted her. She also wanted a baby to prove that she would be a better mother than her mother was to her. They had so much in com-mon.

Asia wanted to know more about Samir's dreams and plans for the future. "I don't really have any plans for the future," Li'l Samir lied.

"Samir, you have to have at least one dream," Asia said.

"Well, a'ight, but you betta not say nothing. I want to one day be a rap artist."

"Are you serious? I dreamed of being a singer. If you spit something I'll sing your hook."

"What!" Samir said.

"I'm serious, I'll start. It'll be fun I promise." Asia sang:

> *Baby boy, I think I'm in love*
> *I'm really feelin' you*
> *So tell me what's up, my baby boy, my baby boy*

Li'l Samir said:

> *Baby girl, I know it ain't easy, fallin' for*
> *a nigga like me*
> *A gangsta by blood*
> *Hustlin' every day in da streets*
> *New York, New York, the only place I'll*
> *eva know*
> *Chillin' wit' my girl Asia, and smokin'*
> *dat hydro*
> *Yeah, I know it ain't easy, to be Bonnie*
> *and hold down Clyde*
> *But I promise I'll stay by yo' side, but*
> *only if you down to ride, my baby girl,*
> *My baby girl*

"Samir, that was tight. I think you got what it takes to make it. I swear you do."

"Talking 'bout me, ma; you can sing."

"Yep, and maybe we can do it together," Asia said happily.

"Maybe, but the only way that would happen is if I stop selling. And the only way I'll stop sellin' is if I had a child or something. I don't want my child to grow up and I might not be there, dead or in jail. I know how that shit feel and I ain't having it."

"I feel ya," Asia said yawning. She dozed off as Li'l Samir played in her hair.

Li'l Samir couldn't sleep. His mind was racing with all the thoughts of everything that could go wrong. *I am my father's son.*

Chapter 6

The next day, Li'l Samir walked Asia home. They had to walk right past Kiyah's house, and he prayed she wouldn't come out starting drama. Unfortunately, God must not have been listening to his prayers that day.

"Samir, who is that bitch you walking with?"

"Kiyah, get back in the house, man. I don't got time for yo' shit."

"So this the bitch you broke up with me for. Really though."

Asia stood in disbelief.

"Kiyah, you already know why we broke up so stop with the dramatics. You can't blame anybody but yourself."

"Forget you, Samir. You ain't the only nigga I can get," Kiyah said pointing her finger and poppin' her neck.

Kiyah was so angry with Li'l Samir she tried to attack Asia. "You dirty ho!" Kiyah screamed while lunging straight for Asia. Li'l Samir grabbed Kiyah just in time.

"Kiyah, look, I am trying to be civil considering all the shit you done, so stop. I ain't trying to dawg you like that. We can be friends but you need to calm down and go back in the house."

He and Asia walked off leaving Kiyah feeling foolish.

Li'l Samir walked Asia home and she invited him in.

"Asia, where have you been? I've been worried sick about you. I kept calling your phone, but you didn't answer. Who is this?"

"Mom, calm down. I told you I was spending the night with Stacy and my friend Samir walked me home," Asia lied. "Mom, this is Samir. Samir, this is my mom."

"Nice to meet you," Samir said nervously.

"Nice to meet you too. Thanks for walking her home. How did y'all meet, Ms. He Walked Me Home?"

"Uh, he's Stacy's brother's friend and he was kind enough to walk me home, Ma, dang."

Asia's mom raised her eyebrow knowing that her daughter was lying. "Asia, there's no need to lie to your mother."

"Ma'am, I know I was wrong for having your daughter out. I should have come to you and introduced myself first," Li'l Samir said putting his hand on his chest.

"So what you are saying? You are dating my daughter?"

"Yes, ma'am. I know I was wrong, but now I am making it right. I really care about her. My mom always says if you care about a woman then you would do things the right way no matter the cost."

"Well, your mom seems like a very intelligent lady. I don't appreciate you having her out all night and especially not knowing where she is. But, I can appreciate your honesty. Don't let it happen again. As for you, Asia, I will deal with you later."

Li'l Samir knew it was time for him to head out and handle his business. "Asia, I'll talk to you later. I have some errands to run. Call me later." Li'l Samir looked over to Asia's mother. "It was nice to meet you, ma'am."

"Okay, see you later, Samir," Asia replied.

Li'l Samir headed to the spot to handle his business. Time flew and his pockets were just like he liked. He had been saving to get a ride that would knock D-Money's ride off its feet, or a ride like the one that was pulling up in front of him right now. This ride was tight. It was a black chromed-out Cadillac Escalade sitting on thirties. The driver rolled down his window as Li'l Samir looked to see who this was rollin' up on him.

"Yo, li'l homie, come here."

"Who you, nigga?" Li'l Samir said, still trying to get a glimpse of the guy in the killer ride.

"Man, just come here. Damn, nigga, you scared?"

"Hell nah, nigga, fuck that," Li'l Samir said walking toward the truck. When Li'l Samir got close to the window he didn't know whether to run or stand his ground.

"Get in the truck, li'l nigga."

"Hell nah, son. You must be crazy."

"Man, I ain't gon' hurt you. I need to talk to you, on the real."

Li'l Samir didn't know what he should do. Big Samir was pressuring him to get in the truck and he didn't want to look like a punk in front of his dad. Li'l Samir thought about it for a moment, wishing he was strapped. He really did need to talk to him, but he didn't know what to expect after jumping on him in the club. Li'l Samir jumped in the truck anyway. Big Samir started his truck and headed down the block.

"You know I could have killed yo' ass at that club," Big Samir said with fire in his eyes.

"Likewise," Li'l Samir said in return.

"You got a lot of heart, my li'l nigga, that's why you need to be down with me."

Li'l Samir had a hoodie on so Big Samir couldn't look at him the way he wanted to. Big Samir had a lot of questions for his possible son.

"So you know word on the street is you my li'l nigga," Big Samir said with a smirk.

"I don't got no father, so you ain't got to stress yourself 'bout dat, dude."

"Is Shaniyah yo' motha?" Big Samir asked.

"Yeah, and I don't appreciate you disrespecting her either. And what's yo' point, man? What do you want from me? I got shit to do."

"How old are you?" Big Samir asked.

"Eighteen. Why?"

"Uh-huh, so what's ya name, kid?"

"If you my father, ain't you supposed to know that?" Li'l Samir said angrily.

"A'ight, I'll take that," Big Samir said nodding his head. "What has your mother told you about me?"

"Just that you lied to her," Li'l Samir said now feeling uneasy about the conversation. He had wanted answers, but now that he was about to get them, he wasn't sure that he was ready to hear them.

"Look, yo motha didn't hold me down like she should have. I lied to her when I told her I had quit dealing. I knew I was dead wrong for not telling her what I was doing. Just like you ain't tellin' her what you doin'. I—"

"How you know I ain't tell her about what I do?" Li'l Samir cut him off.

"Because I know if your motha knew what you were doing out here in the streets she woulda killed your ass already." Big Samir chuckled. "Now, as I was saying, I wanted her to feel safe. I didn't want her to be around that shit. I wanted a better life for us. Hustling is all that I know. Then some dumb bitch set me and D-Money up 'cause I didn't want to be with her."

"I can understand why she was upset and turned from you. You should have told her the truth. You knew the consequences of sellin' and look how long you been gone. Of course she was hurt, man. You trippin'."

"I understand that, li'l man, I do. I was dead wrong and that is why I wanted to talk to you. I wanted you to hear the truth straight from me. When I got out, I had to start from scratch so I moved to the big shit that niggas cravin'. I know you tired of the li'l money you make with D-Money; that's chump change. You can't trust that nigga; look what he did to me, and now he using you against me."

"No! You turned me against you. Man, I don't even know you."

"I broke my damn neck to make your mom happy. The only wrong I did was hustlin' and that same shit can happen to you, but this time

I'ma play my shit smart. You gonna get busted quick rollin' wit' D. Whether it's true or not that you're my son, I'll always have love for your motha and so I'ma look out for you," Big Samir said with sincerity in his eyes.

Li'l Samir pulled off his hoodie so Big Samir could get a look at him. He looked Big Samir dead in the eyes. "I'm Samir Rasheed Hicks, Jr. Do I look like I am your son?"

Big Samir couldn't believe his eyes. He saw the resemblance in the club, but it wasn't like being close up. He was looking at himself dead in the mirror. Big Samir was speechless.

"Damn, man, you look . . . Never mind."

"Nah, say it," Li'l Samir said with tears in his eyes. "Man, I needed you. You don't know how this shit feel to have a father who don't give a fuck about you!"

"Samir, calm down, son. I do care about you. Man, I didn't know. Yo' mother never contacted me or told me nothing. I'm here for you now and that's what matters." Big Samir stopped the truck, scribbled his number on a piece of paper, and stuck it in Li'l Samir's jacket. He grabbed Li'l Samir and held him.

"Nah, man, fuck that!" Li'l Samir yelled pulling out of his father's embrace. He jumped out of the truck and ran down the block toward home.

His father yelled for him until his voice was no longer in Li'l Samir's distance. Once Li'l Samir got home, he headed straight to his room and called Asia.

"What's up, baby?"

"Hey. I miss you already."

"I miss you too. Did I get you in trouble?"

"Not too much. My mom fussed me out, but I guess your honesty helped out a lot. What have you been up to?"

"Well, while I was working on the block I ran into my dad."

"Really? Baby, are you okay?"

"Yes. I am good. But I just ain't feeling him like that." It felt so good to have someone he could open up to about his dad.

"What happened?"

"Nothing really. Once I told to him that I was his son he had the nerve to think I was gon' forgive him for not being there for me. That dude put my mom through too much shit. She had to raise me by herself."

"Well, I mean, I know you are angry with him. And, I understand it will take time, but eventually you will have to forgive him."

"Did you forgive your real mom for walking away from you and your dad?"

"Samir, that's not fair. That's messed up to reverse your situation on me."

"Baby, I'm sorry. I didn't mean it like that, but you of all people know that shit ain't easy. I just don't know who to trust. I know D-Money ain't someone I can depend on either. I should have never got into this shit with him."

"I agree. I really think you should forgive your dad and get out of this mess with D-Money. I know your dad wasn't there for you, but we all make mistakes. The biggest thing is he's your dad. I'm sure he feels guilty so he's gonna try to make things up to you. He will be there to protect you and look out for you; however, with D-Money there could be an ulterior motive. I don't trust him. The way things went down at the club, it almost seems like he's using you to get at your father. And if it's true what you said your dad told you, then it proves that he is not loyal."

When he and Asia got off the phone everything Asia had spoken played over and over in his mind. He knew she was right. It was definitely time to end things with D-Money, but giving in to his father was not so easy. He still resented him for all the trouble he caused him and his mother. For now, Li'l Samir would keep things as they were until he could learn to forgive his dad. In the meantime, his time was spent with Asia planning for their future together.

Chapter 7

Months rolled by without Li'l Samir hearing anything from his father. He continued to work the block for D-Money. Li'l Samir spent most of his free time enjoying Asia as their love for one another continued to grow.

The couple enjoyed a nice lunch at their favorite Italian restaurant in Manhattan. Asia finished the last of her entrée. She looked up from her plate and noticed Li'l Samir was not eating, but looking down at his plate deep in thought.

"What's wrong, babe? You're not hungry?"

"Oh, nah. I'm just thinking about something."

"Do you mind sharing with me what's on your mind?"

"It's nothing. I'm serious."

"You still haven't spoken with your dad?"

"Nope." Li'l Samir sighed.

"I really think you should. You would feel a lot better."

"I don't know. I'll think about it. You ready to get out of here?"

"Okay. I have some things I need to do for my mom anyway."

That night Li'l Samir lay in bed unable to sleep. He debated back and forth about calling his dad. He remembered the balled-up piece of paper in his jacket pocket with his dad's number on it. He jumped out of bed and searched through his closet for the jacket.

Once he found the number he sat on his bed with his cell phone in his hand. He dialed the numbers hesitantly. His dad picked up on the third ring.

"Hello," Big Samir answered into the phone.

"Yeah. It's me, Li'l Samir."

"What's up, son? I've been waiting on your call."

"Well, I almost decided against it."

"I can understand that. What made you change your mind?"

"I don't know, man. I got a lot of resentment in my heart right now. You weren't there for me. I'm thinking about giving you a chance to make things right. I'm trying to learn to forgive you for myself. I have to because the anger is killing me inside."

"I understand you need time."

"Man, I remember as a kid watching other dads at the park throwing balls with their sons and wishing you were here to do those things with me. I craved having a father just to spend time with me and do shit with me. Every time I think about that shit I get so fucking mad." Tears rolled down Li'l Samir's face as anger continued to build inside.

"Son, there is nothing I can do to get back the time that is lost, but we can do our best to build a relationship while we have the chance. I can't go on knowing that you won't let me be a part of your life. Don't keep this anger in your heart because of me. Don't let more time go by and I not be there for your future endeavors. I want to be there when you get married. I want to be there when my first grandchild is born. I couldn't be there before, but I want to be here now. That should count for something."

"Man, I don't know."

"Think of all we can be, son. We can run this thing together. You will be able to live life the way you always dreamed. My plan is working for me and I want you here for the ride, man. Father and son. We can do this. But, you have to let bygones be bygones. I'm here now. Let's do this shit."

After the conversation between Li'l Samir and his father they took the time to get to know each other and build a father-son relationship. In the beginning, Li'l Samir had moments of wanting to still be angry with his father but over time those wounds began to heal. The more Li'l Samir talked to his dad the closer they became.

Li'l Samir was happy to have his father in his life, but he knew his mother would not like it at all when he would tell her. Shaniyah had just finished preparing dinner. She and Li'l Samir sat at the table and caught up. She had been working a lot lately so she wanted to have mother-son time with Li'l Samir.

"I'm glad we are finally able to sit down and have dinner together. Just like old times. Seem like I am missing out on so much. But I guess it's safe to say Asia is keeping you entertained." She laughed.

"Ma, there you go."

"What? It's true. I hardly ever see my baby anymore. I'm starting to get jealous."

"Ma, you know that you are the first lady of my life. No one can take your place. But things with me and Asia are getting serious. I've never met anyone like her."

"Um, hmm. It seems like my baby is not such a baby anymore."

"Nope. I'm far from it."

"Well, you will always be my baby. I am glad to see the happiness in your eyes though."

"Ma, I want to ask you something."

"Sure. You know you can ask me anything."

"I doubt that, but I'll shoot for it anyway. When are you gonna talk to my dad? After all, he is my dad. I think it is time we do what's right."

"You can't be serious. Samir, I am not trying to hurt you, but your dad will not be a positive influence on your life nor mine. I wish things were different so that you could have a relationship with him, but he is still a product of the streets. I'm quite sure of it."

"But what if he is trying to change? Would you ever consider trying to get back together with him?"

"Hell naw! It's best when we are not together because I make horrible decisions when we are."

"Ma, you are not so innocent in this. You knew who my dad was before you decided to be with him! Now you want to blame him for everything!"

"Excuse me? Where is all of this coming from?"

"Never mind. I just wish you to would at least talk to him and build some kind of relationship for me! I'm the innocent one in this mess y'all made." Li'l Samir got up from the table upset.

"Wait, Li'l Samir. You are right." Li'l Samir took his seat back at the table. "The truth is I am hurt. I let this anger I have for your father keep you from having any kind of relationship with him. I admit that. But the damage has been done. I want you to be the man I raised you to be. I am looking out for your well-being. Your father is not the man you need in your life right until he can prove that he is ready to come out of the streets."

"But, Ma—"

"No buts, Samir. I don't want you around him right now. You have to respect that. I am only looking out for you." Shaniyah left Li'l Samir at the table not wanting to discuss his father any further. The guilt of knowing he had already started spending time with him against his mother's wishes tore through him deeply. But it was too late.

Li'l Samir and his dad stood in front of the pizzeria. They both ordered a slice of pizza. Then, they headed to a bench nearby and ate.

"So, how is your mother doing? I bet she still look just as a good as when I first met her."

"She doing good. She just been working a lot."

Big Samir looked off in the distance and laughed.

"What's so funny?"

"Man, I remember the first time I met your mother. My brother and I had just moved to North Carolina right next door to her. She came over and introduced herself. She was the prettiest girl I had ever laid eyes on."

"It seems like you are still in love with her."

"Man, I will always love Shaniyah. She lived a hard life. Your mom is one of the strongest women I know. Her mother was never there for her. She was too busy running the streets. I took her under my wing and eventually we became a couple. I wasn't perfect, but I would do anything for her. We have so much in common. We have shared things with one another that we have never revealed to anyone else."

"Dad, I really wish there was some way I could get her to talk to you. I'm sure she still loves you too. I have tried reasoning with her, but she won't hear anything I have to say. Everyone makes mistakes. I found a way to forgive you so I'm sure she can too."

"I don't know. I'm afraid I fucked up beyond repair. I want her back so bad, but I know she ain't having it. Plus, I can't bring her into this street life I'm living right now. That's the reason she left me in the first place. I have put her through enough already."

"Well, why don't you get out of the game? I know that's what I am trying to do."

"Trust me, I want out. I have to get some things set up first. One thing is for certain, you have to stop rolling with D-Money."

"I know."

"I mean now. And I am dead serious."

"What happened between you and him? I thought y'all were best of friends before all of this."

"We were. When I was in North Carolina we were like brothers. When I got all that time I thought he would at least have my back. I found out the hard way that the whole time he just wanted my spot. I honestly believe that he had something to do with me getting set up. I want out of the game. But, I want revenge on him more."

"What he did to you is messed up. He could do the same thing to me. I'm done with him and if you need me to help you handle the situation with him I gotchu."

"Son, I don't know if I am ready to take you into this business. After getting closer to you I'm afraid to get you caught up in this mess."

"Once I drop him I know I'll already be caught up in it."

"That's true, but best believe I ain't letting shit happen to you."

"You said it yourself that we can do this, so let's get it done."

"All right, man, if you are sure this is what you want to do."

"As long as you promise when we get to where we need to be and handle D-Money we done with this illegal shit."

"Sounds like a plan."

A week later, Big Samir met his son on the block. Li'l Samir jumped into the truck with his dad. It was time for Li'l Samir to learn the business. They pulled up to an old, shabby, run-down house.

"Where we at?" Li'l Samir asked.

"Just follow me and don't say nothing."

"Gotcha," Samir said wiping his eyes.

Big Samir and Li'l Samir entered the run-down house. It was getting kind of late and Li'l Samir had promised Asia he would come to her house and spend time with her; however, he knew the business between him and his dad was very important.

Once inside, Li'l Samir took mental notes of everything. He was learning the drug trade and everything about it. He learned so much in one night. He watched his father re-up and flip his money. Li'l Samir was amazed. There were like fifteen dudes doing their own thing. His father schooled him on how to make real paper.

When Li'l Samir and his father got back in the truck, Big Samir handed him a bag from the back seat. "You take this and treat you, yo lady, and ya motha to anything y'all want." Then he grabbed one of the bags he had just got from the house. "You take this bag and get on ya job. Welcome to the team and play smart. I'ma always be around, especially when you least expect it."

"Don't forget, Pops. You really need to try to talk to my mom."

"Maybe later. I can't get her involved right now. I'ma look out for y'all, but I know yo' mom can't go back to this lifestyle. That's why you need to get yo' own space and handle your business, but still look out for her. She don't need this shit."

"I hear ya, man. Can you drop me off at my girl's house? After a day like this I need something wet to get in."

"Ha, a'ight, man. You gonna end up gettin' her pregnant. You don't know what you doin' anyway."

Li'l Samir laughed. "Did you? Nigga, you must not know me. I am my father's son."

"You damn straight."

Big Samir dropped his son off at Asia's house. Neither of them noticed the black Mercedes that had been following them the whole time.

***

Over the next couple of months, Li'l Samir was living it up. He had finally gotten his own space, kicked D-Money to the curb, and was spending time getting closer with his dad. He had learned the business with his father and they were doing well. He and his dad were packing real money. They were becoming some of the top hustlers of New York. The cops tried to stay on them, but came up short every time. Together, they were unstoppable.

Shaniyah wasn't too happy with her son moving, but she knew it would come sooner or later. She feared for her son's life. Her intuition was telling her that her son was in the streets doing the very thing she had kept him from. It was déjà vu all over again for her. She knew her son couldn't afford the lifestyle he was living unless he was dealing. He wouldn't admit it, and she knew she had to let him make his own mistakes. How could Li'l Samir grow up to be just like a person who was never around him? Little did she know, Li'l Samir knew his father very well by now and had been around him for months.

Chapter 8

Li'l Samir was in his perfectly decorated crib thanks to his mother and Asia. He had rented a one-bedroom loft and he couldn't be happier. *This is what life is about,* he thought as he and Asia watched movies and ate pizza together on the couch. He and Asia were still in love. Some people say things always get tougher once you've been with someone for more than a year but that wasn't the case with these two. She made him happy and he was utterly in love with her. She was sweet, honest, sexy as hell, and she gave Li'l Samir what he wanted, which was love and affection.

"Samir, I have to ask you something," Asia said nervously.

"Well, ask it then," Li'l Samir said stuffing pizza in his mouth with one hand and pausing the movie with the other.

"Samir, do you love me?"

"Girl, you know I care 'bout you. Damn, you making me miss the movie," he said as he reached for the remote to play the movie.

Asia turned the TV off and backed away from Li'l Samir.

"Girl, what is wrong with you?" Samir said getting up.

"Do you love me, Samir? Yes or no? Tell me for real, babe."

"Man, you know I love you more than anything. Why you trippin'? Girl, you play too much!" Li'l Samir said as he pulled her in toward him. That's when he noticed her eyes welling up with tears. "Babe, what's wrong?" he asked genuinely concerned. Just a minute ago, they were both fine watching the movie.

"I'm pregnant!" Asia blurted out crying into her hands.

Li'l Samir was in total shock. So much started going through his head: baby, drugs, jail, and death. He didn't want to take the same route his father did. He also didn't want to hurt or lose Asia.

"Baby, stop crying. How long have you known? You know I'm here for you. I would be happy for you to have my son. You know that."

"I have known for a month now, but I am two months pregnant. I told my mom last night. She told me to come back and get my stuff because I can't stay there anymore. I thought my dad would at least have my back, but he was more disgusted than my mom." Asia began to cry uncontrollably.

"Don't worry 'bout it, Asia. You staying here with me."

Li'l Samir was in the truck rolling with his father. He had told him about Asia and the baby. He was so shaken up and didn't know whether he was coming or going. He needed his father's advice before he made any more dumb decisions.

"Man, I don't know what to do. I want out. I can't go down that same road you went down. I can't risk not being in my child's life, man, for real."

"Man, I know the feelin'. Even though this is all I know, I miss yo' mother bad, man. I feel like this shit is getting old. I still need to stack some more money though. Hell, when I retire, I wanna make sure I'm set for life. I got some money stashed for you too, son. I want you to live your life. Maybe it's time for me to up and leave this shit."

"Well, I got paper stacked too. I been saving ever since I first started. Now with Asia being pregnant maybe I should pull in overtime for a few months and then get out."

Li'l Samir was talking his father to death while his father was spittin' rhymes:

> *Life is a bitch, tryin'a live dope boy dreams*
> *Stackin' dis papa, man, sellin' crack to fiends*
> *Wanna leave da game, but dis da only life I know*
> *Iced out, gear tight, crusin' in the Escalade real slow*
> *Life is a bitch the money real good in da hood*
> *Got everything you ever dreamed, but without a wife it's no good*

Li'l Samir stopped his father and started bustin' his freestyle:

> *Life is a bitch tryin'a live hood rich*
> *Tryin'a do ya own thing, poppin' niggas talkin' slick*
> *I am my father's son, hustlin' by any means*

Made love to my girl and now I done planted my seed
Now shit is real, I got to get out the ghetto
Gotta find a way out befo' 5-0 come knockin' down my front door
Life is a bitch

"Damn, boy. I didn't know you could flow like that," Big Samir said in shock.

"Man, I been flowin' since I could talk. I guess I'm too much like you. It's always been my dream to put out my own album."

"I guess the apple doesn't fall far from the tree. Rappin' was always one of my dreams too. I always wanted to run my own record label. I got my own studio at the crib. Maybe we can make something happen. Who betta to do it with than my son? I have faith in your talent."

"Damn you got yo' own studio? Well, what are we waitin' on? This could be big!"

"I'm down, but you know what I really been thinkin'?" Big Samir said. "I really been thinkin' about bustin' in D-Money's hideout and robbin' his ass. It's time I see that nigga for real."

"Come on. Pops. I know I promised to be down with helping you get revenge on D-Money, but you talkin' 'bout takin' a big risk here."

"I know, man, but I gotta shut that nigga down for what he did to me, man."

"Damn. Well, I got yo' back. When and where?"

"I'ma keep peepin' his spot and seeing when he in and out. I gotta make sure everything legit. I got to find out when he gon' be packin' the most dough. Then, I'ma let you know when we gon' be ready to bust in."

"A'ight, man. If you sure you want to do this, then I'm down."

"I'm sure, my nigga. Then after this, we can quit the game and be in the studio full time."

"That's what's up."

Li'l Samir and his father were making big plans when a familiar Mercedes drove by full speed and started shooting at Big Samir's truck. Li'l Samir reached in his pants and shot back at the Mercedes. He recognized D-Money as he turned on the next street and sped off. Big Samir looked at his son and said, "You all right?"

Li'l Samir nodded.

"It's on. It's time for payback, my li'l nigga," said Big Samir as he sped off down the street.

Chapter 9

Li'l Samir lay on the couch waiting for Asia to get out of the shower. He was watching a video. He was imagining the day that his family would watch him on TV. He couldn't wait to live a normal life with his family. Li'l Samir wanted to prove to himself that he could do something positive with his life. He wanted to make a new start, so he decided that he would move his family to Atlanta.

Li'l Samir dozed off on the couch. Asia came out of the room dressed in lingerie, with her little belly poking out, and her curly hair hanging down her back. She climbed on top of Li'l Samir and planted light kisses all over his face and neck. Li'l Samir woke up grinning fully aroused. He picked Asia up and carried her to their bedroom.

Li'l Samir laid her down gently on the bed and undressed with a quickness. He spread Asia's legs and licked her thighs as she moaned his name. Asia's legs were so soft and thick. Li'l Samir made his way up her thighs and began to taste her sweetness. Asia's moaning increased as she arched her back and Li'l Samir raised her hips to feast deeper. Li'l Samir looked up to see the pleasure on her face, which aroused him even more. Asia's legs started trembling and he knew then that she was about to cum.

"That's right, baby," Li'l Samir said in a low tone. Asia was moaning uncontrollably as she began to softly whisper Li'l Samir's name. He stood up and climbed on top of Asia, entering her slowly. He started off stroking her gently. He couldn't believe how good Asia's wetness was to him. His slow stroke increased as sweat dripped from his muscular body. "Damn, baby, I love you," Samir said.

Asia screamed, "I love you too," as both of them were drawn into ecstasy.

Li'l Samir woke up the next morning and stood on their stoop as Asia slept peacefully. A platinum-colored, chromed-out Cadillac Escalade pulled up with twenty-six-inch rims and a red bow on the front. Big Samir got out and came up on the stoop with his son.

"Damn, man, when did you get that?" Li'l Samir asked.

"It's for you, my man. Just like mine, just a different color. You got TVs, a game system, and everything, not to mention a bangin'-ass stereo sound system. Let's go check it out."

"Word, man, that's what's up. Thanks, Dad."

Li'l Samir was like a little boy on Christmas as he ran down the stoop to check out his new ride. He pressed every button he could find. He started blasting the radio and nodding his head when he noticed Asia at the door rubbing her eyes. Li'l Samir turned off the car and motioned for Asia to come outside.

"Dad, this my wifey Asia. Asia, this is my dad, Big Samir."

"Hey nice to meet you, boss," Asia said shyly.

"Nice to meet you too. Samir, you didn't tell me she was this gorgeous. Samir got his taste from his dad," he said grinning at Asia. "Wow, and I see your li'l stomach is starting to poke out. Y'all about to make me a grandpop," Big Samir said.

"Yep, it looks that way," Asia replied as she rubbed her stomach. "Well, I'ma head back inside and make Samir some breakfast. Would you like some?" Asia asked Big Samir.

"Nah, I'm good. Nice meeting you."

Asia went back in the house as Li'l Samir continued to look at his new truck. "Damn, baby boy, seem like you picked a good one," Big Samir said.

"Yeah, that's my baby," Li'l Samir remarked proudly.

"The real reason I came through is because I got some good news," Big Samir said.

"What's good, Pops?"

"I am officially the owner of Big Money Records. That's what's good."

"Stop lying, man. When did all this happen?" Samir asked excitedly.

"I got on the job the day we first talked about it. I had the studio, but I hadn't put the money in to start the business. After talking with you, I hopped right on it. Guess who my first artist is gonna be?" Big Samir said grinning.

"It betta be me."

"Yep, so get ya shit together, 'cause you about to be famous."

"That's what's up," Li'l Samir said excitedly.

Li'l Samir spent the next few months in the studio with his dad putting his tracks together. He was slowly coming up. He was signed to Big Money Records, and his dad was making all the right moves to get Li'l Samir's song, "My Father's Son," on the radio. Big Samir was also putting out a mix CD locally, to give New York a feel of his son. Everything was looking good.

During the day, they were working in the studio, laying down tracks and working on the album; and at night they were working on finalizing their plans on getting their revenge on D-Money. They had been studying his every move. They had his entire schedule down to a science. They knew where he went and at what time. They knew where his drops and pick-ups were. They even knew what time the man took a shit every day. Now all that was left was for them to pick out the day they'd finally make their move.

Things between Li'l Samir and his mother had taken a bad turn. When he and Asia invited her over for dinner and gave her the news of the baby on the way, she didn't react the way they'd hoped. She became angry with both of them for not being careful and not using protection. She felt they were too young to have a kid and they still had their entire lives ahead of them.

"Ma, you were young when you had me too!" Li'l Samir protested.

"Yes, I was young when I had you. And look how tough it was having to raise you on my own. Having a child is not easy." She pleaded, "It's not what they make it out to be on TV where you're playing in the park and pushing a stroller with a happy baby holding a balloon while the mom and dad smile at each other and walk into the sunset!" she yelled. "Having a child is nothing like that!" she continued. "It's not being able to sleep and getting up at all hours of the night. It's changing shitty diapers and not having any time for yourselves."

"But we'll be ready for when the baby comes," Asia said nervously.

"Asia, I know you two will do your best. I just feel like you two are way too young to have a child," Shaniyah said, calming down a little bit.

"I understand that, Ma. And I get that it was hard for you but things are different for me and Asia," Li'l Samir reassured her.

"How? Please tell me how, Samir?" Shaniyah felt herself getting riled up again. "How are things going to be different? What can you offer this baby if you never even started college because your ass is hustling out there in the streets!" she said as the tears ran down her face.

Samir hated to see her cry. He didn't expect the conversation to go down like this. He wanted to tell her she was wrong and that he wasn't in the streets but, deep down, he knew he couldn't lie to his mother's face.

And what he didn't know was that she knew the truth whether he told it to her or not. A mother knows her son. And she knew he was just like his father. When she found out about Big Samir's release, she knew it would just be a matter of time before father and son came together. As much as she had tried raising Li'l Samir to be a good boy, the streets were in his blood. He was still a good boy in his heart; he just had some bad habits as far as she was concerned. What broke her heart the most was knowing that her son had grown up to deal the same drugs that had destroyed her mother. It sure was a fucked-up circle of life.

As much as it pained her to walk away from her son, she didn't want to hear of him getting locked up, shot, or killed. So she once again decided to walk away from the man she loved. Li'l Samir was hurt when his mother stopped taking his calls. He thought about going to look for her, but he decided to leave well enough alone and give her time and space. Nonetheless, he missed his mother and he hoped that they would talk again one day.

All too soon, the day had come for Li'l Samir and his father to make their big move. After that day Li'l Samir hoped he and his father would never speak of it again. He also prayed that he would live through it and that it wouldn't ruin his life.

"Samir, tomorrow night is the night, my man," Big Samir said.

"Yup. You ready, Dad?" Li'l Samir asked.

"Hell yeah, I'm ready!" he said excitedly. "Tomorrow night we take D-Money and his crew. That's the night they gon' be packing the most dough. Now, we've done our homework so you already know how it's going down. His whole crew gon' meet up at his spot. Now it's time to put in the real work. You feel me? It's time to shut down D-Money's whole operation."

"A'ight. I'm down."

That night came quick as ever. Li'l Samir kissed Asia and told her to stay in the house and lock the doors. He promised her that he would come home to her. He promised tonight was the night he would end all of his illegal business. He was ready to be there for her and with her, full time. All his talking could not erase her fears. Because the truth was Asia was worried that Li'l Samir wouldn't return. She couldn't stand losing him, especially with her baby being due soon.

Big Samir rushed into Li'l Samir's house ready to handle his business. Li'l Samir was beyond scared, but he wasn't going to let his dad see it. He wanted to back out, but he didn't want to let his father down. Li'l Samir kissed Asia one last time before heading out the door with his father.

When Li'l Samir and his father got outside, Li'l Samir didn't see his father's black Cadillac Escalade. There was a red Mustang parked out front instead.

"Whose car is this, man?" Li'l Samir asked.

"It's borrowed. Look, don't worry about that, I ain't 'bout to risk them noticing my shit," Big Samir said.

Big Samir parked across the street from D-Money's spot. He watched as D-Money and his crew headed out of the abandoned building and drove off. Big Samir passed his son a ski mask before they both got out of the car. They headed to the side of the building. Once out of sight, they put on their ski masks and gloves. Big Samir busted the window and let his son in first. Once inside the building they went straight to work. They loaded their bags with money, jewelry, and weed. Then they proceeded to tear everything up in sight.

Once they were done, they stood in a corner with the lights out waiting for D-Money and their crew to return with the big money.

Thirty minutes later, D-Money and his crew returned. They turned on the lights laughing and talking. They looked around in shock. Big Samir held a gun to D-Money's head.

"Hand over the fucking money!" Big Samir screamed.

"Man, what the fuck is this?" one of D-Money's members said.

Li'l Samir hit the dude on the head with the end of the gun and repeated, "Hand over the fucking money!"

"Man, give 'em the money," D-Money said nervously.

D-Money's crew handed Li'l Samir the money. Big Samir noticed one of the dudes pulling out his gat. He took aim and shot the dude in his chest. That's when everything went wrong.

D-Money elbowed Big Samir and started blasting toward Li'l Samir. He ducked and started blasting every dude in sight, except Tray who was in a corner, scared to death. Everybody was down except Tray. Big Samir pointed his gun toward him and blasted as Li'l Samir screamed, "No!" but it was too late.

They both ran out and headed for the Mustang as police cars came out of nowhere. Big Samir and his son got away just in time.

D-Money was still able to move since the bullet only grazed him as he noticed his cousin, Tray, lay dead in a puddle of blood that was seeping from his mouth. He looked around at the rest of his crew and noticed two of the dudes were okay.

"Man, y'all niggas got to get up. Five-oh on the way, man," D-Money said as the sirens came closer.

"Man, I can't move," one of D-Money's goons responded.

The two dudes managed to get up. D-Money had already made it out the back door. It was too late for the other two guys. The cops crammed inside the building, yelling for the boys to stop and put their hand up.

Asia was at the house on pins and needles. She couldn't sleep. It was two o'clock in the morning and Samir still hadn't gotten home. She walked back and forth from the window to the couch.

Hours later, Asia finally heard Li'l Samir fumbling with his keys as he opened the door. She rushed over to him and jumped into his arms.

"Where have you been? Are you okay? I've been worried sick about you," Asia said happy and angry at the same time.

"I told you I would be back, ma," Li'l Samir said bending down to kiss Asia and then her belly. "I'm about to jump in the shower. You can go to bed now and stop worrying your pretty self to death. I'll be there when I'm done."

"Okay," Asia said as she headed to bed exhausted.

Li'l Samir jumped in the shower thinking about what he had just done. He hoped that it was all over. From this moment forward, all that mattered was his family and his rap career. That's all he wanted to think about. He jumped out of the shower, threw on his boxers, and slid into the bed, pulling Asia close to him as he fell asleep.

Li'l Samir was awakened by his cell phone. He wiped the cold out of his eyes and reached over Asia to grab his phone from the nightstand.

"Hello," Li'l Samir said sleepily.

"What up, li'l nigga?"

"Dad, what you doing up this early?"

"Samir, it's twelve in the afternoon," his father replied. "I got some news for you, my man. It's all in the papers and on the streets. The cops got two of D-Money boys, but they still looking for him. Six of them dead, yo."

"Whattt? You mean to tell me D-Money still alive, man? What the fuck we gon' do?" Li'l Samir said whispering and walking out of the bedroom.

"Don't stress it, man. He ain't about ta do nothing. He knows his limits, but we will keep an eye out just in case."

"Whatever you say, man. The first time that nigga act up, I'm takin' him out. No question."

"That's what's up. You need to come by the crib so you can get in the studio. I got a couple more artists lined up."

"A'ight, man. I'll be there in a little bit."

Chapter 10

Li'l Samir met his father's new artists, Kejuan, Zay, and Mike. They were the new singing group Magic Touch, and they had skills. They sang the hook to one of his songs. Big Samir was sure it would be a hit. Everything was working out great. Li'l Samir was just waiting for his first song to hit the radio.

Li'l Samir headed home after a six-hour studio session with Magic Touch. He was exhausted, and he didn't like leaving Asia at home for a long period of time. When he finally got home, he spotted his mom in the kitchen.

"What are you doing here?"

"Boy, what do you mean, what am I doing here? Look how long you lived off of me and you got the nerve to ask why I'm here," Shaniyah complained.

"Ma, don't try to act like everything is cool between us," Li'l Samir said with a hint of attitude in his voice. "You've been ignoring my calls for months and all of a sudden you pop up at my house and wanna act like everything is flowers and pearls."

"Are you saying I'm not welcome in your house?" Shaniyah asked. The tension was so thick you could cut it with a knife.

"I never said that, Ma. It's just that the way things ended up in our last conversation, I didn't think you wanted anything to with me for a while," he said as he looked over at his mother.

"I apologize for ignoring your calls. I thought I could walk away from you, but I realized I could never just let you go how my mother did to me," she said as she took a seat at the kitchen table. "Besides I have a grandbaby on the way and I'll be damned if I miss out on that!"

"You're absolutely right about that!" Asia cut in on the heavy conversation. "For your information, Samir, your mom took me to my doctor's appointment and cooked me something to eat. She was taking care of me while you was out doing only God knows what," Asia explained.

"And for the both of y'all's information, while you jumping at me, I was in the studio. I had to meet my dad to meet his new artist."

Shaniyah was shocked when Li'l Samir blurted out that he'd been with his dad. He'd finally admitted to it. The house went quiet for what seemed like hours. He didn't know if his mom would faint, beat the mess out of him, or disappear for a few months again.

"So you finally admit to hanging out with your dad? How long have you been rollin' wit' his no-good ass?" You could almost hear Shaniyah's heartbeat. "Unbelievable. You are going to end up just like him," Shaniyah said with tears in her eyes.

"Mom, there is nothing wrong with me spending time with him. It just sort of happened. He really misses you. He didn't mean to hurt you, but you have to realize that he is my father. Please don't make a big deal out of this. He really wants to make things right between y'all."

"I don't want to hear shit about him. And I don't want you around him. I'm the one who raised you and took care of you, not him. He was locked up, remember?"

"You did a good job raising me, Ma. But I still deserve the chance to get to know my father. You right. I'm just like him and I can respect that. But, you have to understand he tryin' to change. He doing music now and we gon' make it. Matter of fact we have made it. And little do you know he quit the streets and did it for you!"

Asia didn't know what to do. So, she just listened to Li'l Samir and his mother go at it back and forth about Big Samir. She was definitely not getting in the middle of this one.

"Well, it's a day late and a dollar short. I didn't ask him to change for me now! He should have changed a long time ago. Mark my words, son, he is bad news and you shouldn't be anywhere near him!" Shaniyah was so angry she got her things and stormed out of the door.

Li'l Samir felt bad for his mom. He wished that she would at least give him and his dad a chance to prove they could do something good. Something that didn't involve anything illegal. Truth be told, Shaniyah was still in love with Big Samir, but she was too afraid to admit it. And, as far as she was concerned, she didn't want any more downfalls in her life.

Li'l Samir sat next to Asia with his face in his hands. He didn't think speaking the truth would upset her as much as it did. Now he wondered if she would stop talking to him again. He loved his mother and had missed her terribly these past months that they hadn't talked. And, honestly, she was the one who had been there for him since day one. He just wished he could get out of New York with his family. Everything would be okay and he knew just the person to call.

"Hey. What's up, Dad?"

"Nothing much, wassup?"

"I got home and Ma was here with Asia. We got into it because I accidently told her that we been kicking it. Now she's pissed at me."

Li'l Samir told his father the whole story. He really wanted his dad to figure out how to make things right with his mother. It was either now or never.

"Man, I'll talk to her, but shit, she'll probably try to kill my ass, man. I know shit gotta change though. And, to be honest, I can't see her with nobody else."

"Well, you gotta do what you gotta do. I'll probably head over to her house tomorrow after she cool off, man."

"Well, I'm about to go handle some business. I'll catch up with you later."

"A'ight, Pops. Oh, man, have you heard anything from D-Money?"

"Hell naw, that nigga MIA. He betta hope the cops catch him before I do. I gotta keep an eye out for that nigga 'cause he might try to retaliate on some sneak shit."

"Damn straight. I'ma keep an eye out too. A'ight, I'll holla. Later, Pops."

"A'ight, man."

Li'l Samir spent the rest of his day at the crib with Asia trying to figure out his next move. Time was slippin' away and he knew he had to have everything figured out before Asia had the baby.

The next day Li'l Samir headed to his mother's house in hopes that he could talk to her. He knew she was off because she never worked Sundays. He didn't bother knocking at the door. Instead, he used his key. He looked around at the quiet house, because it appeared as if she wasn't home. Li'l Samir headed to his mother's bedroom and opened the door. He couldn't believe his eyes. His mother was laid up in the bed with some thug-looking nigga. Li'l Samir was so angry, without even thinking he attacked the dude. His mother could barely get Li'l Samir off of him.

Li'l Samir stormed out of the room. Shaniyah threw her robe on and ran after him.

"What the hell are you doing just walking up in my house?" Shaniyah said angrily.

"Sorry, Mom. I came here to talk about what happened at my house yesterday. I didn't know you was gon' be in here fucking like some young slut," Li'l Samir said sarcastically.

"Oh, so you wanna talk to me like we're on the same level? Have it your way, Samir." She said as she tightened her robe, "First off, I am a grown-ass single woman and I can do what and whoever I want. And last time I checked I was your mother, not the other way around. I don't say shit about what you do in the street so don't even come at me with no bullshit."

"Man, whateva. I don't wanna hear that shit. I want that nigga out of here."

The thug-looking dude exited the bedroom and stood beside Shaniyah.

"Mothafucka don't you ever try to jump on me again. It's obvious you don't know me, young blood. I'll fuck yo' shit up. You just lucky you Shaniyah's son or I woulda bust a cap in yo' ass."

"You bitch-ass nigga. You wouldn't have done shit. Like I said, I want you the fuck out of here."

"If Shaniyah ain't got a problem then I don't think you got shit to say."

"You don't have to go nowhere, Derrick. This is my house," Shaniyah said.

"We'll see about that," Li'l Samir said leaving and slamming the door.

Shaniyah was so annoyed by her son's actions, but that didn't stop her from doing what she wanted to do. She was his mother; he wasn't hers.

Li'l Samir was so mad, he could spit fire. He wasted no time calling his father and telling him the news. Li'l Samir's father was even angrier. He was more than ready to move that nigga out to get back with Shaniyah. It was definitely time for a change.

"Man, I know that mothafucka from somewhere. I just can't put my hands on it," Li'l Samir said to his father.

"And you said his name was Derrick?" Big Samir asked.

"Yeah, man. I gotta do a background check on this nigga for real. Man, I know his ass ain't right. If he don't be gone the next time I pay my mother a visit, I'm gon' straight cap his ass no matter what."

Something is up for real and, if I ain't mistaken, D-Money had a nigga in his crew name Derrick. I'ma head on over there and handle this shit myself."

Li'l Samir was riding around the hood, talking to his father on the phone when he heard his song play on the radio. It was like everything his father was talking about was bouncing off the top of his head.

"Yo, Pops, turn on the radio, man!" Li'l Samir was so excited he could barely get the words out.

"Nigga, how you gon' interrupt my conversation like that?"

"My bad, man. Just turn on the fuckin' radio."

Big Samir was even more excited than his son when he heard their song playing on the radio. They knew they were in big business.

Chapter 11

So much had happened in the past month. Li'l Samir was happy and down at the same time. He had been working mad hard in the studio. Jealousy was creeping through New York fast as ever and the ladies were offering their bodies on every end, but Li'l Samir remained focused on his work. He had just done the video for his song "I Am My Father's Son," which quickly moved to the top of the charts. He had received contracts for several endorsement deals. The money was definitely no problem for Li'l Samir. More importantly, he and his dad had finally quit doing illegal business. And, they were able to live their dream. The last thing to make it complete was handling D-Money. Then they would leave New York and build their empire in Atlanta.

Li'l Samir was in the studio going over a couple of tracks with his father. His album would be released in a month, which was also Asia's due date. The people couldn't wait. Li'l Samir had all the tracks he needed, but he still spent most of his time in the studio. He was working on a song with his father that he knew would be hot. Li'l Samir and his father were in the studio recording their song titled "New York's Most Wanted." They both threw a hot beat together and got in the booth. Li'l Samir rapped:

> *Danger, mothafucka, it's real in these streets*
> *It would take a whole army to get rid of a nigga like me*
> *Since I was a li'l man I knew I was a gangsta*
> *Grew up in NY and started pushin' for chump change wit' gangbangas*
> *Neva knew my pops until he got out of jail*
> *Two hustlas on the block openin' the gates of hell*
> *I blew off my old crew and told 'em I'll catch ya lata*
> *Started rollin' wit' my pops makin' maja paper*
> *Jealous mothafuckas started tryin'a take ova da block*
> *Couldn't trust no nigga so I held on to my Glock*

Then my baby girl tells me I done planted my seed
  I knew then I had to get outta the streets
  Me and Pops stacked that dough, laid low, and hit the studio
  Robbed the biggest niggas in the streets tryin'a stop our flow
  The main nigga got away, but we got our eyes on ya
  Come out to play D-Money so I can drop that nine on ya

The hook was:

  It's hard in these streets
  Gotta make that paper, man
  It's hard in these streets
  Gotta make that paper, man
  New York's most wanted
  Everything we on it
  Gat fully loaded
  Got a limp in my walk when I tote it
  It's hard in these streets, man
  New York's most wanted

Big Samir rapped:

  Yeah, it's me, mothafucka, fresh out the pen

It's amazin' my worst enemy was my best friend

I got locked up, lost my girl and my son

Got out, stacked paper, reunited with my fam, and I'm still numba one

D-Money what, nigga? You thought you brought me down

You think you king well I got hollows that will knock off yo' whole crown

I know you didn't think you would last forever

That was a magical moment, you takin' ova is like neva

And if you try I'll be back to jack ya shit again

Step up in ya operation screamin', "Say hello to my li'l friend"

I know y'all jealous, mothafucka. I can see the envy in yo' eyes

I was gone for a minute, but came back and took ya pride

I'm the kingpin of these mothafuckin' streets

And my mini me is the king of holdin' the heat

D, if you want it wit' me come out and play

'Cause I would love to shoot the shells wit' yo' bitch ass all day

Li'l Samir and his father were all up into their new song, and they couldn't wait to blast it through the hood. And they did. Shit got around on the block in no time and D-Money was sure to get the message. The Samirs were getting mighty brave with taking their music to another level. But they didn't care because this situation was beyond music.

Big Samir felt good about how things were going. He'd finally quit the drug game, he and his son were the best of friends, and he had a grandchild on the way. Despite all that though, his life didn't feel complete. He still hadn't talked to Shaniyah to try to mend things with her. He knew from talking with Li'l Samir that she was still carrying a lot of hurt and anger from what had gone down between them; but he also knew he needed to talk to her and see her himself.

According to Li'l Samir, she was still seeing this guy Derrick. Li'l Samir was pretty pissed about it and he wasn't talking with his mom anymore. The only reason he knew Shaniyah was still seeing the guy was because she and Asia talked almost every day.

Big Samir woke up that morning and decided he couldn't put things off between him and her any longer. He wasn't expecting her to get back with him, but he was at least hoping that they could have a conversation. He knew it was now or never, while his adrenaline was flowing. He had sent a message to Li'l Samir that he was going to visit his mother and Li'l Samir wished him good luck. *I'm gonna need it.*

Big Samir headed straight to Shaniyah's place ready for a much-anticipated conversation. He was nervous as ever when the elevator door opened and he stepped off heading toward her apartment. Samir was about to knock on the door when he noticed it was slightly open. He called out her name but there was no answer. *Maybe she stepped out and forgot to lock the door behind her.* He was about to walk back toward the elevator when he heard a faint sound coming from inside the apartment. If he wasn't mistaken it sounded like moaning. *What if she's in there fucking that Derrick nigga?* The thought made his blood boil. He followed the noise down the hallway. He could hear Shaniyah's moans coming from behind a door that he assumed led to her bedroom. He wasted no time bursting the door open.

He couldn't believe his eyes. Shaniyah was laid out in the floor. The words PAYBACK IS A BITCH were written in lipstick across her mirror. Big Samir knelt down and picked up Shaniyah's limp body. She was bleeding from mouth and nose and she had bruises all over. He rushed her to his Escalade and rushed her to the nearest hospital. Once hospital attendants had rushed Shaniyah into a trauma room, he managed to call Li'l Samir from the waiting room to tell him the news.

Li'l Samir was so nervous he could barely drive. He parked his car and flew through the hospital doors. Asia was trying her best to keep up with Li'l Samir, but her big belly was weighing her down. They finally made it to the waiting area where Li'l Samir was greeted by his father.

"Man, what did the doctors say?" Li'l Samir said in tears.

"Nothing yet, man. They been back there with her for a minute. I'm starting to get impatient. I can't take this shit. I know D-Money has something to do with this," Big Samir said as he paced the floor.

"I know, man. We gon' get them mothafuckas. No matter what," Li'l Samir chimed in.

"I know y'all are not about to go out there and do nothing stupid. That's the reason we in this mess now, Samir. I can't handle something happening to you, and you know we have a son on the way. Is this the lifestyle you want for him?" Asia asked, worried.

"Stay the out of this, Asia! Ain't nothing else happening to nobody so just shut up! I gotta do what I got to do," Li'l Samir said angrily.

Asia rolled her eyes, as she walked over to the other side of the waiting area. Her hands and everything else were shaking. This stress was too much for a pregnant woman and Asia was about to lose control.

Li'l Samir noticed how bad she was shaking, so he walked over to her and wrapped his arms around her. "Everything is going to be all right, Asia. I ain't letting nothing happen to you or my child. I promise."

Asia was crying uncontrollably, when the doctor came out to greet them. "Shaniyah was barely conscious when she first got here, but she is going to pull through. She has some serious bruising and we have her on pain medication right now so we're going to keep her here overnight for observation. She is very weak at this time, but you all are welcome to go in and see her."

Li'l Samir was even more hurt when he saw how badly his mother had been beaten. He knew that he had to get D-Money for pulling some shit like this. Li'l Samir looked over at his father who was in tears and thinking the same thing.

After hours of heartache and trying to figure out his next move, Li'l Samir and Asia left the hospital. Big Samir continued to stay by Shaniyah's side. He wanted to be the first person she would wake up to. He had a lot on his mind. He wanted to tell her exactly how he felt before he went on his mission to handle D-Money and Derrick for what they had done.

Li'l Samir dropped Asia off at their crib. He knew he should have waited on his father to make a move on D-Money and Derrick, but he was too angry and couldn't wait. Li'l Samir instructed Asia to go in the house and lock the door. He promised to return. Asia was so afraid of what Li'l Samir might do, but she knew better than to speak on the situation again, so she went in the house and did what she was told.

Li'l Samir went cruising around the block trying to think of where D-Money might be hiding out, but he came up short. He was mad as hell. He made a couple of stops, asking dudes on the block if they had heard anything from D-Money, and to send word that he was looking for him. Li'l Samir got so caught up in his anger that he was going to niggas' spots, threatening them if they didn't give up any information. He was really losing it.

He didn't get home until around one o'clock in the morning. Asia was in bed sound asleep. He kissed her on her forehead and headed for the shower. Li'l Samir was nowhere near tired so he plopped down on the sofa and flipped through the channels on his big-screen TV.

Two hours later, Li'l Samir had dozed off and woke up his phone going off.

"Hello," Li'l Samir answered with a raspy voice.

"Wassup, bitch? Heard you was looking for me."

"Bitch, I'ma fuck you up! Stop hidin', mothafucka. Tell me where you at?"

"Don't worry, li'l homie. You'll find me when the time is right. Payback is a bitch," D-Money said before hanging up the phone.

That was the last straw. Li'l Samir knew he had to do what he had to do. He knew at that moment D-Money had to die. He couldn't risk his family being in danger. His mother had already been hurt. He couldn't let anything happen to Asia and the baby.

By this time D-Money had called two of his cousins from North Carolina, and told them everything that had gone down with him in New York. His cousins, Loco and Tyreek, wasted no time coming to rescue D-Money. They formed a plan to hit Li'l Samir and his father where it would hurt the most, and it was perfect. They wanted to take things slow and let everything cool off. D-Money would make his move when Li'l Samir thought everything was good, and after Li'l Samir's baby was born. That would be the best time to move in on them.

In the meantime, D-Money went back to North Carolina with Loco and Tyreek for a couple of weeks to regroup. Loco stayed on the same block as Tyreek with his girl, Monique. Tyreek stayed alone, so he volunteered to let D-Money shack up with him. The cousins were both small-time drug dealers, but they made a decent living.

D-Money was cruising around with his cousin, Tyreek. Tyreek wanted to show D-Money a good time, so he took him to a club called Club Passion. Club Passion was a local club where all the ballers and fine women hung out. D-Money and Tyreek were high as a kite when they entered the club.

Angel, the finest stripper in the club, noticed D-Money and Tyreek at the bar. She was a smart girl trying to make her way through college. Living alone with no family, she had to do what she had to do to pay for school. So her girl Nikki turned her on to the strip club. She hated the job, and couldn't wait to finish medical school. She had just finished giving a lap dance. But, before she could make her way over to D-Money, she was summoned by another club patron. Angel instantly became attracted to D-Money when she saw him come through the door.

D-Money was sitting at the bar with Tyreek blowed as hell. He couldn't keep his eyes off the chinky-eyed Puerto Rican chick who kept looking his way.

"Yo, Ty, man, who dat chick who keep looking at me?" D-Money said curiously.

"Who, man? I know you ain't talkin' 'bout that ho, Angel. She a stripper here at the club. She think she betta than half the chicks up in here 'cause she in college. She still a ho, though," Tyreek said laughing.

"Damn, man. What's yo' beef with the chick?"

"Dat li'l stuck-up bitch act like she can't give a nigga no play. She just a li'l strip ho anyway. Don't even waste yo' time with the li'l sack chaser."

"Man, you trippin'. You just ain't got no game. Watch and learn, my nigga," D-Money said jumping off the barstool.

Angel was giving an ol' head a lap dance, taking all of the man's money when she noticed D-Money heading her way. She tried to act like she didn't see him, as he made his way over to the table beside where she was dancing.

"Why you wastin' yo' time with this ol' mothafucka when you can be givin' a fine nigga like me a lap dance?" D-Money said.

"Who da fuck you calling a ol' mothafucka, nigga?" the dude said standing up.

D-Money pulled out his piece and aimed right at the dude's forehead. "I called you an ol' mothafucka. Now sit the fuck down and mind yo' business, mothafucka."

"A'ight, man, you can have the trick. I don't mind keepin' my money in my pocket."

D-Money laughed at the punk and pulled Angel to an empty table. "Now give me my lap dance," he demanded.

You'd think seeing a man pull a gun on somebody would scare Angel away but that's not at all how things went down. Angel was so turned on by D-Money's look and bravery that she did what she was told. She'd never enjoyed giving lap dances, let alone had she gotten horny off of them, but D-Money had her mind gone.

D-Money slid Angel's thong to the side and slid his fingers inside her wetness. Angel didn't even put up a fight.

"You know, you're not supposed to touch the dancers," said Angel as she licked her lips.

"Do you want me to stop?" D-Money asked knowing she didn't want him to.

"No, baby, please don't."

D-Money had Angel in another world as she ground on his fingers to T-Pain's cut "I'm in Love with a Stripper." D-Money was horny as hell with how wet Angel's pussy was. He pulled out his fingers and quickly poked his dick through the zipper of his pants. He shoved Angel down on his rock-hard shaft.

"Damn, baby, that feels so good!" Angel screamed as a couple of people looked in their direction.

D-Money gave them a look that said, "Mind your fuckin' business," and they all turned back around. Angel was riding D-Money real slow to the music. D-Money started playing with her clit as she moved her body in sync with the music. Angel's moans grew louder. For a moment, she felt like they were the only two in the club.

Tyreek took notice of what was going on and screamed to them, "That's my nigga. Handle yours, cuz!" D-Money waved him on as he continued to play with Angel's clit.

Angel had never taken a risk like this before especially at her job. She increased her speed until she reached her climax. She could feel D-Money's breath on her neck as he came inside her. They both got up and laughed like nothing happened. D-Money whipped out five grand and placed it in her thong.

D-Money headed back to the bar with Tyreek. He could tell by the look in Angel's eyes that she was whipped. He knew that she would be back, so he played it off like he wasn't even thinking about her anymore.

"Damn, man. How you pull that off, my nigga?" Tyreek said with excitement.

"I told you, you ain't got no game. I betcha she be back over here in five minutes."

"Make that five seconds," Tyreek said as they both turned their heads and noticed Angel making her way over to D-Money.

"So what's up wit' you? Can we talk in private?" Angel said.

"Man, he gon' tell me what y'all talked about anyway," Tyreek said heading toward the dance floor.

"So what's up? What you wanna talk about?" D-Money said.

"You. I know you thinkin' I do what I did to you often, but that's not true. For some crazy reason, I'm just attracted to you. I know you probably got a girl, and you probably think I'm a ho because I work in a strip club, and we just sexed at first sight. But, truth is, I'm just tryin'a pay my way through school."

"Slow the fuck down. Ain't nobody said you was no ho. But it is hard to take a stripper seriously. I'm just keeping it real. I don't have a girl and if I did I wouldn't want her working in no strip club," D-Money said.

Angel lowered her head in guilt. "I figured that," Angel said while getting ready to walk off.

D-Money pulled her back toward the bar. "Maybe that's why you should quit and come back with me to New York."

Angel was totally amazed by D-Money's boldness. "But I can't quit school and just come with you. I don't even know you."

"Well, let's head back to my cousin's crib and I'll tell you all about me."

Tyreek left the dance floor and made his way back to the bar where he noticed D-Money getting ready to leave with Angel. "Man, where you going?" Tyreek asked.

"She gon' take me back to your crib."

"A'ight, man, don't wait up for me. I might get a room with Candy," Tyreek said grinning.

"Who da fuck is Candy?" D-Money asked.

"That li'l thick stripper back there with the pink on. Man, she said she gon' give me a private dance."

D-Money laughed. "A'ight, man. I'll holla."

D-Money and Angel headed to Tyreek's crib. They talked into the night as he told Angel everything he had gone through with Li'l Samir and his father. This didn't scare Angel. If anything, it just turned her on more. And just like that, she had fallen so deep for D-Money that he knew that she wanted to stay by his side no matter what, even if she had to quit school.

Angel and D-Money were having a nice conversation, getting to know each other while listening to the radio. D-Money leaned over and started tonguing Angel down when Samir's song "New York's Most Wanted," started playing through the stereo. Angel popped up and started dancing. "That is my song!"

D-Money grabbed her by the arm and slung her on the couch. "Nigga, what the fuck is wrong with you?" Angel said confused.

D-Money realized the whole time he was telling Angel what happened to him in New York, he didn't mention the names of the ones who had caused him so much trouble, or the fact that they had made a song threatening him. D-Money became angrier and angrier as he heard the words.

Angel was still trying to figure out what was wrong with D-Money. He looked as if he was in another world. Then she heard the words to the song: "D-Money what, nigga you thought you had brought me down/ you think you king well I got hollows that will knock off ya whole crown."

Angel's mouth dropped to the floor. She started putting two and two together. "Oh, my God, D. I didn't even know. You should have said something," Angel said.

"It's all good. Me and Tyreek got the perfect plan for his ass. Soon as his bitch have her baby."

"I hope y'all ain't gonna do nothing stupid."

Anger filled D-Money's eyes. "What the fuck you mean you hope we don't do nothin' stupid? This mothafucka tryin'a ruin me. Eitha you gon' be down with me or you can take yo' Puerto Rican ass back to the strip club."

Angel could tell D-Money was upset. She stood in front of D-Money and kissed him all over his face. Then she unzipped his pants and took his mind off of all his problems.

Chapter 12

Shaniyah was finally released from the hospital about a week after she woke up with Big Samir right by her side. She looked at him with no words. She wanted to curse him out, but she declined the idea.

"What are you doing here?" Shaniyah asked.

"I couldn't leave your side. Don't worry. I'ma get that nigga for what he did to you. I promise you that."

"See, that's why we never made it, because you couldn't leave the drugs and street life alone. After all that we have been through you still haven't learned a thing."

"I'm sorry for everything I put you through. I know I was dead wrong for keeping secrets from you, but I was only trying to protect you."

"Protect me? Because of your bad and stupid decisions, you got locked up. And, I had to take care of Li'l Samir alone. You promised me that you were done with selling drugs and yet you were still doing it behind my back. I believed you when you said you'd stopped everything. I thought we would get married and live happily ever after, but that all came crashing down when your ass got locked up. I haven't even seen you in close to twenty years and when I finally do it's because you got me caught up in some shit again. And if I got dragged into this without me even talking to you, I know you got our son Li'l Samir caught up even worse than me!"

Big Samir sighed. "I know. I beat myself up every day for the pain I caused you and Li'l Samir. I can't say I am sorry enough. I don't know why I keep messin' up. I want badly to do right. That's why I'm pushing so hard. I love you and Li'l Samir more than anything. I am not giving up on us. I know you are mad, but I am going to win your heart back."

"It's not about winning my heart back, Samir. You will always have my heart. I have always loved you. But I forced myself to get over you because I was sure that our fairy tale was over. Then, when I heard you were out of prison I continued to try to keep you out of mind out of fear that I would hear about you being killed in the streets."

"Shaniyah, I'm not trying to come into your life to ruin you. I am only working on the music business right now. I'm done selling drugs. You can ask Li'l Samir if you don't believe me. I gave it up because I want to do right by you. I can't be without you. I need you."

"How can I be with you? Whatever mess you and Li'l Samir have gotten yourselves into has resulted in me being in the hospital. There is no telling what will happen next. I just can't go down that road with you. You have put both me and Li'l Samir in danger."

"Give me a chance to make it right. I will handle this. Nothing will happen to Li'l Samir. I'll make sure of that. He is a man now. He needs to know what it means to defend himself as a man and protect his family at all costs. I am no longer selling, but I refuse to let D-Money go after what he has done to you. I'm sorry, but I'll never forget the night you came to my house hysterical after what happened at your mother's house. I promised I would never let anyone hurt you again. I broke my promise, but I'm gonna make it right."

Shaniyah hated hearing about the night she was attacked and raped. That was something she had put away from her mind forever. It was hard to fathom all that she suffered on that night. As Shaniyah thought back on that night, she could vividly remember how Samir took care of her. Though he was rough around the edges he had always been there for her. He took her away from the pain that she lived in at home with her mom. That alone was enough for her to realize Samir was like the air that she breathed.

For a long time she had felt suffocated by the fact that while locked up Samir would no longer be in her presence. And it killed her inside. But now he was right there standing before her once again. There was no denying that no one had ever taken care of her the way that Samir had. With all the heat that was coming Samir's way she knew that giving him a second chance would be a huge risk. But for once it was time that she be there for him the way that he had been for her.

"Samir, you have always been here for me. We were both young, but even still you protected me. No one is perfect, but you are perfect for me. Please promise me you are done with dealing drugs."

"Baby, I promise you that I am done with that. Shaniyah, I love you. I want us to be together, but I can't promise you that I am not going after D-Money. I have to because if I don't he will come for us. I can't sit back and do nothing. You have to understand that this is something that has to be done or I could lose one of you for good."

"Samir, are you sure getting rid of him is the only way? Can't we just go to the cops?"

"If we go to the cops it will be a waste of time. What would we prove? It could also cause heat to fall on me and Li'l Samir. We have to put an end to D-Money. It is the only way."

Shaniyah sighed. "I can't believe I am saying this. But if it will keep us safe then I guess you have to do what you have to do."

Big Samir stood up and hugged Shaniyah and whispered, "Baby, everything will be all right. Let me and Li'l Samir worry about D-Money. In the meantime, we have a lot of catching up to do." Big Samir leaned in and planted a soft, wet kiss on Shaniyah's lips. Then Big Samir said, "I loved you before and I love you now. I never stopped loving you and I never will stop loving you."

Just then their son along with Asia walked in the door. They were so happy to see that everybody was finally in accord.

Shaniyah was released from the hospital with Big Samir, their son, and Asia right by her side. At home, Samir and his father waited on Shaniyah hand and foot. When they had to work on their music, interviews, and everything else, Asia would stay with Shaniyah. Everything seemed to be back to normal with no sign of

D-Money. But, both Samirs continued to look for him.

Big Samir spent all day looking around New York for clues as to where D-Money might be. Nobody in the hood was talking. It frustrated him that he didn't know where he was. He decided to go back home and spend quality time with Shaniyah. On the way home, he stopped to pick her up a dozen roses. He was glad that Shaniyah was getting better. He hadn't been with her intimately since before he went to prison.

When he got home he found Shaniyah lying on the couch watching TV. He walked over to her with a huge smile on his face. She looked just as beautiful as when they were teenagers. He walked over to her and handed her the roses.

"These are for you, beautiful."

Shaniyah took the roses and stood up to kiss Big Samir. "Thank you. What have I done to deserve this?"

"You keep loving me even when I don't deserve your love."

"I'll always love you. You are my first love and my everything."

Big Samir looked into Shaniyah's eyes. After all those years they were still madly in love with one another. There bond was undeniably sealed for a lifetime.

"Baby, where is Li'l Samir and Asia?"

"Li'l Samir and Asia have been relieved of their babysitting duties," he said taking a seat on the couch next to Shaniyah. "They're out on a romantic date."

"So that means we have the place to ourselves."

Big Samir wrapped his hands around Shaniyah's waist pulling her closer to him. Just being so close to her aroused him. They kissed with such hunger wanting more of the other. Shaniyah grabbed a hold of Big Samir's hand and led him into their bedroom.

Shaniyah helped Big Samir out of his shirt. After they had fully undressed one another, they stood admiring each other's physique. Big Samir zoned in on her beautiful, perky breasts. They fell back onto the bed. Big Samir flipped Shaniyah onto her stomach. He grabbed some massage oil off the dresser. The feeling of his hands caressing her thighs made her moan in approval. He massaged his way up to her soft, plump ass. He continued to caress her body until he craved to be inside her pussy. Shaniyah stayed in position on her stomach. She opened her legs wide as he pushed his long, thick dick inch by inch into her soaking wet pussy. His pelvis slapped against her ass with each thrust. She screamed his name in pleasure. She tightened her walls around his dick making him groan loudly.

Big Samir pulled out and turned Shaniyah onto her back. He climbed on top of her, but she wanted control. She rolled over on top of him and turned around. Big Samir enjoyed the view of her ass as she rode him backward. The headboard banged against the wall as Shaniyah bounced her ass up and down on his dick. The sounds of moaning and Big Samir's dick pounding into Shaniyah's wet pussy echoed through the room. Shaniyah felt herself about to climax as she reached between her legs and massaged Samir's balls. Shaniyah came all over Big Samir's dick as he erupted inside of her.

Shaniyah eased off of Big Samir. Then snuggled up beside him.

"Damn, baby. You got me all messed up now."

Shaniyah laughed. "Well, I'm not the same little inexperienced girl you grew up with."

"You have definitely developed into a full-grown woman."

"I really hope we'll be okay. I wouldn't be able to stand losing you again."

"Baby girl, don't think about that. Let's just enjoy the rest of the night. When I am with you everything is all right."

"I still think you look like Morris Chestnut." Shaniyah giggled.

"Shut up. I don't look like that dude."

"I love you, Samir."

"I love you too, baby."

Li'l and Big Samir had just come from the studio. They were so happy with the surprise they had planned for Asia and Shaniyah. Shaniyah was doing well. She was back on her feet and cooking a huge dinner for her family when Li'l Samir and his father rushed into the house. Li'l Samir grabbed Asia by the hand while his father grabbed Shaniyah.

"What are y'all fools doin'?" Shaniyah said.

"Ma, just be quiet damn," Li'l Samir blurted out.

"Boy, have you lost your mind talking to me like that? You may be grown, but I am still your mother."

"She's back to normal," Samir said making everybody laugh.

"Asia, you know I love you with all my heart. I would never do anything to hurt you and I promise to always protect you," Li'l Samir said after getting on one knee then looking at his father.

Big Samir stood in front of Shaniyah and got down on one knee. "And, Shaniyah, you know that I have always loved you. I promise to always be honest with you and never leave your side again. I want you to be mine forever," Big Samir said.

"Will you marry me?" Big Samir and his son said in unison.

Shaniyah and Asia both started crying as they said yes and hugged their future husbands.

"All right, let's pack this shit up and be out," Big Samir said excited.

Asia and Shaniyah looked at each other puzzled as Big Samir and his son ran out the door. They came back in with big boxes packing up everything that looked valuable to Shaniyah.

"What the hell are y'all doin' with my stuff?" Shaniyah said confused.

"You and Asia staying at my crib until we can end this shit wit D-Money," Big Samir said.

"That's right," Li'l Samir said in agreement. "Asia, I packed up your stuff from our house too."

"How y'all gon' just move us out without our consent?" Asia said.

"Look it ain't safe here. Y'all will be safer at Pop's crib. There y'all will have security and everything. Plus, y'all get to see us in the studio," Li'l Samir said.

Shaniyah smiled and said, "Sounds good to me."

Li'l Samir and his father moved Shaniyah and Asia into Big Samir's house. They seemed comfortable and content. And, so far neither Li'l Samir or his father had any word on D-Money.

Big Samir was following his son in their Escalades to a spot around the block, when he spotted Derrick coming out of a corner store with a forty in his hand. Big Samir called Li'l Samir on his cell.

"Yeah, what up?"

"Look to your left at the corner store," Big Samir said.

"Bingo!"

Li'l Samir wasted no time pulling his Cadillac Escalade to the side and pulling a ski mask over his face. He had been keeping a ski mask within arm's reach just in case anything popped off in broad daylight. His father followed right behind him. Derrick was so busy drinking his forty, he didn't notice Li'l Samir and his father come up. That was until Li'l Samir banged him with the butt of his pistol. Big Samir dragged Derrick a few feet down the block and threw him in the back of his truck. The father-and-son team got back in their vehicles and headed to find a dark alley to handle their business.

Big Samir threw Derrick out of the truck onto the cold asphalt and poured the remainder of the forty in his face. Derrick looked up with fear in his eyes.

"Man, what the fuck you want from me?"

"Why the fuck did you beat my mother and leave her in the house? That's my first question, bitch," Li'l Samir said with his gun pointing in Derrick's face.

"I didn't do it, man. I was just told to pretend I wanted to be with her. I didn't beat her, man. Please don't kill me!"

"Who told you to do this shit?" Big Samir asked already knowing the answer to his question.

"D-Money, but you already know that, man."

"Oh, so you know that makes you a part of this shit, right?" Big Samir said stomping him.

"Come on, man, I had to do it or he would have killed me. At first I was just supposed to sleep with her and find out what I could about you two; but, when he called, he said he had a new plan. That's when he came over and jumped on her. I didn't know what to do so I ran. I was nervous, man. I didn't know he was gon' do that to her. I swear."

"Nah, fuck that shit, nigga. Where's D-Money? You was a part of this shit so don't give me that 'I don't know' bullshit. Where he at? Tell me or swallow one, nigga," Li'l Samir said angrily. Li'l Samir cocked his gat and waited for Derrick to answer.

"I don't know where he at, man."

Li'l Samir put his gun in his pants and pulled Derrick up. He repeatedly punched Derrick in his face causing blood to splatter everywhere. Big Samir kept the gun aimed and laughed.

"Now I'ma ask you again; where the fuck is D-Money? That nigga ain't here to save you now so you may as well tell me," Li'l Samir said.

"I said I don't know, man."

"Li'l Samir, get back." Big Samir pushed his son back and shot Derrick in his knee.

"Ahh! Fuck, man! Why y'all doin this?" Derrick screamed in agony.

Li'l Samir laughed.

"Next time you won't be so lucky," said Big Samir while putting his gun up to Derrick's head.

"A'ight, man! He was with his cousin in North Carolina. He told me to keep a lookout for y'all while he was gone, but I didn't listen. I didn't want to be a part of this anymore. Last I heard he back and he staying in Brooklyn in his dead cousin Tray ol' crib with some chick named Angel."

"Damn. Why the fuck didn't I think to look there?" Li'l Samir said to his father.

Derrick said, trying to spare his own life, "Y'all niggas don't know who y'all dealin' wit', man. Y'all just need to make things right with D-Money man for real. I think he got something real good planned for y'all. All I got to say is you betta watch out for y'all's family."

"Man, fuck you. D-Money don't know who the fuck he dealin' wit', so I guess I got to make an example out of you then, huh?" Li'l' Samir said then unloaded the clip on Derrick.

Li'l Samir and his father bagged up Derrick's body and threw him in Big Samir's trunk. They both jumped in their rides and headed to Brooklyn.

When they reached Tray's old crib where D-Money was supposed to be, they parked on the opposite side of the street and Li'l Samir jumped out of his car. He told his father to stay in his ride and look out.

"Hell naw, nigga! You ain't gon' in there by yourself."

"Man, I got this, trust me. Just watch my back," Li'l Samir said as he headed to the house. He knocked on the door and waited for somebody to open it. He pulled his ski mask back over his face and pulled out his gun.

"Who is it?" a female's voice asked.

"It's Derrick," said Li'l Samir.

When the door swung open, Samir burst the door open and closed the door behind him aiming the gun at the girl.

"You must be Angel," Li'l Samir said. "Where the fuck is D-Money?"

"He in the back, so you better leave now," Angel said.

Li'l Samir grabbed Angel by the hair with the gun at her head and searched the house for D-Money. D-Money was nowhere to be found.

"Where the fuck D-Money at, bitch? And if you lie this time I'ma put a bullet in your throat."

"He not here! He went back to North Carolina with his cousins to take care of some business," Angel said shaking and crying.

"Is that right? He probably planning on doing something to me and my family, but that shit ain't happening."

Li'l Samir opened the door and pulled Angel out with him. He threw her in the back seat and drove up right behind his father.

"Pops, go in the house and take Derrick's body inside. Then take him out of the bag and make it look real pretty in there," Li'l Samir said.

Angel started screaming and hitting Li'l Samir in the back of the head. He turned around and slapped her with his gun, knocking her out cold. Big Samir laughed and went to decorate D-Money's house with Derrick's body.

Inside the house, he had Derrick seated with his back turned to the door and a note in his lap. Big Samir was pleased with his work. He walked back to his truck proudly and the duo drove off together, heading back to his crib.

Chapter 13

Li'l Samir and his father burst in the door with Angel over Li'l Samir's shoulders. Asia and Shaniyah gave Li'l Samir a startled look.

Asia stood up ready to fight. "Who the fuck is that bitch?"

"Man, shut up. It's D-Money girl. We still can't find him so we'll make him come to us," Li'l Samir said.

"Have y'all lost y'all damn mind? This is going too far! Both of y'all are going to jail. Samir, baby, you're gonna mess up your music career," Shaniyah said crying.

"We ain't going to jail. After we find D-Money this will all be over so you two ladies are going to have to ride this out until then," Big Samir said.

Asia and Shaniyah both shook their heads in anger.

"Look, if we don't do this he gonna try to hurt all of us and I ain't having that. I love you both and we have to do what we have to do to survive," Big Samir said.

Li'l Samir threw Angel on the couch. She was still knocked out.

"What are we supposed do when she wakes up? There's got to be another way to handle this. Why can't we just move?" Asia said.

"Then he will find us and we'll always be running. He's not gonna stop until he finds us," Li'l Samir said. "So, please, just shut up and let me and Pops handle this," he continued as his frustrations began to show.

Angel started moving and her eyes opened. She wanted to scream, but Big Samir had taped her mouth shut.

"Well, well, the dead has risen," Li'l Samir said.

Asia and Shaniyah left the room disgusted.

"Now I'll take this tape off your mouth if you promise not to scream or try no funny shit. If you do, I will unload this clip on yo' ass like I did to Derrick. You got that, bitch?" Li'l Samir said then yanked the tape off Angel's mouth.

"Ouch! You bastard!" Angel yelled.

"What the fuck I say? You think I'm playin'?" Li'l Samir said.

Big Samir just sat on the couch. He chuckled as he flipped through the channels on his seventy-inch flat screen.

"Why are you doin' this to me?" Angel said.

"We ain't doin' nothin' to you, yet," Li'l Samir said with a smirk.

"Don't worry. D-Money will come for you. That's if he cares. Either way he gettin' murked," Big Samir said laughing.

"Fuck both of y'all. I hope D-Money kill all y'all includin' your dumb bitches."

Asia and Shaniyah both came back in the room when she said that. By this time Li'l Samir was ready to punch Angel dead in the face.

"Samir. No!" Asia yelled. "That's enough! I understand y'all beefin' with D-Money, but putting her through this is not necessary. And, lady, I understand you are terrified and upset, but calling us out of our names when we had nothing to do with this is also unnecessary."

"I agree. There has to be another way to get to D-Money without hurting this poor girl. I don't like this. Samir, you told me that you would change, but I am starting to regret forgiving you more and more. We could all go to prison on kidnapping charges if we get caught and it'd all be thanks to you. You need to let her go," Shaniyah said.

"Shaniyah, for once stop trying to run away every time some shit go down. Trust me, we have tried every way we can think of to get to D-Money. I don't want to have to do this. Yes, I fucked up. I should have never started this war, but now it's too late. We have no choice. Once this is over we can leave New York and put this all behind us. Can you at least ride it out until then?" Big Samir asked.

Shaniyah sighed. She turned and went back into the kitchen. The situation had Asia very upset and she was experiencing mild contractions. Li'l Samir was trying to calm her down when Angel tried to make a run for the door. Big Samir jumped up just in time before Angel could reach the knob. "I wouldn't try that if I were you," Big Samir said.

Angel was terrified. "Would y'all please let me go? I don't have anything to do with this!"

"I have had enough of you." Li'l Samir dragged Angel down the hall and threw her in the dark downstairs basement and locked the door.

D-Money was on his way back from North Carolina. He had been calling his house for over a week and Angel wasn't answering the phone. D-Money was almost at home. He had a gut feeling that something just wasn't right, so he called his cousin Tyreek.

"Hello," Tyreek answered sleepily.

"Man, something ain't right, man. You and Loco need to get over here, for real."

"What's the deal, man? How you know something's wrong when you ain't even home yet?" Tyreek questioned.

"I'm almost home, and Angel still ain't answerin' the phone. I bet Derrick been runnin' his fuckin' mouth. That nigga been actin' real funny lately. When I see him I'ma take his ass out."

"Well, me and Loco will be there by tomorrow morning. I told you not to trust that nigga or that ho-ass bitch Angel. She probably left yo' ass and came back to North Carolina. I'ma check the club before I head to you, my nigga," Tyreek said.

"Call me when you find out something," D-Money advised.

"A'ight, man," Loco responded.

D-Money pulled up in the front of Tray's crib. He had his Mercedes shipped to Tyreek and had he had driven Loco's BMW back to New York, just in case Li'l Samir and his father were looking for him.

When D-Money got inside the crib he saw Derrick sitting in front of the TV with his back turned toward the door. There was a foul smell that filled the house. It was so strong it almost knocked him down.

"Mothafucka what you doin' here and where is Angel?" D-Money said, pulling out his gun.

Derrick didn't say anything back. When D-Money looked down he saw blood all over the floor. He turned Derrick's chair around and saw the multiple shots on Derrick's body. He noticed the letter in his lap and started reading it.

What up, bitch. You finally decided to bring yo' ass home. Well, surprise! You should watch who you trust. It was so nice of Derrick to tell us where you were hidin' out and we were more than happy to show our appreciation. By the way, we got yo' bitch, so the best thing for you to do is call and let me know where you want to meet and settle this. If we don't hear from you soon, next time yo' bitch gon' be sitting in the chair. Until next time, my nigga. Better the cops find you than us.

D-Money tore the letter up in anger. "Derrick, you stupid bitch!" D-Money yelled. He knew Derrick was dead, but he was so angry he started kicking and unloading his clip on Derrick's rotting and stinking body.

Within a matter of minutes, D-Money heard the sirens in front of the house. He flew out the back door escaping the cops again. D-Money felt the world was closing in on him, but he refused to let Li'l Samir and his dad get the best of him.

Big Samir and his son had just come home from a video countdown show where they debuted their new video for the song "Stick 'Em Up." They were exhausted. Asia and Shaniyah were in the kitchen eating dinner. Big Samir sat at his usual spot on the couch and flipped through the channels.

"How was the show?" Shaniyah asked Big Samir.

"It was a'ight. My hand tired as hell from signing autographs. It was definitely a long four days."

"When is it going to air?" Asia asked.

"Sometime next week," Big Samir answered.

"Where D-Money girl at?" Li'l Samir asked.

"In the basement where you left her," Shaniyah said.

"Has she eaten anything?"

"Unless you fed her, naw. I ain't fixin' to go down there and y'all blame me if she run away," Shaniyah said.

Li'l Samir headed to the kitchen and fixed Angel a plate. He grabbed his gun and headed for the basement. The basement was stinking and Angel was knocked out. Li'l Samir threw water on her face and she woke up weak and looking half dead.

"Here, eat this," Li'l Samir said handing Angel the food.

The food was gone in no time. Li'l Samir looked at his prisoner and started to feel sorry for her. He passed her a cup of water and she gulped it down like a dog.

"Look, man, I'm sorry 'bout all of this, but I gotta do what I got to do."

"Why me? I haven't done anything to y'all. I mean why do you hate D so much? He a good person," Angel said almost unable to speak.

Li'l Samir looked at her like she was stupid. He began telling her everything about the real D-Money all the way back to when he left his dad hanging and took over his spot. Angel was speechless.

"I can't believe I fell for that nigga. Now he got me in this shit. I should be in med school right now. Now look at me," Angel said in tears.

"Well, look you don't have to die if you just follow my directions and don't try nothing funny."

"I promise I won't. If I get out of this I'm done with D-Money's ass for sure. I just want to go back home," Angel said sobbing.

Chapter 14

Asia woke up in the middle of the night in a puddle. Her stomach felt like it was in knots. The contractions were coming back to back. She screamed for Li'l Samir to wake up.

"Baby, what's wrong?"

"My water just broke. And, I am having contractions. Get me to the hospital, now!"

Li'l Samir jumped out of bed. He ran to Shaniyah and Big Samir's room. "Get up! We got to take Asia to the hospital."

"Is everything okay?" Big Samir asked worried.

"Yes. She is getting ready to have your grandson. Now let's go!"

Everybody rushed to the truck. Asia screamed from the pain. Li'l Samir held her in his arms trying to keep her calm. Big Samir sped off toward the hospital.

They pulled into the hospital entrance. Shaniyah and Angel helped Asia out of the truck.

They rushed into the hospital and got Asia in a wheelchair.

"Somebody need to take care of my fucking girl! She fixing to have my son!" Li'l Samir yelled.

Nurses flew over to Asia as the family along with Angel followed.

In the room, Asia was throwing everything she could get her hands on at Li'l Samir while cursing him out.

"Baby, please calm down. I love you," Li'l Samir said. He was just as terrified. His sweet Asia had turned into a madwoman in the blink of an eye.

"This is all your fault!" Asia screamed.

Li'l Samir just shook his head as the doctor went to work.

After hours of labor, Asia had finally dilated to ten centimeters and was ready to start pushing. She then started cursing out the doctors. Li'l Samir didn't care as long as her anger wasn't pointed toward him anymore. Asia continued to push.

It was like music to Li'l Samir's ears when he finally heard his baby boy crying.

"You have a beautiful baby boy," the doctor said.

Big Samir and Shaniyah were in awe of their first grandson. Li'l Samir cut his baby's cord.

He was happier than ever. So much so, that he actually forgot about his crazy life for a moment.

"What's up, my li'l man?" Li'l Samir said to his son.

Finally the doctor asked, "What are you planning to name him?"

Samir looked at Asia and said, "Samir Rasheed Hicks III."

Everybody was so caught up in the adorable baby.

"Gosh he looks just like both Samirs," Angel said.

After a couple days in the hospital, the family returned home with the new baby. Two days in the hospital had the whole family exhausted. Angel went and took a nap in the guest room, Asia went to bed with the baby, and Shaniyah went to her bedroom to take a nap as well. Big Samir plopped down on the couch. He fell asleep watching TV.

Everyone seemed to back to their normal routine except Li'l Samir. He was feeling nervous, excited, and anxious about being a father. He was about to sit down on the couch when he heard his newborn son crying. He went into the room where he and Asia were staying and picked up baby Samir.

"Babe, I just fed him and changed his diaper. He probably just wants to be held," Asia said as she fluffed her pillow. She looked exhausted.

"Don't worry about him, Asia. I got this. You lie down and get some rest," Li'l Samir instructed her. He kissed her on the forehead and went back into the living room. He sat down on the couch across from the one his father had fallen asleep on, and he cradled his son in his arms. Tears ran down his cheek as he looked down at his beautiful baby boy. Baby Samir slept peacefully in Li'l Samir's arms. He held him as if it would be his last day with him. The situation with D-Money was breaking him apart. The birth of his son made him realize that he should have made better decisions. But, now, it was too late.

Li'l Samir finally stood to his feet and walked over to his baby's crib. He gently laid him down and placed the small teddy bear he had bought him close beside him. Then he went into his bedroom and watched Asia sleeping. He grabbed a blanket nearby and covered her. With tears still running down his face he climbed into the bed beside Asia and pulled her close to him. Finally, he drifted off to sleep.

***

D-Money woke up in an alley, dressed like a homeless person. New York was hot and he knew he had to find a way out quick.

Meanwhile, Tyreek and Loco were almost at D-Money's crib. They were supposed to be there that morning. They hadn't heard from D-Money in days but figured he'd probably been busy. If they had bothered to watch the news they would've known how bad things had gotten for their boy.

It was late when Tyreek and Loco finally pulled up in front of their cousin's house. The cops came in from all angles. "Get out of the car!" one policemen yelled. Tyreek and Loco put their guns under the seat and got out of the car with their hands up. The police were putting the two in handcuffs when Li'l Samir and his father rode by. Li'l Samir was driving. Tyreek noticed the front plates on the Escalade that read SAMIR. He looked Li'l Samir dead in the eyes as Li'l Samir aimed his hand in the shape of a gun at them and mouthed the words, "Bang bang." They continued down the block as the cops shoved Loco and Tyreek into the back seat of their car. They hadn't really done anything wrong, but they'd been arrested because they were driving D-Money's car and the cops suspected they were involved with D-Money's dealings.

Inside the police station, the cops put Tyreek and Loco in separate rooms and began questioning them about who they were and the whereabouts of De'Mario Hayes. They also asked them why they were driving De'Mario's car. Neither one of them opened their mouths as the cops threatened them. The cops knew the guys knew more than they were telling, but they had nothing on them, so they had to let them go.

D-Money had no phone on him and he needed to find his cousins. He walked around the block and saw some young boys on a corner thinking they were thugs.

"Do either one of y'all got a cell?" D-Money asked.

"Yeah, but you ain't getting it, you homeless nigga." The boy laughed.

D-Money pulled out his gun and aimed it at the boy's head. "Don't let these mothafuckin' clothes fool you, li'l nigga. Now where is yo' phone?"

The other boys took off running. The young boy was so nervous he pissed on himself wasting no time giving up his phone. Then he took off running leaving the phone in D-Money's possession. D-Money dialed Tyreek's number.

"Hello," Tyreek answered.

"Man, where the fuck you at?"

"Nah, nigga, where the fuck are you?" Tyreek thought for a second. "Don't answer that. I'ma call you back in a few." He hung up before D-Money even had a chance to say one word. He and Loco were walking around Brooklyn, shook. They found the closest payphone and dialed the number back D-Money called from.

"Hello," D-Money answered.

"Man, I had to call you from a payphone. These mu'fuckin' cops is hot. We went by yo' crib looking for you when the cops closed in on our asses. We just got out. They been questioning us all day. Neither one of us said shit, so they had to let us go. Man, where the fuck you at? If we don't find you in the next hour we leavin' yo' ass and headin' back to North Carolina."

D-Money told his cousins where he was, and waited on them to pick him up. Tyreek and Loco were hesitant to take his car back to pick up D-Money so they decided to get another car. With Loco lookin' out for the cops or anybody else suspicious, they got their guns and headed down the block in search of a ride.

They spotted a silver Mercedes coming down the block and flagged it down. The girl rolled down her window.

"What's up, fellas, y'all need a ride?" the girl said with seduction.

"Damn, ma, you fine as hell. You can start by giving me your number," Tyreek said forgetting his reason for stopping the car.

Loco looked at Tyreek like he was crazy. "Mothafucka, is you crazy?" Loco said.

"Oh, my bad, man," Tyreek said laughing. The girl looked puzzled. Loco pulled out his gun and told the girl to get out of the car. She was so scared she did what she was told. Loco hopped in the driver's seat and they took off leaving the girl standing in the cold cursing.

They pulled up where they thought D-Money said he would be. They saw a homeless-looking dude walk up to the car looking in the window. Tyreek rolled his window down.

"D, man, is that you?" Tyreek said laughing.

D-Money jumped in the car and they took off heading back to North Carolina.

Li'l Samir and his father watched as D-Money got in the Mercedes, and took off with his cousins. They had been watching D-Money's cousins since they left the police station knowing that was their only way to find D-Money. They followed them but didn't get too close behind. The time they had been waiting for had finally come.

"Yesss! We gon' finally get this nigga!" Big Samir said.

"I'll be so glad when this shit is over."

"It won't be much longer now, son. The time has come to put an end to him for good."

Chapter 15

Li'l Samir and his father followed D-Money and his cousins to North Carolina without being noticed. They watched as Loco dropped off Tyreek and D-Money at Tyreek's house. They assumed that's where D-Money would be staying.

In the meantime, Li'l Samir and his father found a nice hotel and got a room. They discussed their plans to get rid of D-Money.

D-Money laid low with his cousin Tyreek. He was in too deep and was trying to make sense of everything going on. Meanwhile, his cousins were getting high, laughing, and making their own plan on how they were going to get rid of Li'l Samir and his father. *These mothafuckers think it's really that simple.* D-Money felt himself getting mad at how his cousins were sitting there as if they didn't have a single care in the world.

"Man, this shit got me stressin' like a bitch. Even if I kill Li'l Samir and his dad, I'm still gon' have the cops on my ass. Shit, I'll go to jail for life if I get caught out there. If I'm gonna go down, I'm taking those mothafuckers down with me. I refuse to let them niggas rule my streets and stay on top. I gotta remind theses niggas that I ain't no a little bitch. I got something for their asses, nigga," D-Money said as Tyreek nodded.

"That's what's up, my nigga. Don't worry, me and Loco gotchu, but we gotta come up with a plan quick. If they murked Derrick, that nigga probably snitched and told them the spots you been staying at. So we gon' have to keep a lookout for them niggas in case they come sniffin' around here."

"Yeah, and you know them mothafuckas got Angel? I wouldn't be surprised if they have turned her against me. Fuck that bitch. I hope they don't think she gon' make me come running. Fuck that. Matta fact, I can go to the club right now and find me anotha bitch," D-Money said laughing, high as hell.

"Man, shut the fuck up. You up here got the cops and these two niggas looking for you and all you can think about is gettin' some ass. Nigga, you wildin'," Tyreek said laughing.

"Man, fuck this. I need to get out and relieve some of this stress. Let's go to the club. Nigga, you down or what?"

"Shit I'm down," Tyreek said, hitting the blunt one last time.

***

Li'l Samir and his father had come up with the plan to burst in on D-Money and his cousins the next morning, take them all out, and head back to New York before anything went down with the cops. They were going to leave drugs in the house to make it look like a drug deal gone bad.

They stayed up most of the night trying to figure out how things were going to go down.

"Man, I miss my girl and my son. This shit betta be worth it. I can't risk losing everything I have on this bullshit. I wish I had listened to Mom and never got caught up in these streets," Li'l Samir said feeling doubtful.

"Son, don't start trippin' now. After this is all over we can get on with our lives. But this shit ain't going ever end if we don't handle them mothafuckas. I know something that will get your mind off this bullshit for a while."

"What's that?"

"Let's head down to the club. We passed a spot called Club Passion or some shit like that. I need to get toasted anyway. So what you say? I'm down if you down," Big Samir suggested.

"Yeah, I'm down," Li'l Samir agreed hesitantly.

Li'l Samir and his father headed to Club Passion. They pulled into the parking lot and saw a few cars parked outside. The building looked run-down and dingy. They walked in, hoping things would look better on the inside. They took a quick look around and headed straight for the bar.

D-Money and his cousin Tyreek were in the back of the club getting a table dance from a stripper named Issys. D-Money and Tyreek were enjoying themselves taking time to zone away from their troubles when they saw two familiar faces come through and head to the bar.

"Yo, D-Money, ain't that them niggas there?" Tyreek asked.

"Well, well, well. They came to the wrong spot," D-Money said to himself with a smirk on his face.

"Ay, we should blast these mothafuckas right here and right now," Tyreek said reaching in his pocket to pull out his piece.

"Nah. Nah, man. Not here. We gon' chill right here and see where they head when they leave. The last thing I need is to draw attention to myself by blasting these niggas in the club. I ain't tryin'a have the cops on my ass in NY and North Carolina."

"Yeah, that's true, dawg. I feel ya."

D-Money and Tyreek waved the dancer out of the way and continued to watch Li'l Samir and his father's every move. About an hour later, Li'l Samir and his father headed out of the club with D-Money and Tyreek following right behind them. They had no idea they were being watched and followed.

D-Money and his cousin watched as Li'l Samir and his father headed into their room at the hotel.

Li'l Samir and his father stepped into their hotel room exhausted and drunk. They were laughing at how they pictured D-Money's face looking when they decided to put their plan into effect.

"Man, I can't wait 'til tomorrow so we can put an end to this shit. Then we can move on with our lives and marry our beautiful women," Big Samir said while lying on the bed, eyes barely open.

"That's what's up. I miss my li'l man so much, but I got to do this. I can't risk D-Money coming back and hurting my family. But for real though, that Club Passion would be a hot place to shoot a video," Li'l Samir said.

"You ain't never lied. After this is over, we have to make us a club joint. That shit gon' be hot, too."

After hours of Li'l Samir and his father discussing their future plans, they both finally passed out on the bed. They had no idea that their plans were all in vain since D-Money was already on to them.

The next morning, Li'l Samir woke up to find his father lying on his back snoring. Between his father's loud snores and the thought of Asia and his son on his mind Li'l Samir couldn't go back to sleep, so he decided to ride out to get some fresh air and clear his head. Samir exited the door not realizing that he was being watched. He got in his Escalade and drove around, going nowhere in particular. Li'l Samir picked up his cell phone and called home. He lit his blunt as he waited for Asia to answer. He bobbed his head to the beat of his song blasting on the radio.

"Hello," Asia said angrily.

"Hey, baby girl. How is my son?"

"He doing good, but he would be doing better if his father was here. Where are y'all? Me and your mom have been up all night wondering where you guys went. We were starting to think something bad had happened and y'all were locked up."

"Baby, we in North Carolina. We out here handling our business, but we will be home soon. Just hold on, baby. Everything gon' be all right. I promise."

"Please be sure to come home and be careful, Samir. Me and the baby need you."

"I'm coming home, girl. How is Ma doing?"

"She right here. I'll give her the phone."

"Hello," Shaniyah answered madder than ever. "Where is yo' father? And why hasn't he called me? Asia and I have been worried sick."

"Everything is fine, Ma. We gonna be home soon, I promise. Where is Angel?"

"Oh, I knew I had forgot to tell you something. She took off and ain't came back yet. I don't know where she is. She must've snuck out at some point last night."

"What? Y'all make sure y'all keep a close lookout for her. I knew I should have killed her when I had the chance. If anything go wrong, Ma, there is a gun in my bedroom underneath my mattress. Don't be afraid to use it. I got to go check on Pops. Love y'all."

After Li'l Samir hung up the phone, he headed back to the hotel. His father's truck was still parked so he figured he was still in the room fast asleep. Li'l Samir used his room key to go inside quietly trying not to wake his father. Inside the room, his father was nowhere in sight, but there was a note lying on his bed. Samir picked up the note that read:

Well, well, well. Guess it wasn't such a good idea for you to come looking for me after all. I guess your plans to kill me ain't gonna work. Payback still is and always will be a bitch! I got your pops, mothafucka! If you're just a little bit smart you won't try to find me. What you need to worry about is that beautiful family of yours. I got what I want and that's payback! Just be thankful you survived, bitch!

"Fuck!" Li'l Samir shouted. He didn't know what to think. He felt like the room was spinning in circles. Samir grabbed the keys to his truck and flew out of the hotel parking lot. He couldn't even think straight with his family on his mind. He prayed that D-Money was bluffing. He had to hurry back to New York before it was too late.

Eight hours later, Li'l Samir finally made it home and everything looked okay from the outside. It was dark so Li'l Samir made sure to watch his back. He prayed that his family was okay. He knew that he couldn't have been more than an hour behind if D-Money had come there with his dad.

He burst into the house and he could hear his son crying in his crib. Li'l Samir rushed to the crib and grabbed his son. Baby Samir stopped crying as soon as his dad picked him up. The house was silent and that made Samir nervous. He looked in every room but Shaniyah and Asia were nowhere to be found. Samir didn't know what to do so he grabbed some of Baby Samir's things and rushed to Kiyah's house. He hadn't talked to Kiyah since they'd broken up and he'd gotten with Asia, but desperate times called for desperate measures. Luckily Kiyah was home and she answered the door.

"Boy, what the hell is wrong with you? You got the nerve to bang on my door just to show me the baby you had with that bitch? Well, don't worry. I already heard."

"Kiyah, please. I don't have time for your shit. I just came to ask you a huge favor and you know I've never asked you for nothing. My family may be hurt and I have to go help them. Please keep my son here. I promise I will pay you."

"Samir, what kind of trouble that bitch got you in? That's why you should have stayed with me. And I don't know shit about watching no baby."

"Kiyah, please, I'm begging you. I promise I'll pay you back big time."

"You sure are," Kiyah said reaching for the baby who was drooling all over everywhere.

"Thanks, Kiyah. Please take care of my son," Li'l Samir begged before heading down the street.

Chapter 16

Li'l Samir headed back to his house. Still, there was no one in sight. He didn't know who to call or where to look for his family. He thought about it and decided to call his father's cell phone. Li'l Samir heard the phone going off so he followed the sound of his father's phone. The cell phone was lying on the floor in front of the basement door. Li'l Samir could see his hands shaking as he opened the basement door. The basement was dark and cold. When Li'l Samir got to the last step he turned on the lights.

"Shit!" was all that Li'l Samir could say when he saw his girl tied up, and his mother and father stretched out on the floor in a puddle of blood. Asia looked terrified as she shook her head from side to side and tried to say something through the tape over her mouth.

"Behind you!" she yelled out as soon as he removed the duct tape. He ducked just in time to square off with D-Money. During the tussle

D-Money slipped in Big Samir's and Shaniyah's blood and hit his head on the cement floor. Li'l Samir stood over him to make sure he was knocked out cold. Just as he turned to face Asia, he saw Loco coming out of the corner ready to aim for him, but Li'l Samir was quick. He shot Loco in the head and he fell dead.

Li'l Samir rushed to Asia's side. Her eyes were puffy and red. "Asia, are you okay?" he asked staring into her panic-stricken eyes.

"He's got a gun!" Asia screamed.

Li'l Samir turned his body to try to shield Asia. He aimed his gun at the dark figure coming toward him, but he wasn't quick enough. Tyreek shot at Li'l Samir hitting him in the arm. Still Li'l Samir managed to let off a shot and caught Tyreek right in the chest. Tyreek dropped his gun and fell on his back. You could hear a gurgling sound from him trying not to drown in his own blood.

Asia was terrified. Li'l Samir looked at his girl. "Everything is going to be just fine now," Samir said.

"I don't think that's possible," Asia said crying.

Li'l Samir looked at his mother and father who were surely gone for life and he broke out crying. Then, Li'l Samir just snapped. He pointed his gun at D-Money who was coming back out of his unconscious state.

"You mothafucka! You killed my parents!"

"Go ahead and kill me. I did what I came to do. I ain't got shit to live for anyway," D-Money said laughing.

"Oh, you ain't got shit to live for? What about me?" Angel said from the top of the basement steps.

Angel startled Li'l Samir as he pointed his gun toward her. Angel ducked, screaming for her life. "Please don't shoot. I'm pregnant!"

"Where the fuck you been, bitch? I told you not to go nowhere," Li'l Samir said.

"Mothafucka, that's my bitch. You can't tell her shit."

"Well, nigga, you won't see ya bitch or ya baby no time soon mothafucka." Li'l Samir started pointing his gun back at D-Money with fire in his eyes.

"Freeze!" The cops came rushing down the steps once again startling Li'l Samir as he pointed his gun at the cop.

"Drop your weapon now!" the police officer screamed.

Li'l Samir dropped his gun just like the police officer instructed him to. He threw his hands up in the air. No one saw when D-Money pulled out his gun. One of the officers saw what D-Money was up to and shot at him. As D-Money's gun fell to the ground, a shot went off, hitting Asia in the chest. Li'l Samir rushed to Asia screaming. Everything else was a blur after that.

That day was the hardest day of Li'l Samir's life. He lost his mother, father, and girl to the violence of the streets. D-Money died from the shot that was fired at him by the cops. Life as Li'l Samir knew it was over.

Chapter 17

The bars closed in as Samir was left alone in a holding cell, forced to think about all that he had lost. He felt as if the world was closing in on him. He wanted desperately to get out and get to his son. Tears fell from his face, as he thought about how his mother and father looked as they lay motionless in a pool of blood. It was like a nightmare that he couldn't wake up from. Then, instantly, he broke down from the flashback of Asia being shot. They were supposed to get married and live their happily-ever-after fairy tale with their new baby boy but everything came crashing down. He had no one to blame but himself. *I should have listened to my mother and never gotten caught up in the streets. Now I've lost everything.*

After being in a holding cell suffering for several days, Samir was finally released. Paul Reid, the attorney his mother had worked with for so many years, represented him. He argued that the police didn't have anything to hold Samir.

The murders were not committed by Samir, as De'Mario Hayes was the one who broke into the house and was holding the family hostage. From the outside looking in, it looked like a robbery that led to a hostage situation. No one would ever know the truth except for the one person who lived through it. Now, thanks to Paul, Samir was released with no charges pending against him.

"Thank you so much for everything." Samir sounded like a broken man. "Send me the bill and I'll be sure to pay you every penny of it."

"No need to repay me. This was pro bono. Your mother was a good woman. She worked for me for many years," he replied. "I knew how much she loved you. This was the least I could do."

"Good looking out. I really appreciate that."

"Now, Samir, I have some good news, and I have some bad news," Paul said as they walked to his car.

"Go ahead with it. Things can't get any worse than they are now." Samir sighed. He hadn't slept in days and it showed all over his face. His eyes were bloodshot, his face looked inflamed, and he'd started to grow a messy five o'clock shadow.

"The good news is I was able to hold your mom and dad's funeral until tomorrow, so you will be able to attend. The bad news is Asia's parents refused to talk to me about Asia's funeral arrangements. They picked up her body and moved as soon as you were put in jail. We have no information on them at all."

"What?" Samir cried. *So not only did I miss my fiancée's funeral, but I won't even know where she is buried to visit the site.*

Samir broke down right in the parking lot. He wished God had taken him instead of Asia. He didn't know how he was going to make it through.

"Samir, it will be okay. Asia knew how much you loved her, and that's something her parents can never take away. Pull yourself together," Paul encouraged Samir.

"Did they take my son with them?" Samir was scared to hear the answer to that question, but he had to know.

"No, they didn't." Paul took a deep breath. "They wanted nothing to do with him. They said they couldn't bear to look at him and have a constant reminder of their daughter's murder."

Samir was relieved to hear those words, but he was still unable to control his emotions from feeling the loss of his parents and his girl.

"You've got to pull yourself together, Samir. Your son needs you. You are all that he has."

Samir wiped his face, and got into the car. He looked out of the window, and wondered where he would go from here. Paul was right. His son needed him more than anything now. He was determined to find the strength to pull himself together for his baby. One thing was for certain: the street life was over for him.

The funeral of his parents was almost unbearable. When the caskets closed Samir knew he would never see his parents again. The reality of it left him torn inside.

After his parents were laid to rest, friends and acquaintances who showed up offered their condolences. It never bothered him that he and his mother didn't have family growing up, but during this difficult time, he wished to God he had an aunt, uncle, or somebody to help him through it. He'd never felt so alone in his life. He just stood by the gravesite sobbing. It pained him even more thinking about Asia.

"Nephew, you good, man?"

Samir turned around puzzled. For a second he thought it was his father standing there. The guy looked so much like Big Samir. "Who are you?" Samir asked, confused.

"I'm your Uncle Sedrick. I've been trying to meet you for a while. Your dad kept saying he was going to bring you and the family to visit, but he never got that chance." Sedrick sighed.

"It's crazy because I never thought about my dad's family, or my mom's family for that matter, until now. I was starting to think there wasn't anybody," Samir whispered, in a state of shock.

"Well, I am all the family your father had. We never knew our father, and our mom died of a drug overdose when we were teenagers. I just hate I have to meet you under these circumstances."

"Yeah, me too."

"So who's the little one?" Sedrick asked bringing his attention to Baby Samir.

"This here is your great-nephew, Samir Rasheed III."

"Damn, he looks just like you," Sedrick said, reaching for the baby's hand. "Head full of curls and all."

"That's my pride and joy. The reason I live, man."

"Well, how you holding up?" Sedrick asked concerned.

"To be honest, I don't know. I can't believe they're gone. Everything happened so fast. I also lost my fiancée, Asia. The last memory I'll always have of her is watching that bullet hit her. I can barely sleep at night. I keep hearing her cries from that night. And her parents just picked up and left. I don't know what happened with her funeral, where she was buried or anything. I have asked as many people as I can think of, but no one knows anything."

"Her parents blame you, huh?"

"Pretty much."

"Well, look I got to get back home to North Carolina. You and li'l man welcome to come stay with me. It's gon' take you some time to get yourself right with everything going on. You can't handle this on your own."

"Thanks for the offer, but as bad as it is, I gotta keep it moving for my baby boy. It hurts like hell, man. I can't even describe the pain," Samir said as he broke down crying again.

Sedrick placed his hands on Samir's shoulders, and waited patiently for him to pull himself together. Samir wiped his hands over his face, and took a deep breath. "My dad died trying to put an end to his demons, so he could get me and the family away to start a new life in Atlanta. And that's what I am going to do. I'ma head straight to ATL. Me and baby Samir," he said as he pulled the baby out of the stroller and into his arms. "We gon' start fresh in a nice place."

"Are you good financially? I'll help you in any way I can."

"Man, I don't have no problems in that area. My dad and I had plenty stacked to start fresh. I got an appointment to meet with my lawyer in the morning, to go over what my mom had for me. My dad had already given me ties to everything that he owned." Samir was trying to fight back tears. "After that, me and my son hitting the highway and never looking back. It's just so messed up, because it was supposed to be all of us."

"It will be okay, nephew. Things will get better. It may seem hard to believe now, but it will get better. Just keep doing what you doing, and everything will work out. Your breakthrough is on the way."

"Thanks, man. It was good to finally meet you, Unc," Samir said. He put Baby Samir back in his stroller and leaned in to give his uncle a hug.

"You too, man, and don't forget, if you need anything here's my number. I'm just a phone call away," he said as he handed Samir his card with his information on it. "Hey, Rasheed? Do me a favor and take care of your daddy for me, okay?" he said as he knelt down toward his great-nephew's stroller and grabbed his hand playfully. Baby Samir just smiled up at him.

Chapter 18

Two and a half years later

Samir Jr. sat on the bench watching his son playing at the playground. He smiled at his son as he yelled, "Weee!" while coming down the slide. After everything Samir went through with losing his fiancée, mother, and father, he realized just how precious life really was. He was proud to live a life free of drugs and violence. He loved being able to watch his son grow up. It was hard not having Asia around to enjoy the ride, but he vowed to be the best father he could be for Baby Samir.

"Daddy! Daddy! Come shhlide wif me!"

"A'ight, baby boy! Here I come!" Samir got up from the bench, and met his son at the top of the slide. He grabbed his son, sat him on his lap, and down they went, until they reached the bottom. Baby Samir giggled with joy. Samir chased his son around the playground. He caught him and lifted him into the air. They were having the time of their lives.

A beautiful woman watched from a distance in awe of their father-and-son relationship. She walked up to the duo with her son in hand.

"Wow! He is so adorable," she said.

Samir looked up, and immediately noticed the beautiful woman standing before him. He stood up and smoothed out his clothes, after just getting off the ground from rolling around in the grass.

"He a'ight," Samir joked. The lady laughed at his comment. "I'm just kidding. Thank you. Your son is adorable too, just like his mom," he said as he gestured to the little boy holding her hand.

"Thank you." She blushed.

"I'm Samir, and this is my pride and joy, Baby Samir. But, I call him by our middle name, Rasheed."

"Samir and Rasheed, okay. Well, I am Chanel and this handsome boy is Jaylin. He turned two yesterday."

"Happy belated birthday, Jay," Samir said, "Rasheed, can you tell Jay happy birthday?"

"Happy birfday!" Rasheed yelled.

"That's so sweet." Chanel smiled. "And how old are you, cutie?"

"I two," Rasheed replied holding up four fingers. Samir and Channel both chuckled.

"He will be three next Friday. As a matter of fact, I am taking him to Kids Play Land for his birthday. We would love for you to come and bring Jay, that's if your husband or boyfriend won't mind."

"I like how you slid in the whole husband, boyfriend thing, but, unfortunately that's over."

"Oh, wow, I'm sorry to hear that."

"It's all good. But we would love to come. Sounds like fun."

"Okay, that's what's up!"

"Now, I'm not gonna have to worry about any baby mommas or girlfriends, am I?"

"Nah, I'm a single dad," Samir replied. He didn't want to go any further on the topic.

Chanel waited to see if Samir would elaborate on why he was single, but he didn't, so she didn't push the subject. "Well, put my number into your cell, so you can call or text me the details or to let me know if anything changes. We look forward to helping you celebrate Rasheed's birthday."

Samir pulled out his cell phone, and saved Chanel's number in his phone. "Take mine down too."

"Oh, okay," Chanel replied. She took her phone out of her purse, and punched in Samir's number. Chanel waved good-bye, and headed to her car with Jaylin tagging along.

Samir lifted Rasheed into his arms. It was time for them to head home as well. His heart felt heavy from thinking about Asia now. He tried not to think about her too much, but he couldn't help it since Chanel asked about Rasheed's mother. He never liked to talk or mention anything about her because it just served as a painful reminder that she was no longer by his side. He knew he needed to move on though. He wanted badly to just get on with his life. After all, it had been two years, and he had barely spoken to another woman. But, for the sake of his son, he had to keep moving forward.

Chanel stood against her apartment door begging for her ex-boyfriend to leave. He continued to bang on the door. Jaylin stood, terrified, in the middle of the floor. He cried out to her, as she motioned for him to go back to his room.

"It's all right, Jaylin. Go to your room, and close the door. I promise, everything will be okay, baby."

Jaylin ran to his room, sobbing.

Chanel continued to beg for Cam'ron to leave. "Please go, Cam! If you don't go, I'm calling the police!"

Cam'ron burst through the door, breaking the chain lock. Tears ran down Chanel's cheeks. She had broken up with Cam'ron months ago because of the way he treated her. He was abusive, and he ran the streets nonstop. But, he refused to let her go, and as far as he was concerned, if he couldn't have her no one would.

"I told you, Chanel, you will never get rid of me. Jaylin is my son, and if you try to keep him from me, I'll take him."

"He is scared of you!" Chanel cried.

"Shut the fuck up!" Cam'ron hit Chanel so hard she fell to the floor. Blood dripped from her lip. When she tried to crawl away, he grabbed her by her long hair, and dragged her across the floor. "You are mine! Don't you forget that. And don't you ever disrespect me!" he screamed, while he landed punches and kicks all over Chanel's body. Chanel just balled herself up to try to shield herself from the menacing blows.

Jaylin ran out of his room crying, "Momma! Momma!"

"You see what you made me do? You brought this on yourself for thinking you could leave me!"

Cam'ron looked down at his son. Enraged, he let Chanel go, and slammed the door behind him. Chanel struggled to sit up. She grabbed little Jaylin, and embraced him.

The next morning, Chanel woke up early and got herself and Jaylin dressed. She put on her Louis Vuitton shades to hide her dark eyes. She did her best in applying makeup to cover her battered face. Then, she left the apartment, closing the door behind them. When she got outside, she unlocked the doors to her red Honda, and buckled Jaylin into his car seat.

Chanel was tired of the abuse and heartache. She couldn't go another night having to watch her son crying and being terrified of his father. She drove straight to the police station demanding to talk to someone.

She approached an officer, and explained the situation.

"Ma'am, why didn't you call the police when he was beating on your door?" the officer asked.

"Because I was too busy trying to hold the door to keep him from coming in. I was terrified, and then he broke in, and beat up on me."

"We can't arrest him, because you're coming to us after the fact. We weren't called the night that it happened. But, you can file a restraining order against him, and if he comes back you call us. We'll be able to arrest him after he breaks the order."

"But for how long?"

"It all depends. But, hopefully the restraining order will keep him away."

"Hopefully? What if he ignores the restraining order then kills me?"

"Lady, just file the restraining order, and call us if he shows up at your house."

"He is also threatening to take my son. What should I do about that?"

"That's a different matter. You will have to go to court to gain full custody of your son. Otherwise, there is nothing we can do. After all, he is his son too."

Chanel felt defeated. She couldn't understand why the police didn't seem eager to want to help her. Wasn't it their job to serve and protect after all? With very few options, she filed the restraining order, and returned home. She called the landlord to change the locks and to fix the chain on the door.

That evening, Chanel put Jaylin to sleep, and decided to take a lavender bath. Her body was achy all over from the beating she took from Cam'ron. She was grateful that she hadn't bruised up as bad as she expected so she wouldn't have to worry about people asking her what happened. She hated having to lie every time and say she fell down the stairs or some crazy story.

After her bath, she climbed into her bed and did a mental tally of her and Jaylin's plans for the next day. She remembered they were supposed to celebrate Rasheed's birthday that afternoon. She grabbed her mirror off the nightstand. Her face had almost cleared up, except for the dark spot under her left eye. She decided it would be best to call Samir and cancel. She sadly picked up her phone to break the news.

"What's good?" Samir answered into the phone. His voice was deep and sexy.

"Hey. How are you?"

"I just put my li'l man to sleep. He's excited about tomorrow. I practically had to trick him to go to sleep." Samir laughed.

"I'm sure he is going to have a blast. I wish we could be there, but some things came up."

"Uh-uh. Nope. You gotta come. Rasheed's been running around all day saying, 'I can't wait to play with my new friend from the park.' What happened?"

"I'm so sorry. I just have a lot going on right now. It's kind of complicated."

"Do you want to talk about it?"

"Not really." Chanel sighed.

"It sounds like you are going through a lot. I think coming to help us celebrate will take your mind off your troubles. And when you feel like talking about what's going on, I'm all ears."

Chanel could tell Samir was not going to give up. She reluctantly gave in. "Okay. We'll see you tomorrow."

"Great, see you then."

Chapter 19

Samir helped Rasheed into the bouncy house. His son was dressed cute in a red IT'S MY BIRTHDAY T-shirt, a red and white New York fitted cap, denim shorts, and matching Js. Samir was dressed the same, except he sported a red and white T-shirt that read BIRTHDAY BOY'S DAD. Rasheed giggled and screamed as he jumped up and down in the bouncy house. Samir watched on and laughed at his son enjoying himself.

Samir glanced at the door, and did a double take when he noticed Chanel and Jaylin walk in. Chanel was just as beautiful as the day he'd met her at the park. His eyes scanned every inch of her body as she walked toward him. She was wearing a long gray skirt with a plain white tank top. On her chest lay a simple gold chain with a cross hanging from it. The skirt hugged her hips perfectly and he could see the outline of her perfectly round breasts through her shirt. He could tell she was wearing a lacy black bra. It was such a simple outfit yet she looked stunning in it. Her long, shiny black hair swung off her shoulders. With her sexy smile and cocoa skin, Samir couldn't help but notice how much she resembled Tika Sumpter, the actress who portrayed Candace Young in Tyler Perry's *The Haves and the Have Nots*. It wasn't a show Samir cared to watch, even though he remembered his mother, Shaniyah, watched it faithfully. He licked his lips as he looked her up and down, admiring what he was seeing. It had been a long time since he felt attracted to a woman. It was a feeling he didn't think he'd ever experience after Asia died.

Chanel looked around the roomful of kids, and found Samir standing by the bouncy house. He looked as if he should have been on the cover of a magazine. His fine, silky hair was pulled back into a neat ponytail, with his fitted cap tilted to the side. The attire he wore was fresh from head to toe. There wasn't a spot or blemish on his handsome face. Chanel admired his muscles bulging from the sleeves of his shirt. His light skin glowed, just as much as the diamond Rolex on his wrist.

Jaylin ran up to Samir and pointed toward the bouncy house, as Chanel made her way over to them.

"Wait, Jaylin. Mommy will help you up there."

"Nah, I got it," Samir said. He bent down to take off Jaylin's shoes. Then, he helped Jaylin into the bouncy house. Jaylin joined in on the fun bouncing up and down with Rasheed.

"Thank you," Chanel replied.

"You don't have to thank me. It was my pleasure. Thank you for coming."

"Of course. They sure are having a lot of fun."

"Yep. The joys of being a kid."

"The good life." She laughed.

Chanel and Samir walked over to a nearby table so they could talk and watch the kids play. Chanel acted uneasy. She didn't want to look Samir straight in the face for fear he would notice the bruise on her face.

"So, do you plan on taking off the shades so I can see those beautiful brown eyes?"

Chanel thought she felt her heart jumping out of her chest. "Um, no, I'm good."

"Ah, come on." Samir reached over and pulled the shades from her face. Chanel quickly turned her head.

Samir immediately noticed the dark spot under her right eye. "What happened to your eye?" he asked curiously.

Chanel tried to laugh it off. "Jaylin was playing with one of his toy trucks. He threw one, and it hit me right under my eye. You know how it is with boys."

Samir raised his eyebrow. He wasn't buying her story at all. "Chanel, what's going on?"

"What do you mean? I already told you what happened. I'm serious."

"So you really expect me to believe that's what happened?"

Chanel turned, and faced him. "I'm serious. Jaylin hit me with one of his toys. End of story."

"Okay, if you say so. Well, what's the story with Jay's dad, if you don't mind me asking? Is he still in the picture?"

"Like I told you before, we broke up. He comes around sometimes to see Jaylin. As for us, things just didn't work out."

Samir studied her closely. He could tell she was nervous about the conversation, but he didn't want to pressure her, since they barely knew one another.

They both looked toward the bouncy house to make sure the boys were still inside playing.

"Since you are questioning me, where is Rasheed's mother?"

Samir wasn't expecting her to reverse things on him. Samir inhaled, and then exhaled deeply. He looked into Chanel's eyes. She was waiting for him to respond. He cleared his throat.

"Well, Rasheed's mother passed away about two years ago."

Chanel hated that she'd asked. "I'm so sorry."

"It's cool. I'm making it. Just trying to move on with my life, but she will forever be in my heart, along with my mother and father."

"Wow. You lost your parents as well?"

"Yes. I lost all three of them on the same day," he said. "I'm getting by though. Some days are better than others."

Chanel could hear the sadness in his voice. She decided not to ask for details. She preferred to wait until he was comfortable to tell her on his own. Just then, the kids ran over to them.

"I want ice queem, Daddy!" Rasheed yelled, jumping up and down.

"Okay, son. Ice cream it is."

"Me choo! Me choo!" Jaylin raised his hand.

Samir laughed. "Okay! Okay! Let's get you two some ice cream."

Chanel stayed at the table, while Samir took the kids to the counter. They each came back carrying an ice cream cone. Samir handed a cone to Chanel. Rasheed sat down, and slid to the corner of the booth. Samir took a seat beside him. Chanel patted the seat next to her for her son to sit down.

"No." Jaylin pointed toward Samir. "With him," he begged.

"No, Jaylin. You can sit next to Mommy. Let Rasheed sit with his dad."

"It's cool," Samir interjected. He helped Jaylin up, and sat him on the other side of him.

"I think he likes you a bit too much," Chanel said, a bit worried.

"I like li'l man too. Is that a bad thing?"

"Yes, it is if he starts getting attached. We barely know each other. Maybe this wasn't a good idea." Chanel was starting to regret the whole play date.

"Well, that's why I want to get to know you. I don't just let anyone around my son either. If I hadn't gotten a good vibe from you at the park, you wouldn't be here today," Samir answered nonchalantly.

"Oh, is that so?" Chanel asked in a teasing kind of way.

"That's how it is," Samir said with a smile and a wink.

After the fun was over, Samir walked Chanel to her car. Rasheed was seated on Samir's shoulders. Jaylin pointed up toward Rasheed. "Me choo," he said.

Samir laughed. "All right, li'l man." Samir let his son down, and hoisted Jaylin onto his shoulders. Chanel was afraid Rasheed would get upset, so she held out her arms to him. He happily ran up to her, as she lifted him onto her hip. As he watched his son in Chanel's arms, Samir began to feel warm inside.

"When can I see you again?" Samir asked.

"I don't know. I really like you, and I love how great you are with my son. I just have so much going on. I don't want to drag you and Rasheed into my chaos."

"I'm a big boy. I have most likely been through worse than whatever you got going on, so whatever it is, I'm sure I can handle it. I have to see you again, and I won't take no for an answer."

Chanel smiled. "We've got each other's numbers, so I guess we will just have to see where it goes."

Samir opened the car door, and strapped Jaylin into his car seat. Then, he opened Chanel's door, and took Rasheed from her arms. Chanel seated herself in the car, and smiled at them.

"Talk to you soon, beautiful," Samir said. Then, he looked over into the back seat. "See you later, li'l man."

"Bye bye," Jaylin said, smiling from ear to ear.

Samir watched as they pulled off. Then, he and Rasheed headed home.

"Asia!" Samir screamed. The horrible nightmare woke Samir out of his sleep. His body was drenched in sweat. It had been almost a year since he'd had that nightmare. For some reason, the dream had returned, leaving him in a bad head space.

Samir threw off the covers, and stepped out of bed. Tiptoeing into the kitchen, attempting to not wake his son, he poured himself a glass of water. The time on the microwave read ten o'clock. He walked into the living room, and sat down on the couch. There was no use in going back to bed. Reaching for the remote, he turned on the TV, and stopped the channel on *Good Times*. "Ha-ha! That damn J.J. Evans is a fool!" he said to himself.

Suddenly, Samir heard his cell phone ringing in his bedroom. He turned off the TV, and quickly ran to his room to answer the phone so it wouldn't wake Rasheed.

"Yo, who is this?"

"That's no way to answer the phone."

"Chanel?"

"Of course. How many other women do you have calling you?"

Samir smiled. "Trust me. You are the only one. So what's up?"

"I just had you on my mind, and thought I would give you a call. Did I wake you?"

"Nah. Actually, I couldn't sleep. I was up watching TV."

"I haven't heard from you. I thought you had forgotten about me."

"I could never forget you. I was just giving you your space. I know you been going through some things, and I didn't want to seem pushy."

"I appreciate that, but I think Jaylin misses you and Rasheed."

"Is he the only one missing us?"

Chanel blushed. "No. I miss Rasheed too."

"Ha-ha, so you got jokes?"

"I'm just kidding. I miss you too, silly."

"Well, how about we take the kids to see a movie tomorrow?"

"I don't think Jaylin will do well in a movie theatre."

"We could go to the drive-in."

"That could work. But what time? Because I have to work tomorrow."

"Oh, where do you work?" Samir asked.

"At the hospital. I'm a physical therapist."

"Well, what time do you get off?"

"I get off at five."

"I'll pick you up at six then."

"Okay. That sounds like a plan."

"All right. Good night, beautiful."

"Good night," she said, before hanging up.

Samir smiled to himself. The thought of seeing Chanel again took away all of his frustrations. He slept all night, without any bad dreams.

Chapter 20

Samir and Rasheed knocked on the door to Chanel's apartment. Samir held Rasheed's hand as they waited for Chanel to come to the door. The door opened, as Chanel stood in the doorway looking absolutely breathtaking.

"Don't you two look handsome?" Chanel said.

"And you are stunning." Samir's eyes shot to Chanel's thighs, as she did a model spin in her cute strapless romper shorts. Her hair was pinned into a neat bun on top of her head.

Chanel threw her hands on her hips and smiled. "You like?" she asked.

"I love," Samir replied, licking his lips.

"Me too!" Rasheed blurted out. They both burst out laughing.

Jaylin popped his head out of the door. "Shamir! Sheed!" he screamed. He ran, and grabbed a hold of Samir's leg. After letting Samir's leg loose, he ran to hug Rasheed.

"Aww, what's up, li'l man?" Samir said to Jaylin. "Everybody ready?"

Samir waited for Chanel to lock up before he grabbed her hand. His affection toward her made her heart flutter. She looked at him, and smiled. It felt good to be with a real man.

When they got to the car, he helped Chanel into his brand new Mercedes-Maybach S600. He strapped the boys into their seats. The fresh scent was intoxicating, and the leather seats were so comfortable.

"Samir, what do you do?" Chanel asked, taking note of the new, flashy ride.

"What do you mean?"

"I don't want you to get the wrong idea about me and think I'm a gold digger or a materialistic person . . ." She hesitated to say her next sentence.

"But?" Samir egged her on.

"But when we met up at the bouncy place, I noticed the pricey Rolex shining on your wrist and now you're rollin' in a brand new Maybach. Really, what do you do?" Chanel quizzed.

"I'm an entrepreneur," Samir answered bluntly. He turned up the radio, as the car drove smoothly down the road. The boys bobbed their head, to the beat of the music. Samir looked into the rearview mirror, and laughed.

Chanel picked up on how he tried to brush her question off and she was not letting him off so easy. She turned down the music, and continued to question him. "Boy, don't play with me. What is it that you do?"

"I just told you." Samir cut off the conversation again, and turned the volume back up to the song on the radio.

After dodging Chanel's questions throughout the ride, they pulled up to the booth at the drive-in movie theatre. Samir paid for the entrance fee, and drove in. He glanced over at Chanel, who had her arms folded and was looking out of the window. It was obvious she was upset that he hadn't answered her question. He turned the radio to the station for the movie, parked the car, and then turned around to get the boys out of their seats. They were both knocked out.

"Damn, we stuck watching a kiddy movie, while these two knuckleheads are fast asleep."

"Well, you can take us home," Chanel said with an attitude.

"Why you mad?" Samir asked, as if he didn't know.

"I'm not going to waste my time falling for another Cam'ron. I won't put me or my son through that again."

"Cam'ron? Is that your ex?"

"Yes, Jaylin's father. He put us through so much. I wanted to believe you were different."

Samir knew he had to come clean. "Chanel, I really like you, and I don't want what I'ma about to tell you to ruin things for us."

Chanel unfolded her arms, and looked at Samir. "Just be honest."

Samir sighed. "The reason I have so much money is because my dad and I were big-time hustlers in New York."

"Unbelievable! Samir, take us home."

"No, hear me out." Samir paused, then began to explain. "We made enough to quit hustling but in the midst of all that, we put out hit songs, which made us more money. I don't know if you ever heard the rap songs 'I Am My Father's Son' and 'New York's Most Wanted.'

"I'm sorry. I haven't, because I hardly ever listen to rap, but continue."

"Anyway, that's basically how I got so much money. When my dad died, of course, I was left with his portion as well. My mom made sure I was straight, too. To sum it all up, and I don't mean to sound cocky but, I am pretty well off."

"So, you really gave up hustling?"

"Yes. I gave that life up a long time ago, and I will never go back. I'd give up all of my luxuries before I went back to hustling on the streets. That life just ain't worth it."

"Samir, I realize it's a touchy subject for you, but if you and I were to move forward with getting to know each other, I need to know; what happened to your family? I'd want to know if being involved with you will bring any kind of trouble to my doorstep."

Samir laid his head back against the seat. He knew honesty was the best policy in this or any situation. He had learned from what happened between him and his mother that it was better to be straight up and tell the truth than to hide things and lie. And he figured it'd be better to lay all the cards on the table so he could know from jump that Chanel was down for him.

"Man, I don't even know where to start." Samir paused. Flashbacks of the tragedy flooded his mind.

"My mom moved to New York when I was two. My dad was there locked up. She raised me by herself, up until I was eighteen. When my father was released from prison, I resented him for not being there when I was growing up. It took awhile for us to build a father-and-son bond, because I wasn't ready to forgive him. Over time, I eventually grew closer to him, so we both started hustling together. It was stupid, but I didn't realize it at that time."

Samir sighed, then tried to get through the rest of the story. "Well, my father had a best friend, D-Money, who turned on him once he got locked up. He was the first guy I was introduced to when I wanted to start hustling. D-Money is the one who put me on. Once my father and I linked up, I kicked him to the curb. Like an idiot, we planned to get revenge on him for betraying my father. Long story short, it all backfired. He killed my mother and father." Tears filled Samir's eyes. "And . . . and my girl ended up dead too, because of me. It was my fault! And now my son has to grow up without ever knowing his mother!" Samir couldn't hold it in any longer, and he sobbed. The guilt hurt him worse than anything. "I messed up! I'd give anything to take it all back!"

Chanel was in total shock. She leaned over, and hugged Samir, as he cried on her shoulder. "It's okay, baby. Let it out. It's okay. Samir, I am so sorry you went through that. Baby, you have to forgive yourself. People make mistakes. You can't change the past, and I can't take away your pain, but I'll be here to help you in any way I can. Your son loves you, and from what I've seen so far, you are a great father. No matter what happened in your past, it has made you a better man today. Asia would be so proud of you, and so would your mother and father."

Samir lifted his head from Chanel's shoulder. Even though the pain still filled his heart, Chanel's calming voice soothed him. She wiped the tears from his face. He looked her in her pretty brown eyes, and leaned in to kiss her. Chanel closed her eyes, and inhaled the scent of his cologne. The heat escaping their bodies fogged the windows of the car. The kiss lasted longer than expected. Finally, Chanel pulled back.

"Um, I think we better go." Chanel could feel the dampness between her thighs.

"Come back to my place and stay the night with me," Samir said, not wanting the night to end.

"As tempting as that sounds, I can't. We are just getting to know each other. That definitely would not be a good look."

"I don't care about that. I truly believe in my heart you are the one I want to be with. I felt something deep toward you when we celebrated Rasheed's birthday."

"No. You don't know that for sure, at least, not just yet."

"Yes, I do," he said, trying to assure her.

"Let's just go. We have plenty of time to spend with each other."

"Damn, just stab me in my heart why don't you?" Samir said as he clutched his chest.

"You will be okay, I'm sure." Chanel laughed.

"Girl, I'm just playing. But all jokes aside, I understand, and I respect you."

"Thank you, baby."

"I still wish you would stay the night with me though."

"It may happen one day, but not today." Chanel laughed.

"Yeah, yeah. Let's just go."

Samir gave up on a lost cause, and started the car. When they got to Chanel's house, he walked her to her apartment door, and then kissed her good night.

Chapter 21

Months rolled by and things were definitely starting to look up for Chanel. She hadn't seen or heard from Cam'ron in months and things between her and Samir were going great. She was spending every chance she had with Samir and the boys. She'd never experienced the kind of love she felt for Samir. He made it so easy to love him and he was so patient and loving, especially the way he took time getting to know her and Jaylin. The one issue that haunted her was that she hadn't told him about her past with Cam'ron. She tried to keep it in the back of her mind, since she believed Cam'ron had finally gotten the message that she was done with him. Her focus now was to keep working on the blossoming relationship between her and Samir.

Chanel's mom had a tradition of cooking a big dinner every Sunday. Chanel never missed a Sunday. She always looked forward to spending Sunday evenings talking with her mother while Jaylin played in the backyard. Chanel had decided this Sunday coming up would be the perfect day to finally introduce Samir to her mother. She wasn't sure if he would be willing to meet her, or if he thought the relationship was getting serious enough for him to meet her mother, but she knew she was serious about him so she decided to ask him. Much to her surprise, Samir was excited to meet her mom and agreed to come along. She just hoped her mom would like Samir and be happy for her. She wished her father was still alive to meet him, but Chanel's father had died of cancer a few years back.

"Man, I hate this hot-ass weather in Atlanta," Samir complained. "Make me wanna cut this slick-ass ponytail off my head."

The kids sat quietly, enjoying the cartoons that played on the TVs installed in the back seat.

"You are not cutting any of that pretty hair off. Plus, soon enough I'll be playing in it." She smirked.

Samir raised his eyebrow. "Is that right? Well, in that case, I'll just take the heat."

Chanel laughed. "I thought you might change your mind."

The heat wouldn't let up, and the little dress Chanel had on was making him even hotter. If the kids hadn't been in the car with them, he would've pulled over and gotten a taste of her sweetness.

After what felt like forever, when they pulled into Chanel's mother's driveway, Samir quickly got sex off of his brain, and became nervous. "I hope your mom likes me."

"I'm sure she will." Chanel smiled at him reassuringly. "Let's go, boys," Chanel said as she exited the car. The two got the boys out of their seats and headed to the door, where they were greeted by Chanel's mom, Rose.

"Hello, hello! Come on in," Rose said, smiling. She stepped aside as they all entered her cozy home.

Chanel turned and looked at Samir. He wore a look of anxiety. "Mom, this is my friend Samir and his handsome son, Rasheed. Samir, this is my beautiful mother, Rose."

"Nice to meet you, ma'am," Samir replied, sticking out his free hand for her to shake.

"Oh, boy, you better put that hand away, and give ol' Mrs. Rose a hug." She leaned in and hugged Samir, almost squishing Rasheed, who was standing in between his father's legs. "Y'all follow me to the kitchen. I got a nice spread, so I hope you brought your appetite."

They all sat at the table, and enjoyed a nice Sunday dinner of ham, fried chicken, baked macaroni and cheese, turnip salad, potato salad, candied yams, and rolls. Samir thought he had died and gone to heaven.

"This is delicious," Samir said. "Mrs. Rose, this is the best baked macaroni I've ever had!"

"I'm glad you're enjoying it, sugar. And there's plenty more so eat up."

Samir didn't respond because he was too busy chewing on a mouthful of food. Even Rasheed, who was usually very picky with his food, was enjoying his meal.

"Samir, I have heard a lot of great things about you. I'm so glad Chanel worked up the nerves to invite you to meet me. I prayed every night that God would send her a good man. Unlike that no-good devil of a man Cam'ron," she said sternly. You could hear the anger seeping through her words.

"Mom, don't. Not now," Chanel pleaded.

Samir could sense Chanel's discomfort.

"Well, it's the truth. It don't make no sense what that boy put you through. I have to tell it so you won't ever make the mistake of going back to him again. I rebuke it in Jesus' name!"

"Mom, please! We are over, so just drop it!"

Samir cleared his throat. "Well, I don't know much about the whole Cam'ron situation, but, Mrs. Rose, I want you know I have nothing but complete respect for your daughter and your grandson. I'm here now, and I am going to make sure they are both taken care of."

"Amen. You are exactly what she needs. Anytime y'all need to go out or anything, you leave those boys right here with their ol' nana, ya hear?"

"Yes, ma'am." Samir smiled. It felt good for her to include Rasheed, especially since Rasheed didn't really have a grandmother after Shaniyah passed. The thought made him feel heartbroken, but Mrs. Rose made him feel welcome and seemed sincere about treating him and Rasheed like family and that helped his situation out a lot. He could get used to the warm family feeling again.

"Chanel was telling me a little bit about your past. I have to say I am truly sorry about what you and that baby had to go through. I can't replace all that you have lost, but you are welcome to call me anytime you need to talk. I really believe you and Chanel found each other for a reason, and I'll make sure your son has a nana he can look to as well."

"Thank you, Mrs. Rose. That means a lot. I'm sure he will love that," Samir said glancing over at Chanel with a smile.

After dinner, Chanel helped her mother clean the kitchen, while Samir ran around outside with the boys. Things between her and Samir were going well, but she was questioning if they were moving too fast. Even still, she knew she was already head over heels madly in love with him and that scared her.

"Have you heard anything from Cam'ron?" her mother asked, bringing her back to reality.

"Um, no. I think he finally got the point," Chanel said confidently.

"I don't know. I don't trust that fool. I'm afraid that he'll come back and hurt you, Chanel," her mother said worriedly.

"Well, Mom, I have done all that I can. I went to the police. I have a restraining order against him. What more can I do?"

"I guess there's nothing more you can do. You just be careful. I'd hate for something to happen to you. Now tell me about you and Samir. Have you told him about the abuse?"

"Of course not, Ma! I don't need to have him flipping out over nothing. Cam'ron is out of my life, and I am moving on with it. Just be happy for me, Ma."

"I am happy for you, baby. But you have to realize, as a mother I am also worried." Mrs. Rose sighed. "I think you need to tell that young man about your past. He wasn't afraid to tell you about his, and you should do the same."

"I don't know, Ma. I just don't think it matters if I tell him. And, like I said, Cam'ron is gone so I'm not going to stress about telling him."

"Maybe you are right. Maybe he is gone," Mrs. Rose agreed, but you could tell she was still concerned.

Chanel stepped onto the porch, and watched as her man played with the kids. As Samir looked up, and saw her standing there, he motioned for her to come over to him. She went across the yard to see what he wanted. Meeting her half-way, he playfully lifted her into the air spinning her around.

They laughed, and began chasing each other around like two elementary school kids. The boys joined in on the fun. Just then, Mrs. Rose opened the door. "Who wants ice cream?" she yelled.

The boys took off toward the door. Chanel and Samir followed. The boys ran inside with Mrs. Rose. On the porch, he stopped and pulled her to him, and kissed her passionately. His lips, his smell, his taste, everything about him drove her insane. Just the feel of his tongue tangling with hers left wetness between her thighs. He pulled away from her.

"I want you to stay with me tonight," Samir said.

"No, Samir. I can't. I don't want Jaylin to get the wrong idea." Although they had stayed late at his house before, they had never spent the night.

"What idea would that be?"

"If we stay the night at your house, he will never want to leave."

"Then don't. Chanel, I love you. Ain't no sense in hiding the feelings I have for you. You and Jay mean the world to me. Come live with me."

Chanel sighed. "Not yet. Just give me a little more time to be sure."

Samir kissed her forehead. "Okay."

They both headed into the house hand in hand. The boys were already seated at the table stuffing their faces. Their clothes were covered in ice cream.

"Dang, did y'all leave any for us?" Samir joked.

"Nope!" Rasheed and Jaylin giggled.

"Well, I guess I gotta eat yours," Samir said, pretending to take Rasheed's ice cream.

"Nnoo!" Rasheed whined.

"Leave that baby alone. I got y'all ice cream right here," Mrs. Rose said, bringing two bowls to the table.

They continued to talk, and enjoy one another until it was time for them to go home.

Chapter 22

Samir pulled up to his beautiful home, and parked in the garage. After spending hours working out at the gym, the shower was calling his name. He took a quick shower, got dressed, and headed out the door to pick up Chanel and the kids. On the way to his car, an unfamiliar man approached him.

"Hey what's up? I'm Keshawn. I just moved in across the street."

Samir looked up to acknowledge the dark, skinny stranger. "Oh, wassup. I'm Samir."

"Yeah, I saw you coming out, and decided to come over and introduce myself."

"That's cool. You picked a nice neighborhood. Everybody here is pretty nice. So it's just you?"

"Well, me and my wife, Renee. Look, we are planning a cookout next weekend. We're tryin' to get to know everybody and it would be great if you and your wife, or girlfriend, if there is one, could come over. Free food and drinks, you can't beat it," Keshawn persuaded him.

Samir thought about it for a second. "Okay, cool. Me and my girl will try to make it. Nice meeting you, man."

"You too," Keshawn said, before heading back across the street.

While the new neighbor went back across the street to his home, Samir opened the door to his car, and slid into the seat. He dialed Chanel's number, but she didn't pick up. *That's strange. Maybe she's busy with the kids*. He started the car, and headed down the highway toward her house. On the way, he tried dialing her again.

"Who the fuck is this?" a guy answered.

Samir took the phone from his ear, and looked at the number he had dialed. After realizing he dialed the right number, he placed the phone back to his ear.

"Who the fuck is this?" Samir shot back.

Just then, Samir heard the kids crying in the background, and Chanel screaming. Panic struck when the call dropped. Samir furiously increased his speed to get to Chanel and the kids. When he reached Chanel's turn, the car swerved into the parking lot. He put the car in park, and without taking the keys out of the ignition, he jumped out, running into the apartment building. Taking two stairs at a time, he dashed to her door. The sounds of the man screaming at Chanel infuriated him even more. Not wasting another second, he burst through the door. The kids were in the middle of the floor crying, while a man had Chanel against the wall with his hand around her neck.

Like a flash of lightning, Samir grabbed him, and threw him to the floor. Chanel ran, and grabbed the kids, taking them into Jaylin's room. The frightened look in the kids' eyes broke her heart. In a soothing tone, she told them to stay in the room. She hurried back into the living room screaming for Samir to get off of Cam'ron, but Samir was too lost in his rage to hear a word she said. Protecting his loved ones was the only thing he cared about. Flashbacks of D-Money hurting his family filled his head. In his mind, Cam'ron was D-Money, and he wasn't going to stop until he was dead for hurting them. His ears were numb to Chanel's cries. Blood splattered from Cam'ron's nose and mouth.

Police rushed through the door. One officer grabbed Samir, and the other grabbed Cam'ron. Chanel explained to the officer what happened. They arrested Cam'ron, and let Samir go.

"This ain't over," Cam'ron said, looking from Samir then to Chanel.

"Nah, bitch. You lucky the cops got your ass." Samir scowled at him.

"Son, don't say anything you will regret later. Let us handle this. We understand you are upset, but you caught a break so let it go," the officer interjected.

The officers left, with Cam'ron in tow. Chanel broke down crying. Embarrassment and anxiety took over, as she fell to the floor. Her body wouldn't stop shaking. Samir rushed to her side, and held her.

"I'm so sorry, Samir! I thought he had finally moved on! I didn't know he would come back!"

"It's okay, Chanel. I got you. I will never let anything happen to you again. You are a part of me now," Samir continued to console her. "Who was that nigga and how many times has this happened?"

Chanel put her head down in shame. It was time she told Samir the truth. It was all too much for her to handle on her own. Not only was her child put in danger, but Samir's son had been, too.

"That's Cam'ron. Jaylin's dad." She felt ashamed and embarrassed about the whole situation. "I'm so sorry about all of this. I never wanted to bring you two into this."

"It's not your fault, Chanel. You should have told me. I want to be here for you."

"I understand now. I really should have been upfront with you. The truth is, I broke up with Cam because of his cheating ways, his drinking, and abuse. He moved out and he seemed okay with the breakup. But then one night, he asked to come see Jaylin, so I let him. When he asked to get back with me, I simply said no. He went off, flippin' out, and cursing at me like an enraged animal. Then he pushed me to the floor, straddled me, and punched me until I passed out." Chanel was so much of wreck, she could barely continue.

The pain he caused her hurt Samir to his core. "Baby, he will never hurt you again. Everything will be okay." He kissed her on her cheek. "What else happened? You can tell me."

The sincerity in his voice calmed her trembling body. The love and care he gave her was how her father made her feel when he was alive. She continued to tell him everything she had been through. It felt good to finally tell him and let it all out.

"Well, things seemed to get worse, and the beatings continued. Cam would come by, out of the blue drunk, beating on the door, and raising hell. Numerous times he burst through the door, and jumped on me, right in front of Jaylin. Now, Jaylin is terrified of him." Chanel could no longer fight the tears. "I don't know what else to do. I've gone to the police, but they don't really help. I filed a restraining order against him the day we met up for Rasheed's birthday, and I figured it'd worked because I hadn't seen him or heard from him."

So that's why she tried to cancel on me that day. And that explains the bruise she had on her face that day, too. Samir put all the pieces together and now he understood why she was always so reluctant to move forward in the relationship with him. She was probably scared that Samir would turn out just like Cam'ron.

"Tonight was the first time the cops actually did something and locked him up." Samir returned his focus as Chanel went on explaining everything. "But what's going to happen when he gets out?" she asked to no one in particular. "Samir, he threatened to take Jaylin from me! I can't let him take my baby!" Chanel went into hysterics.

"Baby, calm down. Everything will be okay. I promise nothing is going to happen to you or Jaylin. I got you."

Jaylin and Rasheed rushed out of the bedroom, and into Samir's arms. "Daddy! Daddy! I want to go home!" Rasheed cried.

Jaylin ran up to Samir, yanking on the leg of his pants. "Me choo. Me choo!" Samir looked into Chanel's eyes. She looked confused, and hurt. The first thing that crossed his mind was that he would do anything to protect them. He wasn't able to protect Asia, but he'd be damned if he let another woman he loved get hurt again. The look in her and Jaylin's eyes sealed his promise. He vowed to not make the same mistake twice. Protecting his son, Chanel, and Jaylin at all cost was his number one priority, even if it killed him.

"Chanel, go pack you and Jaylin's things. Y'all are coming home with me," Samir said sternly.

"But—"

"No buts. Go get y'all stuff. Now!"

Chanel stood to her feet, and went to pack their belongings. Samir's love for her and Jaylin was evident. No matter how much she wanted to keep Samir from her troubles, he was determined to be there, and keep them safe regardless.

Chanel gave the boys their bath, and put them to bed. Her nervousness kicked in, as she realized it would be her first time staying the night with Samir. In the bathroom adjoining his bedroom, Samir made sure it was to perfection for her. Chanel popped her head in the door.

"The boys are in bed. If you don't mind, I'm going to the guest bathroom to take a shower. My body is a little sore from, well, you know," Chanel said nervously.

Samir walked over to her, and kissed her on the forehead. With gentleness, he unbuttoned her blouse, and let it drop to the floor. Chanel stiffened, as he continued to undress her.

"Samir, what are you doing?"

"Sshh. I told you I got you," Samir replied, in a low tone.

Chanel stood frozen, and unaware of what was about to take place. When Samir had fully undressed her, he stood in admiration of her beautiful dark brown skin. Like a shy virgin showing herself for the first time, she covered her private parts with her hands, and looked down to the floor.

Samir placed his hand under her chin, lifted her head, and looked her dead in the eyes. "You have nothing to be insecure about. You are beautiful." Bruises were printed around her neck, as Samir lifted her head higher to observe them. He shook his head, and tried to refrain from getting angry again. As he pulled her to him, he tilted her head, and kissed her bruises. Chanel's body trembled. Butterflies danced around in her belly, as he grabbed her hands, and guided her into the bathroom.

Once inside, she noticed the white, pink, and red rose petals in the tub. The scent of sweet vanilla bath beads filled the bathroom. Samir picked her up into his arms, and gently placed her in the water. *This man can't be real,* Chanel thought.

"Relax, and ease your mind of everything. I'll be in the guest bathroom," Samir said sincerely. Before leaving he kneeled down, and kissed her.

The bath soothed her aching body. Her mind drifted off into a happy place. The visions of her future with her perfect guy left a smile on her face.

Finally, after blissful imageries and a fulfilling bath, she stepped out of the tub, dried off, and oiled down her whole body. She searched through her bag, and slid into her red lace panties. Then, she squeezed on her black and red corset that pushed her breasts up to full attention. In spite of how nervous she felt, she wanted to please Samir in the same way he pleased her.

She waited patiently on the center of the bed for her sexy man. Her mind was going a thousand miles a minute. *What the hell am I doing? This is stupid.* She wrestled back and forth in her mind about whether she should get up and change into her long gown.

Insecurities flooded her mind, making her wonder if she could give Samir the pleasure he deserved. The fact that her ex was the only man she had been with made her feel inadequate. To top it off, Samir was the sexiest, most intimidating man she had ever laid eyes on. She was afraid to be vulnerable and exposed to him intimately.

At last, she decided to get up and change. As soon as she sat up in the bed, Samir walked through the door. Panic left her frozen in place. Her eyes widened in fear. Fear changed to lust, as she zoomed in on his bare chest. The sight of him was like staring at a god, from his chest muscles to his bulging abs. His arms were so strong, and his body glistened through the candlelight. It was like looking in a magazine of a dream guy she would never get to touch, but there he was, in the flesh wrapped in nothing but a white towel. The word RASHEED was tattooed with baby footprints across his chest.

In that moment, Chanel wished she could disappear, as she sat in the middle of the bed in her pretty panties and corset. Samir looked up, and his eyes widened in amazement of her beautiful glowing skin and her "freak me" outfit. Asia was the only woman he had looked at in that way. Blood rushed from his head and feet to his groin, creating a thick bulge underneath his towel. Chanel tried to look in every direction but his.

Samir sensed her discomfort. As bad as he wanted to run and leap into her hot flesh, he wanted more to make her feel comfortable with being with him.

"Baby, come here."

The sexy sound of his command made her want to run into his arms, though she dared not to. She cleared her throat, and then scooted off of the bed. She took her time walking over to him, trying not to appear nervous.

"What is it?" she asked, standing face to face with him.

Samir rubbed his fingers gently down the side of her face. "Why are you so nervous around me?"

"What are you talking about? I'm not nervous."

"Are you sure about that?" Samir quizzed.

Chanel didn't answer. She looked down, trying not to look him in the eyes. The huge bulge poking through his towel caught her attention. Her panties dampened, and her mind wondered off, as she imagined him sliding his thickness into her tight opening.

Samir smiled. "You want it?" he asked.

Stunned, Chanel quickly looked up. "Huh?" she asked, sounding confused.

Samir chuckled at her childlike innocence. He stepped up to her, and leaned in for a kiss. Her lips parted, as his tongue made way into her mouth. The bulge grew bigger poking right into Chanel's stomach. Her panties were now drenched, as a soft moan escaped her lips.

"Tell me you want it, and it's yours," Samir whispered, seductively. His tongue made a trail down to her neck. Chanel panted heavily, as his tongue flicked on her spot. "Tell me," he whispered again. "I'm not giving it to you, until you tell me you want it."

Samir's towel dropped to the floor. He stepped back, and let Chanel admire his lengthy, thick penis. She couldn't move. Her eyes were fixated on his groin. Her lips parted.

"I, um . . ."

"You, um, what?" Samir teased.

Chanel looked into Samir's sexy eyes. "I want it," Chanel whispered, timidly.

Her response was exactly what he wanted to hear, as he walked up to her, gently pushed her onto the bed, and climbed on top of her. Their bodies collided, as his mouth covered hers, and their tongues tangled together. He trailed his tongue all the way down from her neck, to her breasts, then to her panties. With one swift tug, he tore them off.

"Mmm!" The feel of his tongue lapping away at her sweetness sent her body into a serious frenzy, as he savored every drip. She closed her eyes, and arched her back. Samir kissed her clit, vibrated his tongue on it, and then dived into her juices. He made love to her kitty cat with his long, curvy tongue. Sounds of licking, panting, and moaning echoed throughout the room. Slowly she began to grind on his tongue, while sliding her fingers through his hair. Her body jerked, as she screamed out, and climaxed, sending her juices right into his mouth and down his throat.

Samir flipped her over on her stomach, and eased into her from behind. Chanel gripped the sheets, as he went deeper and deeper into her flesh. He bent down, and licked the center of her back, while penetrating her. With her hands, she fought to push him back, as he slid more inches into her. He grabbed her hands, and pinned them over her head. Chills went down her spine from the touch of his tongue trailing down the back of her neck. The pain of his length sliding deeper and deeper into her tight walls was too much to take in. "Samir, wait!" she screamed.

The teasing continued, as he stroked in and out of her, with just the head of his penis. Juices flowed onto the sheets, while she begged for him to put it all in. In one motion, he flipped her over onto her back, and continued stroking in and out of her, allowing only a few inches. He lifted her upper body with one hand, and watched her pleading look, while taking the other hand and fingering her clit. Her insides throbbed for all of him.

"Please!" Chanel begged.

"You said it was too much," Samir replied, breathing heavily.

"No, baby, please! I want to cum."

Every time Chanel came close to another orgasm, Samir would slow his pace teasing her. She didn't realize he was finally breaking her out of her shell.

"Either you take it all, or you only get a sample. Tell me, baby, what do you want?"

Chanel breathed heavily. Her chest heaved up and down. Her body was on fire, and she wanted Samir to put it out.

"Samir, fuck me!" she screamed.

Samir slid into her inch by inch. Chanel locked her legs tightly around his waist, making sure he wouldn't be able to tease her again. She clenched her pussy tightly around his dick, making him grunt loudly in satisfaction. He pounded into her like a wild animal, sweat pouring from his back. His hands covered her mouth, so she wouldn't wake the boys, as she exploded into another orgasm. After a couple more deep strokes, Samir erupted inside of her. They were both so exhausted they could barely move. Chanel had never been so pleased in her life. She slid over to Samir, laying her head in his arms, and wrapped one of her legs around his waist. They embraced, and caressed each other until they both fell asleep.

In the morning, the sunshine beamed throughout the bedroom. Samir rubbed his eyes, and slid his hand across the empty side of the bed. The roaring sounds of pots, pans, and laughter chimed in the kitchen. The aroma of breakfast being prepared filled the house. He went into the bathroom to brush his teeth, and then opened the double doors of his bedroom. With a smile of pure joy, he stepped into the kitchen greeting his family. The boys were at the table eating breakfast. Chanel brought their plates to the table.

"Good morning, sleepyhead," Chanel teased.

"Good morning, baby," Samir said as he leaned over, and kissed Chanel on the forehead.

"Eeww!" Rasheed said. The boys both laughed.

"Hush, boy, and eat your food," Samir said. "I see you found my robe. It looks hot on you." He winked at Chanel.

They sat at the table, and enjoyed breakfast.

"So now what?" Chanel asked, breaking the silence.

"What do you mean?"

"I mean, what's next with us?"

"You, my lady; and I plan on treating Jaylin as if he were my own. My home is your home now, so don't act like you're in a strange place. I love you and Jaylin and I will always be there to protect you both. You and Jaylin have brought a lot of joy into my and Rasheed's lives. And, I believe the best is yet to come. Did that answer your question?"

"So it's that simple to you, huh?"

"Yes. You love me right?"

"Of course, and I love Rasheed as well."

"Okay, then. Our relationship will continue to grow. I'm in this for the long haul. I just need you to be sure you are too."

"I wouldn't be here if I weren't."

"All right then."

"What about Cam'ron?"

Samir's face turned sour. "Please, I have dealt with worse chumps than him. As long as you're with me, you have nothing to worry about. Baby, you're mine now, and I protect what's mine. Don't worry about that punk anyway. What kind of man puts his hands on a woman, especially the mother of his child? I ain't trippin' off him, and neither should you. Anyway, enough about him. Who wants to go outside and play?"

The boys jumped for joy. The life Chanel had only dreamed of had finally come true.

Chapter 23

After a three-day lockup, Cam'ron was finally released from jail. He rolled through College Park with one of his partners, Brick. Brick was Cam'ron's right hand man. If there was trouble, Brick was definitely the man to call. With the stature of a body builder, his long dreads, and dark appearance, the ladies flocked to him like buzzards on road kill. He and Cam'ron had grown up together and the bond between them was like that of two blood brothers. Their loyalty to each other was unbreakable.

Unlike Brick, people could take one look at Cam'ron and assume he was a pretty boy. Women loved his hazel eyes and caramel complexion. His dark waves glistened in the sunlight. When he smiled, he could light up a room with his perfect pearly white teeth and deep dimples. As easy as it was to mistake him for Mr. Prince Charming, he was nonetheless a coldhearted thug full of anger. He was relentless, and ready to stop anyone in his path.

In the past, Cam'ron was the ultimate heart-throb every female wanted, but he only had eyes for Chanel. She was his high school sweetheart. Chanel knew she had found the perfect guy when she met Cam'ron. He was every female's dream. Not once did Chanel think her first love could hide such a dark side.

After she moved in with him, his dark side started to show. She witnessed everything from his jealous ways to his split personalities. Chanel later found out his change in moods was because he was bipolar. His mother had been on drugs during her entire pregnancy and it had affected Cam'ron's development when he was born. Child protective services took him from his parents; but, when he was a few years old, they somehow got him back and he grew up with a drug-addicted mother and an alcoholic father who would abuse both Cam'ron and his mother. He had an older brother, who he looked up to, but he was killed by a rival gang when Cam'ron was just seven years old.

At first, Chanel stayed with him, and dealt with his ways because she felt sorry for him. But after Jaylin was born, she realized she couldn't stay with a man like Cam'ron. She knew she had to leave him. Cam'ron felt betrayed by her leaving him and he felt like he got bitched out when he learned that she was dating somebody else. If she didn't want to be with him, she was going to be with nobody else as far as he was concerned. Now, Cam'ron was going to stop at nothing, until she got back with him or got laid to rest if she didn't take him back. But either way this new man of hers had to get taken care of, too. The thought of her being with someone else infuriated him. Cam'ron gritted his teeth, while making a vow that this chump-ass new nigga of hers would soon be history.

"Man, I can't believe that mothafucka! That bitch nigga gon' walk into my baby momma house like he King Kong or some shit. Just wait 'til I find that nigga," Cam'ron ranted to his friend.

"Who the fuck is he anyway?" Brick asked.

"I don't know who the fuck he is and I don't give a fuck. He gon' wish he never got in my business. And you better believe I'ma get Chanel's triflin' ass, just wait!" he barked as he punched his fist into his hand.

Brick laughed. "All right, nigga. You gon' get that ass sent to prison. I told you 'bout going insane over these hoes. All my baby mommas know I don't play."

"I thought Chanel knew better by now. She gon' learn real soon. She ain't never had a ass whoopin like the one she's gonna catch from me!

And she got the nerve to have this nigga roun' my son. Hell naw!"

"Yeah, that shit ain't cool. So whatchu gon' do 'bout it? We need to call Dex, so we can handle that punk." Dex was Cam'ron's other right-hand man. He kept tabs on any niggas who weren't handling business. Nothing could get past Dex, and he didn't mind offing anyone who crossed his boys.

"Best believe we gon' get that mothafucka," Cam'ron said deep in thought.

"All you gotta do is say the word, and it's handled."

"In due time. The nigga can breathe happily for now."

"Speakin' of handlin' mothafuckas, when are you gon' handle Perez ass?" Brick asked hoping he'd get Cam'ron to change the subject. He wasn't trying to get stuck talking about baby momma drama all day.

"Man, I know you ain't on that Perez shit again. I told you he good peoples, man. That's my family."

"Cousins or not, that mothafucka playin' you. Everybody turned in their percentage but him."

"Man, that nigga know not to cross me."

"Dex called and told me that nigga rolled through his way in a brand new ride. Some hot shit, too. But he paid you yo' money yet?"

"He got a new whip for real?" Cam'ron asked in surprise.

"For real, for real. You had the rest of us turn our shit in yesterday. You let too much shit slide with him. He ain't tryin'a pay you yo' money. Don't believe me? Call that nigga, and tell to him bring you yo' shit right now. You supposed to be boss nigga of the operation, and that nigga ain't respectin' you. You betta check that shit."

The thought of his cousin running game on him made Cam'ron furious. He hoped his cousin had a reasonable explanation for not getting his percentage to him.

"Don't worry. I'ma look into it. Family or not, if he on some dirty shit, that nigga gettin' handled too."

Samir, Chanel, and the kids headed across the street to the new neighbors' cookout. The aroma of food cooking on the grill filled the air. They headed to the back of the house to join the rest of the party. Keshawn's wife saw them walking and left a group of people to greet them.

"Hey, I'm Renee, and you are?" she said, holding out her hand.

Samir shook her hand. "I'm Samir, and this is my lady, Chanel, and our boys, Rasheed and Jaylin."

"Well, it's so nice to meet you. Keshawn told me about you. I'm so glad you all could make it." She turned her attention to Rasheed and Jaylin. "And aren't you two the cutest."

"I hope everyone likes the pasta salad I made," Chanel said.

"Oh, I'm sure we all will. You can take it to the food table right over there. And, I'll take these two cuties to play with the other little ones, if that's okay."

"That's fine," Samir replied. "You two behave yourselves."

"Make yourselves at home, and feel free to mingle. Keshawn is right over by the grill."

Chanel followed Samir, as he headed to the grill to speak to Keshawn.

"What's up, man? You got it smelling good over here."

"Yo! Samir, right?" Keshawn was surprised he showed up.

"Yes. And this is my lady, Chanel. I would've wanted to introduce you to our two boys, but your wife took them to play with the other kids."

"Okay. Nice to meet you Chanel," Keshawn said, extending his hand. "She is beautiful, Samir. Better not let her get away."

Samir laughed. "Yes, she is. And trust me, she stuck with me now."

"All right now! So do you know any of our neighbors here?"

Samir looked around. "Nah, not really. I recognize some by face, but I don't really know them. I may have spoken to them in passing here and there but that's as far as that goes. Most of our neighbors are older. You 'bout the only one I know of who's around my age."

"Well, we gon' have to link up sometimes after this. And, Chanel, I'm sure my wife would love to get to know you. We are from Florida, so we hardly know anyone here."

"I'd like that. I don't have many friends around here either," Chanel replied.

"Hey, what are you guys talking about?" Renee said, jumping in on the conversation.

"Bae, we were just discussing how we should all get together and hang out just the four of us. I think it would be cool."

"Oh, yes! That sounds great, but for starters, I have better idea. You guys go out, while Chanel and I have a ladies' night." Renee laughed.

"I could sure use that," Chanel replied.

Toward the end of the cookout, Keshawn and Renee said their good-byes to their guests. Chanel took the initiative to help pick up the empty beer and water bottles around the back yard.

"Oh, Chanel honey, you don't have to do that." Renee stepped in.

"It's fine. I don't mind at all. That's what friends are for."

Renee smiled. When everything was picked up and put away Chanel walked to the swings to get Rasheed and Jaylin.

"Well, we really enjoyed ourselves, and thanks again for inviting us. I guess we should head on home so we can get the boys ready for bed," Samir said.

"Yes, and unfortunately I have to get ready to go back to work tomorrow," Chanel added.

"Okay, it was nice meeting you. We definitely will keep in touch. Y'all be safe," Keshawn said.

Samir and Chanel headed back home, carrying the boys in their arms. It felt nice to have neighbors around their age. They were looking forward to getting to know them.

Chapter 24

Samir woke up to find Chanel dressed and ready to head out for work. He hated that she still went to work. He had tried time and time again to convince her to stop working, but she refused to listen. She let him know that she loved her job, and she never wanted to feel like she had to depend on him. He understood where she was coming from and he respected a female who wanted to provide for herself. But that still didn't stop him from wishing she would quit her job so they could enjoy every day together just chilling and spending time with Rasheed and Jaylin.

Seeing how much Chanel enjoyed what she did made Samir consider going into the work field himself. He had never had a real job before so he didn't even know if he'd enjoy it. Up until this point all he had ever done was deal in the streets and with his short-lived career as a rapper. After Asia and his parents died, he lost the drive and passion he had to want to write or rap.

He went into the studio for a few sessions and worked on a few tracks, but his heart just wasn't in it anymore. After a couple of months he quit the music world and hadn't looked back since.

Chanel grabbed her nametag from the dresser, and pinned it to her shirt. She hadn't noticed Samir was awake and had been watching her move around for the last five minutes.

"I know you not gon' leave without kissing me good-bye," Samir said, as he rose up from the bed.

Chanel looked up, and smiled. He walked over to her, and kissed her on the forehead. Forehead kisses were becoming Samir's signature with Chanel.

"I didn't want to wake you up. I have to hurry up, and get Jaylin dressed so I can get him to my mother."

"For what?" Samir asked, confused.

"Because, I have to go to work. Duh."

"He's been staying with me for a week. Why can't he stay with me all of a sudden? That's crazy to take him all the way to your mother when I'm here with Rasheed."

"I didn't want to keep putting him off on you."

"Really? Come on now, Chanel. You can't be serious. That doesn't make sense. I told you, I look at Jay as if he were my own. He is staying here with me and Rasheed and that's it," he said in a stern tone.

"Okay. I won't argue with you."

"That's because you know I'll always win anyway," Samir said, pulling Chanel to him.

"Uh-uh, hug only. You got morning breath," Chanel joked.

"Oh, it's like that." Samir laughed.

"Nah, boo, I'm just playing." Chanel placed her hands around Samir's neck, and planted a kiss on his lips.

Samir finally pulled back. "You better get off to work before you start something you can't finish."

"Yeah, you right," Chanel said, as she grabbed her purse. Samir walked her to the door, and gave her one last kiss before she headed off to work.

Chanel checked the time on her watch. She had been on her feet all day, and was super tired. In just three more hours, she would get to be home with her loves. She walked into her office, and sighed with relief that she was able to sit down and take a break.

As she sat down, her coworker came into the room. "Hey, chick, these are for you," she said, as she placed a lovely bouquet of flowers on Chanel's desk.

Chanel fished through the flowers to find the small card that read:

> *Enjoy your day, beautiful.*
> *Samir*

Chanel blushed. "Thank you for bringing these in Sharon," she said.

Sharon pulled up a chair. "Thank you my ass. Girl, who are these from?"

"My man. Why?"

"Don't play with me, Nel. Who is this new boo? Because I know damn well your baby daddy didn't do this. No offense."

"None taken, but if you must know, his name is Samir." Chanel couldn't stop smiling, as she filled her work buddy in.

"Damn, he must really love you. How come I didn't know nothing about this?"

"Because, I wanted to be sure it was real."

"Well, I'm happy for you, girl. You deserve to be happy, especially after all the bull you-know-who put you through. How long have y'all been dating?"

"We are way past dating. And, to answer your question, almost nine months."

"Yes, honey! I love it! Just make sure I get invited to the wedding."

"Wedding? Chile, cut it out."

"I'm serious. You saying cut it out, but that glow on your face says otherwise."

"Well, I can't deny that I believe I have definitely found the one. He is every woman's dream. And, he is all mine." Chanel blushed.

"I heard that's right! Do he got a brother though?"

"Nope, not that I know of." Chanel laughed.

"Figures. Well, anyway, let me get back to work, and get these few hours over with. I can't wait to get up outta here," Sharon said as she rose up from the chair and put it back in its original place.

"I know right? I'm hoping these last hours go by fast," Chanel said, as she sniffed her beautiful flowers before getting back to work.

Samir was exhausted from a long morning of chasing after the boys, cleaning up their messes, and getting them dressed. Two toddlers running around was a full-time job in itself and it was exhausting. But, he loved every minute of it.

He strapped the boys into their seats, went around the car, and got into the driver's seat. Samir looked into the mirror at them.

"Where do you guys want to go to eat?" Samir asked.

"Burgers!" Rasheed yelled out.

"Yeah! Burgers!" Jaylin replied.

"Okay. Burger joint it is."

The trio walked into the packed Burger King. The boys stood on each side of Samir holding his hand. Once he ordered their food, he guided them to a nearby table. The kids laughed, and enjoyed their meal. Samir happened to glance toward the counter, and saw a very familiar face. He knew if he didn't leave, there was going to be trouble.

"All right, boys, it's time to go."

"No!" Rasheed whined. "I want to play on da shhlide!"

"No, we gotta go!" Samir yelled. He threw away their trash, and headed out the door.

Cam'ron spotted Samir walking out, and headed right in his direction with his crew following him.

Samir quickly buckled the boys in the car. He closed the door, and tried to get in the car himself when Cam'ron and his crew cut him off and surrounded him. Samir did his best to stay out of trouble, but it seemed like trouble always found him. A crowd of people walked by, trying to figure out what was going on.

"Samir, is it? What the fuck you doing with my son in your car?" Cam'ron barked.

Samir tried to remain calm, but his pressure was building by the second. "Look, man, I ain't trying to get into nothing while the kids are around. So you go ahead about your business."

Samir opened his driver's side door. Cam'ron kicked it closed. Samir laughed. *Jesus, I'm trying, but no, this fool did not just kick at my Maybach.* "I'm gon' pretend you didn't just kick my car. Y'all enjoy the rest of your day," Samir said, as he opened his car door again. Cam'ron, once again, kicked it closed.

Samir turned and faced him, looking him dead in the eyes. "Cam'ron, is it? I'ma try to make this plain, 'cause it's obvious you don't know who the fuck I am. I said, 'Have a nice day.' In other words, you and your side bitches need to bounce. You got beef with me, that's cool, but not in front of these kids. Play the man card this one time for your son. He don't need to see this." By now, people had picked up on a possible fight about to go down and were starting to crowd around.

"Man, come on, Cam'ron, before one of these mothafuckas call the cops. We will see that nigga another time," Cam'ron's homeboy Dex said, pulling Cam'ron back.

"That's right. Best believe I'ma see you later, nigga. Remember, Chanel is mine, and if she ain't with me, she won't make it to be with nobody."

"What the fuck you say? You threatenin' her, nigga?" That's all it took for Samir to lose it.

He was seconds from striking Cam'ron when a stranger grabbed him. "It's not worth it, son. You got your boys in the car. Don't do it." Samir quickly came back to his senses. He was grateful to the old man for talking him down. That still didn't change how pissed off he felt. He was so mad his veins were popping out of his neck as he drove home.

There was no way that Samir was going to let Cam'ron come in and destroy his life, after working so hard to rebuild it. When he got home, he put the boys down for a nap. He sat on the couch in silence, thinking about all his family went through with D-Money. He felt like his past lifestyle was coming back to haunt him. Here he was minding his own business building a good, decent and, most importantly, legal life for him and his son and trouble just has to come knocking on his front door.

Chanel walked through the door. She looked into the boys' room, and found them fast asleep. After she closed their door, she looked around the house for Samir. She found him sitting quietly on the couch, with a look of disdain on his face. He was so out of his mind, he didn't notice Chanel standing in the doorway of the living room.

"Hey, baby, are you okay?" she asked, concerned.

Samir quickly snapped back to reality. There was no way he could tell her about what happened between him and Cam'ron. She would be devastated. And, he didn't want to see her stressed out. "Oh, everything is fine. How was your day?"

"It was okay. Thank you for the beautiful flowers," she said, still looking at him curiously.

"Of course. You deserved them." Samir tried to pretend everything was fine, but Chanel could tell it wasn't.

"Samir, did the boys drive you crazy today?" she asked, taking a seat on the couch next to him.

"No. They were fine. Why would you think that?"

"Because, when I came in here you looked angry. Don't lie to me, Samir. What's wrong?"

It killed Samir to lie to her; however, he knew it was for her own good. She continued to question him, because she knew something was wrong. Samir ignored her questions, and focused on changing the subject.

"Baby, I missed you." Samir leaned in to kiss her.

"No, Samir, talk to me, seriously."

Samir pulled her leg onto the couch, straddling her, and then pulled her to him. He climbed on top of her, and flicked his tongue back and forth across her neck.

Chanel tried pushing him up. "Samir, no!" she yelled. Samir ignored her plea, and pulled off her clothes. He was too strong for her to even put up a fight. "Samir, we need to talk!"

Not saying a word, he threw his shirt to the floor. His mouth covered hers, while he slid out of his pants. Chanel pushed him on his chest. He pinned her hands down over her head with one of his hands, as she tried to wrestle them free. Slowly, he slid into her golden spot, causing her to gasp for air. He sucked on her neck, and pinched her nipple, while mastering hitting her G-spot over and over. The heat of passion overcame him, as he panted in her ear, sliding his hands down her thigh, then gripping her perfectly plump ass thrusting deeper into her walls. He knew just where to land to send her into an orgasmic frenzy. Her moans became more intense, as she dug her nails into his back. Like many times, Samir had to place his hands over her mouth, as she screamed in ecstasy. Samir's face became contorted, as he tried to keep from grunting too loud. Seconds later, he spilled into her, breathing heavily.

"Come on. Let's get cleaned up before the kids wake up," he said, after finally catching his breath.

"Okay," Chanel replied. Samir helped her off the couch. Her thighs felt like Jell-O.

"You good?" Samir smirked.

"I think so."

Samir lifted her into his arms, and carried her to their bedroom. He was thankful that he had dodged a bullet. *Now that's how you avoid answering questions.* Samir smirked.

Chapter 25

The cold winter wind swirled around Samir and the boys, as they ran inside the barbershop to keep from freezing to death. He hated to bring them out in the cold, but a haircut for both of them was long overdue.

"What's good, Ralph?" Samir said, as they entered the shop.

"Hey there, Puerto Rican. If it ain't Samir and the tag team."

"Ralph, man, I done told you one time, I ain't no damn Puerto Rican. I'm all black."

"I know Ralph ain't the only one you see," Kita chimed in. She was the braider for the shop.

"My bad, Kita. Hello to everyone," Samir said, sarcastically. "Ralph, I need you to hook my boys up. Don't cut it too close. Last time you almost left them bald," Samir joked.

"The closer the cut the longer it last."

"Well, in that case you shouldn't want to cut it so low, 'cause the longer it lasts, the longer it takes for you to get that nice tip I always leave you."

"That's a good point, young'un." Ralph chuckled. "Don't worry. I won't cut it so low anymore."

"You need to do something to yo' head, Samir," Kita cut into their conversation. .

"Kita, there you go, always trying to get me do something with my hair. I can't even take you serious with all them damn rainbow colors you got all up on your head," Samir shot back.

"Boy, you always talking shit. I'm being serious. That ponytail getting old. Let me hook you up."

"Man, you might mess my shit up."

"I promise you, Chanel will like it."

"Since you put it like that, hook me up. But she better like it or else I'm coming for your ass," Samir said, jumping into Kita's chair.

"Well, damn! You don't need to threaten me." Kita acted like she was concerned.

"So, Samir, how have you and the family been doing?" Ralph asked, while lifting Rasheed into his chair, then putting a cape around him.

"Everything's good, man. I can't complain."

"You ain't heard nothing from that crazy ex of hers, have you?"

"Hell naw. I ain't even tryin' to run into that dude. I'm just tryin' to be a family man, and stay out of trouble."

"That's right. These young punks nowadays don't have no morals. They roam the streets like they untouchable. And, it's those same ones I end up seeing in the obituary when I'm reading the papers."

That comment made Samir think about his dad. "Yeah, it's sad, man." Samir didn't really know how he should respond.

"Anyway, you keep doing what you doing. Don't even pay that fool any mind. You concentrate on keeping that beautiful girlfriend of yours satisfied, before an old man like me come sweep her off her feet," Ralph joked.

"Man, please. All jokes aside though, I'm ready to make her my wife."

"That's what ya need to do," Kita said right before popping her gum for what seemed like the millionth time since Samir had walked into the shop with the boys.

"Nah, what I need to do is pop you in the mouth the next time you pop that damn gum behind my head. That shit irritatin'."

Ralph let Rasheed down, then placed Jaylin in the seat. "I think that's the manly thing to do. I can't stand to see a man shackin' up with a woman for years and years, but can't marry her. I don't get that."

"That's 'cause you from the old school," replied Ted coming in from the back of the shop. Ted was another barber who worked in the shop. He had been folding some face towels in the back but had been listening to the entire conversation.

"And ain't nothing wrong with that," Ralph proudly replied.

Kita finally finished Samir's hair. It was neatly braided in small braids in the front with two long plaits, one on each side of his head, hanging down his shoulders. Samir checked himself out in the mirror. He nodded in approval.

"I gotta give you yo props, Kita. My shit nice."

"You better like it. Shit, it ain't easy braidin' all that slick-ass hair."

"Well, best believe you did yo' thang, fa real."

Ralph finished up with Jaylin. Samir paid Kita and Ralph, then they said their good-byes. They ran back into the cold wind. Samir hit the button on his keychain to unlock the doors, and quickly got the kids into their seats. He blew into his hands, as he rushed to get in the car.

When they got home, they rushed into the house out of the cold. Samir was so glad to be warm again. They met Chanel in the kitchen, as she was just finishing up dinner.

"Awww, don't y'all look so cute with y'all fresh haircuts." Chanel looked at Samir. "Damn, you fine. What's your name?" she joked.

"Ha-ha, real funny. I take it you like the braids."

"I love it! But now I'm jealous, because you never let me do your hair. Who braided it?"

"Kita," Samir replied.

"I'm surprised you let Kita touch it."

"Trust me, I only did it for you."

"Uh-huh, if you say so."

"I'm serious. Now fix yo' man a plate. I'm hungry."

"And what's wrong with yo' hands?" Chanel barked.

"Baby, they're numb. We almost froze outside." Samir tried his best to make big puppy eyes at her.

Chanel giggled. "Boy, you are something else."

"You love me though."

"I sure do," she replied.

The following day, Samir planned a special surprise for Chanel while she was at work. The hospital doors slid open, as he stepped in looking as fresh as always. The women stopped, and stared as he walked down the hall. They were all trying to figure out who this sexy specimen of a man was. He walked over to the receptionist desk and removed his shades before greeting the receptionist sitting at the desk.

"Hey, handsome, can I help you?" she asked.

"You sure can," Samir said, with a smile showing his perfect white teeth. The receptionist blushed. "Can you tell me where to find Chanel Owen, please?"

"Sure. Are you her brother?"

"No, I'm her man actually," Samir said knowing that he had just burst her bubble. "I'm here to see my lady."

The receptionist quickly changed her attitude. "She is on the fourth floor."

"Thank you," Samir replied, heading toward the elevators.

When he got to the fourth floor, he looked around for Chanel. He walked to the nurses' station, and asked for her, then waited patiently for the nurse to page her.

"What are you doing here?"

He turned around, and there she was. "Hey, baby, it's your lunch break right?"

"Yes, it is. Why?" she asked, curiously.

"Well, come on. I have something special planned for you."

The rest of the nurses watched in envy, as Samir grabbed Chanel by the hand to take her out.

"Where are the kids?"

"Your mom volunteered to keep them for me."

They walked toward the elevators, and were stopped midway.

"Damn, is this the famous Samir?" Sharon asked.

Chanel laughed. "Yes, Sharon."

"I see why you stay smiling all the time. He is hot as hell!"

"Samir, this is my coworker Sharon, and, Sharon, you already know this is Samir."

"Nice to meet you, Sharon," Samir replied. "I hate to make this introduction short, but I don't have long so . . ."

"Oh, okay, honey. Chanel, you can give me the details when you return."

Chanel shook her head, and laughed. "All right, girl, see you when I get back."

Samir pulled into the park.

"Baby, it's a little too chilly for us to be at the park," Chanel protested.

He helped Chanel out of the car, and pulled a big, furry blanket and a small basket from the back seat. "Girl, hush up and let me do my thing." Samir smiled at her as he threw the blanket around her.

"Now poke your cute little hand out so I can hold it while we walk," Samir demanded once she was all wrapped up. Chanel did as she was told without saying a single word. She was so curious to see what this man had up his sleeve. They walked through the park hand in hand with Samir leading the way. After a two minutes of walking, Chanel noticed a gazebo up ahead. As they got closer she saw dozens of little tea lights on the floor surrounding a table that had been set for two. A beautiful arrangement of white flowers adorned the top of the table and she could feel a warm draft that came from heating lanterns that hung from the corners of the gazebo. Samir let go of her hand, placed the basket on the table, and proceeded to pull her chair out. "Wow, Samir! This is so sweet. You didn't have to do all this."

"I don't mind going the extra mile for my queen."

"You are too much," Chanel said, giving her Prince Charming a kiss.

"All right now, you have to be back to work in thirty minutes, don't start nothing," Samir joked.

"I'll try not to."

"Well, I brought you here so we can have alone time to talk."

"To talk about what?"

Samir reached into the basket and pulled out two thermos cups filled with hot chocolate. He handed her a cup before answering. "I've been doing a lot of thinking and, well, I think we should go into business together."

"What? Go into business together? Doing what?"

"I would like to open a gym for athletes, and you can do your physical therapy there."

"Are you serious?"

"Yes, I am very serious. I already got some information, and I have been looking at locations. I just need to know if you would be on board."

"Of course! I'd love that. Do you think it could be successful?"

"It will take some time, and a lot of hard work, but I feel it's worth a shot. I just want to do something that will make me feel accomplished. I enjoy being home with the boys but, I'd really like to have my own business. I've been thinking about this for a while."

"Well, we should definitely look into it. There's nothing like running your own business."

"Exactly! I have no experience in the health field, but you do so I really think we'll make a great team. I'll handle the business parts and you can handle the patients. Another thing I wanted to ask, can you take some time off from work?"

"When and for how long?"

"Four days, a month and a half from now."

"I'll put in for it. Where are we going?" Chanel asked, excited.

"I can't tell you all that, nosy." Samir laughed.

"Now you gonna have me wondering what you have planned."

"And, you will be a'ight. Now, let's get you back to work, before I get you fired."

"I'm too much of a good worker to get fired."

"Yeah, right," Samir said as they got ready to head back toward the car.

Samir dropped Chanel back off at work. The ride was relaxing, as August Alsina's lyrics from "Make It Home" played smoothly through the speakers. After the life he lived in the past few years, the song was definitely something he could relate to. The lyrics made him think of Chanel and the boys. His head bobbed in time with the music, as he waited for cars to go by while at the stop sign. When the coast was clear, he took his foot off the brake, and gently pressed the gas crossing the intersection. In that instant a car stopped in front of him. He mashed the break again, wondering why the car stopped.

Cam'ron and his crew surrounded the car. Without hesitation, Cam'ron burst Samir's window, and yanked him out of the car. Standing to his feet, Samir looked around at the guys surrounding him.

"Y'all ain't nothing but some bitch niggas!" he shouted in anger.

Cam'ron stepped up to him with a smirk on his face. "You just bring my bitch home where she belong, or else!"

"She ain't coming home with you! Take yo' loss like a man, bruh. She done wit yo' weak ass."

Out of anger and embarrassment, Cam'ron swung and hit Samir in the face. Like a bolt of lightning, Samir swung back knocking Cam'ron to the ground.

As a result, one of the guys hit him in the back of his head. There was nothing Samir could do. He was outnumbered. The men all took turns jumping on Samir. The only thing he knew to do was to curl up, and protect his face. After cars passed taking notice of what was going on, it wasn't long before the sounds of sirens neared. Cam'ron and his crew loaded into the car, and took off leaving Samir in the road hurt.

Chapter 26

The lights in the hospital room irritated Samir's eyes. He woke up to find Chanel right by his side. His mouth was dry, and his head was thumping out of control. He struggled to move, as pain shot through his body. Bandaged from face to arms, he struggled to get comfortable in the small bed.

"Baby, I am so sorry this happened to you," Chanel cried. She had been an absolute mess since finding out that it was Cam'ron and his crew who hurt Samir like that.

"Stop crying, woman. I'm all right. Trust me."

"No! You are not okay. I shouldn't have brought my drama into your life." Chanel continued to weep.

"You can't let your ex stop you from living your life. I said I'm fine, so stop stressin' over it."

"Stop stressin'? Look at you. You're all banged up, and it's because of me!"

Samir laughed. "I don't think you are that strong."

"Stop playing. You know what I mean."

"It's okay. Next time, I'll be more careful. Don't worry about nothing. I'll handle it."

"Samir—"

The nurse entered, interrupting the conversation. "Hey, how are you feeling?"

"Like shit," Samir answered bluntly.

"Samir, watch your mouth."

"Oh, no, he is perfectly fine. I understand," the nurse interjected. "I have something right here to help with the pain. Hopefully, you will be able to go home tomorrow."

The nurse wheeled her cart over to Samir's bedside. She checked his temperature, and then gave him pain medicine in his IV.

"Yes! The best part of being in here," Samir joked. A minute later, the meds kicked in. He continued to crack jokes to make Chanel laugh. Though she still felt bad about what Cam'ron had done, she was thankful that Samir was in good spirits.

A few minutes later, there was a knock at the door. Keshawn and his wife Renee entered the room. "What's up, man? Whatchu doin' in here?" Keshawn joked.

"I don't know, man. Mothafuckas hatin' as usual."

"Samir, watch your mouth!" Chanel yelled.

"Excuse my language. What I meant to say is, these cornballs out here trippin' like females as usual. You know how it is, man? It's all good though. He will get what's coming to him soon enough."

"Renee, I'm a little hungry. Will you walk with me to the cafeteria?" Chanel asked.

"I sure will. I need something to drink anyway."

Chanel walked over to Samir, and kissed his forehead. "I'll be back in a bit."

"A'ight, baby."

Once Chanel and Renee entered the hospital cafeteria, Chanel found a nearby table and sat down. Sighing, she rested her chin on her hands, and looked as if she was deep in thought. Renee took a seat across from her.

"Girl, I thought you were hungry. Is everything okay?"

"I just needed to get away to talk. Everything is so messed up." Chanel began to sob.

Renee rushed to the counter to get some napkins, and then handed them to Chanel. "Aww, honey, what is going on? What really happened with Samir? You know you can talk to me."

Cleaning her face, she took a deep breath. "It's my ex, Cam'ron. We broke up awhile ago, because he was running the streets and abusing me. Now that I have moved on, he's been threatening to take Jaylin."

"Oh, I thought Samir was his father," Renee said sounding surprised.

"Girl, I wish," Chanel said kissing her teeth. "Cam'ron is the reason Samir is in the hospital. From what I was told, he collided with Samir's car on purpose, and he and some guys who were with him pulled Samir out of the car and beat him half to death. Now I'm afraid it's going to get worse." Chanel started crying again.

"Oh my God, Chanel! I had no idea things were this bad," Renee responded with genuine concern. "Well, have you told the police?"

"Yes, but it doesn't help. They lock him up for a few days then he's right back out, causing havoc all over again. I tried to make things work when we were together, but all he cared about was his red painted car, loud system, and rims. Then the constant female calls and threats were ridiculous. I was contemplating leaving him when I found out I was pregnant. I thought maybe he would change once he found out we had a baby on the way but nothing changed.

Then after I had Jaylin, he started hitting me. Watching the fright in my son's eyes was the last straw."

"I'm so sorry you are dealing with this, Chanel."

"I know, and to top it off, Samir keeps talking about retaliating on him. It's going to end up being one big mess. Samir has been through enough in his past. He worked so hard to get out of the streets, and I hate to see everything come crashing down because of me."

"Honestly, I don't know what to say. This is a dangerous situation. The best thing to do in a situation like this is trust that Samir will take care of it, but at the same time, advise him not to do anything that will put his life in jeopardy."

"I just wish Cam would get the fuck away from me and my family! I'm so sick of this!"

"Calm down. It will be okay. And if ever you need me, you know I'm just across the street, and a phone call away."

"Thank you so much, Renee. You are truly a lifesaver."

"Of course, honey. That's what I'm here for. I may need you one day when Keshawn acting crazy," she joked. "Now come on. Let's go back and see what these men are talking 'bout."

***

Two weeks passed, and Chanel was glad to clock out, and get home to the love of her life. Samir was back to his normal self and in good spirits. Luckily, Chanel was able to talk him out of going on a hunting spree to find Cam'ron.

As Chanel reached out to open her car door, she was approached from behind. When she turned around, her mouth dropped, and her eyes widened in fear.

"Where the fuck you been hidin' at with my son?" Cam'ron barked, as he grabbed Chanel by the arm. The look in his eyes made her fear for her life.

"I, umm . . ." she said, stammering over her words.

"You what, bitch? I want to see my fuckin' son. Your ho ass so busy in bed with the next nigga. If you won't be with me, I promise you, Jaylin won't ever see you again!"

"Please! Let me go. You are hurting me!"

Just then, Chanel's friend Sharon came outside. "Cam, get your fuckin' hands off of her!"

"Bitch, mind yo' fuckin' business!"

"It's okay, Sharon. Just stay out of it." It was bad enough Cam'ron was lashing out at her, but she didn't want Sharon in the middle of it, and end up on Cam'ron's hit list.

"So what's it gon' be, Chanel? You coming home with me, or what?"

"No! You know I'm not coming home with you, Cam. Why can't you understand we are done? You had your chance and you blew it. This is your fault!" Chanel shouted nervously.

"Let her go now, or I'm calling the police!" Sharon yelled, taking her cell phone out of her pocket.

Cam'ron held a tighter grip on her arm. His anger intensified by the second. He looked at her with a deadly stare. "You fucked up, Chanel! You mark my words, this ain't over."

Realizing he didn't want to spend any more nights in jail, he released her arm. His eyes shot back at Sharon coldly, as he walked off, got into his car, and drove away. Chanel was too shaken up to get into her car and drive. Sharon stayed by her side, trying to calm her down.

"I don't know what to do. I am so afraid he is going to try to take Jaylin away from me. Either that, or he is going to try to kill me and Samir!"

"No, don't think like that, Nel. That punk ain't gonna do nothing; otherwise, he would have done it by now. He gets off on scaring you. You know Samir ain't gonna let nothing happen to you."

"I'm not a baby, Sharon. Samir can't be around every time Cam pops up. I know something bad is going to happen, and I can't let Samir go through that again. I wish I had never brought Samir into this."

"Don't say that. You deserve to be happy, and that man loves you. Don't regret being with a man who wants to protect you. None of this is your fault. Now come on. I'll follow you home."

Cam'ron circled the corner, and followed Chanel and Sharon's cars. He was desperate to find out where Chanel was staying. Making sure to stay far behind, he watched as they pulled into a driveway. As soon as she got out of her car that bitch nigga Samir came out of the house. This had to be where they were living. His first mission was accomplished. Now all he had to do was work on his next move now that he knew where she lived.

Samir opened the door to greet Chanel. His smile quickly faded when he noticed the distraught look on Chanel's face. Sharon walked beside her, as they made their way to the door. Samir welcomed them both into the house, as he stood curiously wanting to know what was wrong.

"Chanel, what's wrong. Did something happen to you?" he asked.

"Everything is fine, Samir. I just had a rough day at work. We will discuss it later."

"No, Nel, you need to tell him now!" Sharon argued.

Samir looked from Chanel to Sharon. "Tell me what?"

Chanel didn't respond. Samir folded his arms, and waited for someone to tell him what was going on.

Finally, Sharon broke the silence. "Cam came up to the job today threatening Chanel. He is threatening to hurt her and take Jaylin. Look what he did to her arm."

Chanel looked at Sharon in disbelief. She knew Samir was about to blow a fuse. Sharon ignored her snide look as she reached for Chanel's arm, lifting her sleeve. Cam'ron's handprints were on her left arm.

"Stay here with her," Samir told Sharon. Running to the hall closet, he reached into a shoebox on the top shelf, and pulled out a gun. Sharon's and Chanel's hearts both dropped.

"Samir, no!" Chanel pleaded. "Please don't!"

"Enough! I'm tired of this shit! For months I have listened to you. Every time you beg for me not to do anything, I listen, and now look at you. I promised to protect mine, and that's what I'ma do! This punk mothafucka don't know me, and I'm tired of hiding in his shadow. Fuck that. I'm coming straight from the hood of the Big Apple on these Georgia peach bitches!"

Samir walked out, slamming the door behind him. There was nothing Chanel or Sharon could do to stop him. He made it to the car before he realized he didn't know the first place to look for Cam'ron. Marching back into the house, he looked Chanel dead in the eyes to let her know he meant serious business.

"Where he live at? And don't lie to me," he demanded.

"In College Park," Chanel answered, in almost a whisper.

"Where in College Park?"

Chanel didn't answer. Sharon was in shock. She had never seen this side of Samir. She immediately regretted opening her mouth, and it showed all over her face. The look in Samir's eyes frightened her when he turned, and faced her.

"Where in College Park, Chanel?" Samir asked almost yelling. Chanel just stayed quiet, afraid to speak again. "Sharon, do you know his address?"

She hesitated trying to figure out what to say. "Um . . ." She glanced over at Chanel, who shook her head no. She looked back at Samir. He was serious, and she could not hold it off any longer.

There was nothing more she could do, so she told him Cam'ron's address.

Cam'ron walked into his house talking on his cell phone. The moment he found out where Chanel was staying, he called his boys, Dex and Brick, to tell them the news. Now, all he had to do was make the surprise visit of a lifetime. His plan to get his girl back, or take them down at all cost, would soon be in effect.

"Man, hell yeah. I walked up to her ass like a mu'fuckin' boss. I had her ass shook. It won't be long now," he said into the phone.

"That was some smart shit to follow her home. Now we know where to go to bust in on that mothafucka," Brick replied.

"I don't give a fuck. I'll take a life sentence just to kill that bitch out. And her nigga."

Cam'ron continued to ramble on and on about his plans to take out Samir. Samir pulled up to the house, and walked up to the screen door. His adrenaline was through the roof, and he was ready to show Cam'ron who he was dealing with. He rang the doorbell nonstop.

"Man, I'ma call you back. Somebody ringing my damn bell like they ain't got no fuckin' sense."

"A'ight, nigga," Brick said.

Unaware of who was at the door, Cam'ron cursed loudly, then froze when he saw Samir on the other side of the screen. In a matter of seconds, Samir kicked in the screen door. The door flew open hitting Cam'ron in the mouth. "What the fuck?" he yelled, as blood gushed from his lip.

Samir walked in like the former kingpin he was, and beat Cam'ron with ease. Flashbacks of old times like the day he beat Derrick with his pops crowded his memory, as he continued to beat Cam'ron until he was barely conscious.

"Get the fuck up, bitch! You want to hit a woman? Get up, and hit a man, mothafucka!"

Samir aimed his gun at Cam'ron's head. "Nigga, whatcha gon' do now? Go get yo' goons? I'm in this bitch by myself, nigga. You fucked with the wrong one. You, and yo' weak-ass niggas gon' jump me, but you ain't got enough balls to handle me yo'self." Samir looked down at him, and laughed. "The only time you don't need yo' goons is when you hittin' a woman, pussy nigga?"

Cam'ron lay on the floor helpless, and coughing up blood, while Samir made sure he belittled him in every way possible.

"This is your final warning, nigga. Stay the fuck away from my girl! And if ever you in New York, bitch, ask about me," Samir said, then hit him in the head with the butt of the gun. Like it was nothing, Samir left him lying in the floor, as he walked out of the door.

When Samir returned home, he found Chanel in their bedroom packing her bags. Stress of the situation overwhelmed her, as she continued to throw her belongings in her suitcase. It pained Samir to see her hurting. Her eyes and face were red, and puffy from crying. Samir walked over to her, and tried to embrace her, but she pulled away.

"Chanel, where are you going?"

"I'm going to my mother's house. I can't do this anymore."

"Why are you leaving me?"

"Look at you."

Samir looked down at his blood-spotted tee. "I didn't kill him, Chanel, damn. I'm trying to protect you. I did what I had to do!"

"Samir, no! You did what you wanted to do. I thought you were better than that. Why would you even stoop to his level? Do you even know what he is capable of? I would never be able to live with myself knowing I will be the reason you end up in jail, or dead."

"Chanel, say what you want, but I had no choice. When I played good guy, this nigga still came after you making threats and shit. And let's not forget, I ended up in the hospital behind this nigga. You talk about what he is capable of, but he crossed me, and he has no idea what I am capable of. I promised I would protect you, and Jaylin, and that's what I'm doing. And, you are not going anywhere."

"You are not my daddy. I'm going to my mother's house, and I mean it."

"No, you are not. Listen . . ." Samir pulled Chanel to him, and looked deeply into her eyes. "I love you. I know you are scared and upset, but you are not leaving me. It's not your fault this dude is making threats. You are not to blame for any of this, but neither am I. When I said I was going to make sure nothing happens to you or Jaylin, I meant that at all costs. If something happens to me, all I ask is that you take care of Rasheed. I know you got that no questions asked."

The tears formed like raindrops in Chanel's eyes once again. "Samir, don't say that! I don't want anything to happen to you! Don't talk like that!"

"Baby, I know. I know you don't want to hear this, but please listen to me! No matter what happens, I just want to be sure you will take care of Rasheed. I'll make sure you're financially straight I swear. I'm not saying anything will happen. I'm just saying, just in case. Promise me, you will take Rasheed. Promise me!" Samir said, as tears fell from his eyes as well.

"I promise. You know I'll take care of him, but—"

"No buts. Everything will be all right."

Chanel broke down crying, as Samir held her in his arms.

Chapter 27

"Mothafucka, you thought you could play me just 'cause we blood?" Cam'ron yelled.

"No man! I wasn't trying to play you. I swear! I'ma have yo' money next week, man, I swear!" Perez pleaded, while Brick kept a tight grip on his arms.

"Where the fuck is the product if you ain't got the money?"

"I sold it, man. I swear," Perez cried.

"So where's my fucking money?"

"I spent it, man, but I planned to pay you back! Come on, man. We cousins!"

"I know, and that's why I'm pissed even more at you. How you gon' cross me like that? Out of all the backstabbing mothafuckas, I never thought you would be this stupid, P."

"I told you, man. I'ma pay you back with interest. Please!"

"Hell naw, Cam. Don't let this nigga slide. We ain't even blood and we don't pull that type of shit. We pay our percentage. No questions asked.

This mothafucka rollin' 'round in a mu'fuckin' Audi R8. Fuck that shit!" Dex barked.

Perez was on his knees begging for his life. The crew didn't want to hear anything he had to say. They worked too hard, and never came up short. Brick cocked back his gun.

"What's it gon' be, Cam?" Brick asked, through clenched teeth.

"Off that nigga!" Cam yelled.

"Nnnoo!" Perez pleaded, as urine seeped through his jeans.

Brick pulled the trigger, and a bullet went straight through his head. Cam'ron was relentless, and didn't show any remorse.

"Clean this shit up! That's a prime example of what's gon' happen to the next mothafucka who cross me."

Brick looked at Cam'ron, and shook his head.

"Nigga. Y'all heard the man, clean it up," he instructed the rest of the crew. "Yo, Cam'ron, let's go hit up the bar," he said running after his boy.

"You do know business ain't finished, right?" Brick said. Cam'ron, Brick, and Dex were at the bar having a couple of drinks.

"What the fuck you talkin' 'bout, Brick?" Cam'ron said, downing his third drink.

"Whatcha gon' do 'bout that nigga wit' Chanel? That mothafucka came in yo' house, and fucked you up, and you ain't gon' do shit?"

"You stupid! I woulda unloaded the clip on that bitch." Dex laughed. "Just think, dude bangin' the hell out yo' baby momma. And you just lettin' that shit ride. Couldn't be me."

The guys continued to boost Cam'ron up. His head pounded as the thought made his blood pressure rise. "Man, I got this shit handled. Believe that." Cam'ron turned around, and enjoyed the scenery while his boys laughed and joked about his situation.

He focused his attention on a group of girls at a table nearby. There was one girl in particular who caught his eye, a brown-skinned cutie with chinky eyes. Cam'ron winked at her, and motioned for her to come over.

She smiled, and shook her head no. She mouthed for Cam'ron to come to her. Cam'ron gave her a smug look, and turned his back toward the bar. *Bitch, wait on it.*

"Man, Cam, you better go over there, and wax that ass before I do," Brick said.

"Fuck that. She ain't that damn fine. She shoulda come when I called her. She must think she Nicki Minaj, or somebody."

Brick and Dex burst out laughin'. "Man, you ain't got no chill." Dex chuckled.

"Oh, well." Cam'ron stood up, and walked down the hall of the club to the bathroom. After he took a leak, he washed his hands. As he was drying his hands, his phone vibrated in his pocket. He took his cell out, and looked at the caller ID. After realizing it was his aunt, Perez's mom, he ignored her call, and walked out of the bathroom. The moment he looked down to put his phone into his pocket, he bumped into the chinky-eyed cutie.

"My bad," he said. "Oh, damn, it's you."

"You are such an asshole," the girl replied.

"So I've been told. And your point is?"

"Your mother should have taught you how to talk to a lady."

Cam'ron smirked. "What's your name?"

"Keara. Why?"

"Well, Keara, I think we got off on the wrong foot. How about I make it up to you?"

"And how do you plan to do that?"

He raised his eyebrow, and licked his lips. The girl rolled her eyes, and walked off in the direction of the ladies' room. *Oh, she tryin' to play hard to get.*

Cam'ron waited a few minutes before going into the ladies' room. Keara was in the mirror fixing her long braids when she noticed him come in.

"Have you lost your damn mind?"

"Ssshh," Cam'ron whispered, pulling her into an empty stall.

"What the fuck are you doing?"

"Sshh, be quiet, damn."

He turned her around, lifted her tight dress, and pushed her thong to the side. Before she could protest, he plunged himself inside of her moist flesh. "Yess! You good, and ready for big daddy!"

Keara kept her hands pressed against the door, while he gripped her hips grinding deep into her. The feeling was irresistible despite the fact Cam'ron was a complete jerk. Keara couldn't deny his dick game was on point, as she worked her hips in the rhythm of his penetration.

Cam'ron picked up speed, ready to erupt into her. The toilet from the next stall flushed, and someone came out. Keara's adrenaline rushed from the thought of getting caught. It only intensified their sexcapade. The sink ran as the stranger washed her hands. They both let out a howling moan that made the stranger turn toward their stall.

The stranger shook her head, and left the bathroom disgusted. Cam'ron stepped out of the stall peeping around to make sure the coast was clear. He left the bathroom, and made his way back to the bar with his boys.

"Man, where the fuck was you at? I thought we were gon' have to come look for you," Brick yelled.

"Yeah, we thought Chanel's ol' boy was in there whoopin' that ass again." Dex laughed.

"Man, fuck y'all! I was in the bathroom, damn."

"For that long? What the fuck was you doing?"

Just then, Keara crept through with a guilty look on her face. Brick looked at Dex, and they both turned to Cam'ron.

"Nigga, did you?" Brick and Dex burst out laughing.

"Man, you one lucky mothafucka. I don't know how you be pullin' that shit off."

Cam'ron joined in on the laughter. He knew he was the man. His arrogant ways were never enough to stop females from giving him what he wanted. He was sexy and brave. His sexy brown skin, and built body full of tattoos, made women fall at his feet. The only woman who had ever made him work for her attention was Chanel. There was nobody out there like Chanel. It killed him, not being able to wake up next to her. There was no woman who made him feel as good as

Chanel. She belonged to him and him only. It was time he got back what was rightfully his.

"Thank you, Mommy! We owe you big time," Chanel said, giving her mother a kiss on the cheek.

"Yes, Mrs. Rose, I can't thank you enough."

"Oh, hush up, you two. I told you, I love when the boys stay with their nana. Just enjoy your trip. You both need the break after all you have been through."

Samir kissed Mrs. Rose on the cheek. "You are a lifesaver."

"Did you have that knucklehead locked up for what he did to you?" Mrs. Rose asked Samir.

"No, ma'am."

"Now that's just foolish. Why didn't you have his ass locked up? He gets away with too much."

"Trust me, Mrs. Rose, I handled it. But, right now, I just want to focus on quality time with your daughter."

"If you say so. Y'all have a good time, and be careful."

Samir and Chanel kissed the boys good-bye, then headed down the highway for a much needed getaway.

Chapter 28

Keshawn pulled into his driveway, and stepped out of his truck. He was ready to go into his house when he noticed a car parked a little ways down from Samir's house. He knew Samir and Chanel had gone out of town, so he wondered who the lurker was in the cotton candy–painted car. There weren't too many people in Atlanta driving around in cars like that. The man stepped out, so Keshawn walked over the edge of the yard.

"Can I help you?" Keshawn asked.

"Sure can. Do you happen to know where my boy Samir is at?"

"How do you know him?" Keshawn asked curiously.

"Oh, that's my homeboy. We were supposed to be linkin' up."

Keshawn eyed the man suspiciously.

"I have tried to call him like three times, but he's not picking up his phone," the man added.

Keshawn thought about it for a second. The guy seemed genuine so he decided to let his guard down. "I'm sorry, man, I'm not trying to come off rude or anything like that. You just can't be too careful sometimes. I just wanted to make sure you weren't here to start trouble," Keshawn replied.

"Yeah, I hear that. Samir and I go way back. Glad ol' boy found him a good woman. Chanel, right?"

Keshawn let out a sigh of relief. "Yeah, man. He supposed to be taking her on a cabin trip out on Stone Mountain to propose to her."

"Oh, yeah? Well, what cabin he taking her to? I might need to woo my lady like that."

"I know that's right!" Keshawn agreed with him.

"Well, guess I'll have to catch Samir another time. It was nice meeting you."

"Yeah, same here." Keshawn turned and was almost at his front door when he realized he'd missed something.

"Yo, my man!" he yelled out to Samir's friend.

"Yeah?" the guy screamed across the way.

"What'd you say your name was?"

"Cam'ron," the man yelled as he got into his cotton candy car and drove off.

***

Renee came through the door after working overtime at her job. Keshawn was in the kitchen warming the dinner he made her. She plopped down at the kitchen table.

"Hey, baby, how was work?" Keshawn asked, placing her food on the table in front of her. He kissed her cheek, and then took a seat beside her.

"It was exhausting. I should have listened to you, babe. I should've worked from home today."

"I told you."

"Yeah, but then I wouldn't have gotten any work done."

"True." Keshawn smirked. "Go ahead and eat up so you can take your shower."

"Why you rushing me? You ain't slick." She grinned.

"Just hurry up."

Renee finished her meal, and then purposely took her time in the shower. Still foaming with suds, Keshawn pulled her out of the shower, and threw her onto the bed. He was already naked, and fully erect.

"What the hell? Keshawn, I gotta wash this soap off!" She stood to her feet. Keshawn pushed her back on the bed.

"I told you to hurry the hell up. Next time, you will be obedient." He climbed on top of Renee's slippery body. She pinched his arm, and wiggled away from him. Rubbing his arm from the pain, he jumped from the bed, and raced after her. Renee quickly rinsed the soap off, and was once again pulled out of the tub.

"Boy, you are insane!"

"And you are hardheaded. You know I'm horny. Why you playing?"

Renee giggled, while Keshawn licked all over her wet body. When he got to her nipple he sucked on it hard, causing her to scream from the pain.

"Ouch, Shawn!"

"Ain't so funny now is it?" he said seductively.

"And that's why you not getting any." Renee jumped from the bed, and raced into the kitchen with Keshawn right behind her. She loved teasing him when he wanted sex.

Chasing his wife around the house only aroused him even more. He watched her ass bounce as she ran. He grabbed her by her waist, and pushed her onto the kitchen table.

"No, Shawn! My back be hurting when we do it on this thing!"

"Nah, take it," he teased.

The centerpiece on the table fell to the floor, as he cocked her legs onto his shoulders. The look of pleasure on her face made him throb for more. He looked down at her well-groomed pussy, and admired the low cut Mohawk. Her legs shook from the touch of his thumb on her clit. Tablemats fell onto the floor, as he piled on top of her to suck on her neck. She wrapped her legs tightly around his waist screaming, as she climaxed. His hammering continued, until a loud moan rang throughout the house as his semen mixed into her juices.

"Satisfied now?" Renee joked.

Keshawn helped her off of the table. "Yep, and don't act like you didn't want a piece of big daddy."

They cleaned up, and jumped into bed. "How was your day, big daddy?" She laughed.

"It was cool. I missed you though."

"I can tell. I missed you too," Renee said, snuggling closer to her man.

"I met one of Samir's friends today."

"Oh, yeah, how?" she asked.

"He was at the house looking for him. Seems like a really nice guy."

"How'd you two end up talking?"

"He was parked by their house, so I asked him what he wanted. He said he was looking for Samir."

Renee sat up in the bed. "And that's all he said?"

"We started talking, and I told him Samir and his girl was on a li'l vacation."

Renee could feel her heart about to jump out of her chest. Something about that conversation seemed off to her. "Please don't tell me you told him where they are."

"Why not? It was his friend. It ain't like he gon' crash in on them, or something. What the hell is your problem?"

"By any chance did you get his name?"

"I did, but I don't remember it right now. What's up with the questions? Do you know him?" Keshawn asked sternly.

"Babe, it is very important that you try to remember the guy's name. I have a feeling it might've been Chanel's ex. She told me about him. He is the one who put Samir in the hospital and he's very dangerous." Renee was now very nervous and felt on edge. She had such a bad feeling in the pit of her stomach. Keshawn sat up trying to remember the man's name. What didn't help was that Renee couldn't remember Chanel's ex's name either. The couple lay back down. Both of them were deep in thought. After five minutes Renee sat up.

"Cam'ron! Was his name Cam'ron?"

"Fuck!" Keshawn yelled, and reached for his cell phone to call Samir.

***

Samir and Chanel lay by the fire place sipping champagne. Chanel was in awe of their trip so far. It was everything she imagined it to be. Samir definitely went all out for her. She relaxed on the pallet, spread neatly on the floor, wrapped in nothing but a blanket. The soft sound of jazz played in the background. Samir watched the look of glee on her face, as he turned up his flute, sipping the last of the contents in his glass.

"What did I do to deserve you?" Chanel asked.

Samir looked down at her, and smiled. "You are a beautiful, smart woman. You are one of the best things that has happened to me. The way you take care of my son is remarkable. I'm just so happy we found each other, so I guess the question is what have I done to deserve you?"

"You mean our son."

"What?"

"You said I take care of your son. You meant our son."

"Of course, you know what I meant." Chanel's eyes went from Samir's sexy face to his bare chest. "Turn over."

"Huh?"

Samir pulled away the blanket covering her body. "Turn over," he repeated.

She turned onto her stomach. Samir licked his lips at the sight of her apple-shaped behind. He poured massage oil into his hands and began caressing her back.

"Mmmm, that feels so good. Maybe you need to go into the massage business."

"Ha-ha! That sounds good. Then, I can do this all the time."

"Do it to whom?" Chanel quizzed.

"Nobody but you, baby."

"Uh-huh, that's what I thought."

His hands continued to roam her soft skin. The feeling of her soft ass and thighs aroused him.

"Mmmm, daddy. I swear, you are really good at this."

"Keep moaning like that you gon' start some-thin'."

"Mmmm, ahhh. Yes, daddy, right there," Chanel teased.

He slid out of his shorts, and flipped Chanel over onto her back.

"Why did you stop?" She smiled. Her eyes widened at the sight of his fully erect penis. "Oh, that's why."

She grabbed Samir's arm, and pulled him on top of her. She wrapped her arms around his neck, and gazed into his eyes. "I love you so much." A tear fell from her eyes. "You have suffered so much just to be with me. I can't thank you enough. I wish I could do something to show you just how much I appreciate you."

Samir wiped away her tears, and kissed her on the forehead. He grabbed her hands, and held them down over her head. "There is something you can do for me."

"What is it?"

"Marry me?" he replied. He brought her hand across her chest. Her mouth popped open as she stared down at the seven-carat diamond ring he snuck onto her finger.

She couldn't stop the tears from flowing, as Samir waited for her to answer.

"Yes? No? Maybe?" Samir joked.

"Of course! Yes, baby, I'll marry you!" she screamed.

"I planned to do this a little different, but it just felt right in this moment."

"It's perfect. Everything is perfect."

"Now, what do I get?"

"You get me."

"What else?" Samir teased.

"You are so silly."

"I just want one more thing from you."

"What now?" Chanel asked, pretending to be annoyed.

Without warning, he slid himself into her, and whispered, "Have my baby."

The feeling was far too good to reject. He made love to her in ways he had never before. From the floor to the king-sized bed, her body craved his, as he gave her orgasm after orgasm.

The aroma from the kitchen woke Samir from his sleep. He pushed the pillow from his head, and reached onto the nightstand for his cell phone. *Damn, ten missed calls.* Keshawn and his lawyer were blowing up his phone.

"Uh-uh, not happening," Chanel said, taking Samir's phone and shutting it off.

"Baby, wait! It might be important."

"This is supposed to be our time together. It can wait," she said placing the pull out tray in front of Samir.

"Damn, breakfast in bed. I must've really put it on you last night."

"Yeah, you did a li'l somethin' somethin'."

Chanel climbed in bed beside him.

"You not eating?" Samir asked.

"Feed me."

Samir dropped his mouth. "Oh, so you made me breakfast in bed, so I can feed it to you. That's messed up." He lifted the fork full of his cheese omelet to her mouth. "You lucky I love you."

"Don't act like you don't want to feed your fiancée," she said, shaking her hand in his face to show off her ring.

"Is this what I'ma have to put up with for the rest of my life?" Samir joked.

"Pretty much." Chanel took the fork out of Samir's hand.

"So now you gon' eat it all?"

"Boy, be quiet, and open up." She slid the food into his mouth. "See, I'm tryin' to be sweet, and you runnin' your mouth."

"I'm sorry, baby."

"Uh-huh. So what's on the agenda for today?"

"I was thinkin', we should go fishin'."

"Fishing? I don't know nothin' 'bout no fishin'."

"That's why it will be fun."

"Eeww, I'm not touching no worms."

Samir laughed.

Chapter 29

"All right, now put the worm on the hook like this." Samir demonstrated, by baiting the worm on his hook. Chanel looked disgusted. "All right, now you try baiting your hook."

"Hell naw! I'm not doing that."

Samir popped his lips. "Chanel, just pick up the worm. It ain't gon' bite you."

Chanel twisted her mouth. She reached into the container, and fingered through the dirt for a worm. She felt one moving underneath her fingers. "Eeew eeew eew!" Samir laughed under his breath. "Okay, I got it now! Take it! Take it!" she screamed.

"No, now you have to put him on the hook."

"Uuggh!"

"Just stick it through the hook. Make sure you put him on good, or the fish will snatch him right off, then you'll have to start the process all over again."

"You're enjoyin' torturing me, aren't you?"

"A little bit."

Chanel got the bait on the hook. "Now what?"

Samir guided her hands, and showed her what to do. "Now be quiet, and wait for the fish to bite. When your stopper goes underwater, you have to reel him in." Samir threw his line out. "Now ain't this relaxin'?"

"To be honest, it actually is, minus the baiting the hook part."

"This has been a great trip. I liked whitewater rafting, but I don't think I'll be doing that again."

Chanel's stopper dived under water. "Samir! Samir! What do I do?"

He rushed over to her, and grabbed her hand. With the help of Samir, she brought in a large bass.

Chanel was overly excited, jumping up and down. "Where's your camera, so I can take a picture of you and your first fish?"

"Over by the chair, hurry up!"

She posed with one hand on her hip, and the other holding her rod with the fish hanging on the hook.

"Ha-ha! Why you gotta pose pretty, just to take a picture with the fish?"

"Just shut up, and take the picture."

Samir snapped the picture, then placed the camera down. "All right, now you gotta take the fish off the hook."

"I'm not doing that!"

"All right then, you gon' be standing there holding him all night." Samir walked over to the edge of the lake, and picked up his rod.

"Are you serious?" He pretended not to hear her. "Un-fucking-believable!"

Chanel stepped her foot on the fish, then bent down to wiggle the hook out of his mouth without touching him. Samir peeped from the corner of his eyes. He laughed to himself, as he continued fishing. She finally got the fish off the hook then picked him up by the tail, and literally threw him into the bucket. Water splashed on Samir.

"Damn, Chanel!"

"Good, that's what you get for making me touch that nasty fish!"

Samir dropped his rod, reached in the bucket, and pulled out the fish. Chanel looked up, and ran off with Samir right behind her. "No! Samir, put that thing away!" she screamed.

He laughed, as he continued chasing her around with the fish in his hand. Picking up speed, Samir reached out and grabbed her. She closed her eyes, and screamed when he wiggled the fish in front of her.

"Say, you're sorry!" Samir teased.

"Okay! Okay! I'm sorry!"

Samir threw the fish back into the bucket, and then pulled Chanel to him. "I love you so much."

"I love you too. Now, let's get out of here. The shower is calling my name."

Chanel walked into the bedroom in her nightie, smiling.

"Whatchu comin' in here cheesing for?" Samir asked.

She jumped in the bed next to him. "Today was so much fun!"

"I told you! You have to step out of your comfort zone from time to time."

"I thought you were a li'l city boy."

"I'm gon' always be a city boy, but everybody got a li'l country in 'em."

"Whatever. I'm gon' fix me something to drink. Do you want anything?"

"Nah, bae, I'm good. I'm tryin' to catch the last of this game."

"Boring," Chanel teased, as she exited the bedroom to get her something to drink.

"Yes!" Samir yelled to the TV. When the game went to commercial, he reached over to the nightstand to get the remote, knocking his cell phone to the floor. That's when he remembered the missed calls and texts from the night before.

He reached down to grab his phone, and then pressed the button to turn it on. Texts came through back to back.

He opened one of the texts, and read it quietly to himself: "Samir, you and Chanel need to get out of the cabin. Cam'ron knows where you are, and he may try to come after you. Get back to me as soon as possible." In a state of shock, Samir's eyes widened, and then he realized when the text was sent. *If Cam'ron really wanted to do something, he would have done it by now.*

Samir looked at the clock on the radio. It was ten minutes until eleven. Though it was late, Samir felt the need to return Keshawn's call. With Keshawn's sense of urgency, he didn't want him to be worried. Scrolling through his call log, he hit the phone button to dial Keshawn's number. He answered after the second ring.

"Samir, man, both me and Renee have been walking around on pins and needles. We thought something had happened to one of you. Is everything okay?" Keshawn asked.

"Man, everything is fine. I saw that you had blown my phone up, so I thought I'd give you a call back to let you know everything is okay."

"Are you sure? Renee wants to know how Chanel is doing." Keshawn waited for a response. Samir was too busy drifting off in his mind.

When Keshawn mentioned Chanel, Samir realized she had not returned from the kitchen. Maybe he was over-thinking things. She could have decided to fix herself something to eat, but if that were true, there would be an aroma coming from the kitchen.

"Chanel!" Samir screamed out.

"Samir? Is everything okay? Do you need me to call the police?" Keshawn yelled question after question through the phone. Samir zoned him out, then dropped the phone. He jumped from the bed, hollering out for Chanel.

"Chanell! Where you at, babe?" Samir continued to scream. There was no answer, and his heart pounded faster through his chest. Briefly, the light flickered off then back on. Something was wrong definitely, and Samir could sense it. He ran to his suitcase, and pulled out his gun.

Darkness had covered every room, except the bedroom and the kitchen. Samir made his way through the house in search of his fiancée. Desperately, he hoped she was just playing a trick on him, and would jump out to scare him at any moment.

Time slowly passed, as Samir searched diligently throughout the house. The last place he thought to look was outside. He searched around the whole cabin for Chanel, but still to no avail. Her name echoed into the night air, as he continued to yell for her. Helplessly, he turned, and went back into the cabin. When he walked back into the house, he was stopped dead in his tracks. Right there in the living room area sat Chanel in a chair with her hands tied behind her back, and duct tape over her mouth. Tears streamed her beautiful face.

The sight of her in that state was too much to bear. Flashbacks of when Asia was found in the basement, tied the same way, right before she was shot, played over in his mind. It felt as if demons of his past had come back to haunt him. The fright in Chanel's eyes was the same look he saw on Asia's face when he found her.

Taking out his gun, he looked around, and then took a step toward her. Before he could reach her, he heard a gun cock back. From the dark corner, a figure approached from the shadows. Samir pointed his gun in the direction of the stranger. Stepping into the light, standing behind Chanel, Cam'ron appeared with his gun pointed at Chanel.

"Don't take another step," Cam'ron spoke in a deep tone. Cam'ron looked at Samir with a devilish grin on his face. "Well, well, we meet again."

The demonic stare from his enemy gave him the impression that his life would be over. There was no way he could escape death this time.

"Man, what the fuck is your problem?" Samir yelled angrily.

"Shut the fuck up! I warned you but yo' punk ass wouldn't listen."

Samir's and Cam'ron's eyes pierced through one another. The only sounds could be heard in the cabin were those of Chanel whimpering.

"Man, let her go. Do whatever you want to me, but please let her go!"

"Oh, trust me. I will do what I need to, but the only problem is even when you are gone Chanel still won't be with me, so she may be leaving right behind you," Cam'ron sneered.

"What the fuck is wrong with you? You would kill your own son's mother?"

"I have no other choice! All she had to do was listen, but that's what's wrong with hoes nowadays. They don't fuckin' listen!"

"Nigga, you gotta be the dumbest mothafucka on the face of this earth," Samir spat.

Cam'ron gave him a smug look. "You must not give a damn about your life or hers, talking to me like that. Your mouth gon' cause me to let this trigga loose."

Not caring about the pain, Cam'ron yanked the tape off Chanel's mouth. "Ahh!" she screamed.

"Now, I'ma give you the chance to say your last good-bye to your punk-ass boyfriend."

"You mean fiancé," Samir said spitefully.

Samir still had his gun drawn on Cam'ron. Cam'ron swiftly pointed his gun toward Samir and yelled, "Don't fuckin' play with me! Now put your gun down!"

"Hell naw! I ain't puttin' shit down. You gon' kill me anyway. I ain't stupid."

The two men continued to argue back and forth. While Cam'ron was not paying attention, Chanel wiggled her hands free from the rope tied around them. Samir noticed what Chanel was doing, and continued fussing with Cam'ron, to keep him distracted.

"Okay, obviously you really care about her, so I'll back off. I'll disappear from her life. You can walk away from here with no problems, and she can go home with you," Samir offered.

"Nigga, don't try to insult my intelligence. I know that's just a setup to get me locked up. Now," Cam'ron said through stone-cold eyes, "I said put the gun down."

"Fuck you!" Samir said. He kept his gun aimed at Cam'ron. There was no way he was putting down his gun. He looked at Chanel, whose eyes were dark and wet from crying.

She looked terrified. One thing was for certain, Samir was not going to let Chanel die. He was willing to die, but he was not going down alone. He was going to keep his promise to protect Chanel no matter what. He was willing to die, but not unless he took Cam'ron with him.

Cam'ron's eyes narrowed. He fired his gun hitting Samir in the arm.

"No!" Chanel yelled leaping up from the chair, and knocking Cam'ron against the wall.

Chanel tried to wrestle the gun away from Cam'ron, but her strength was no match for him. With one shove, Chanel fell backward onto the floor.

Pow! Pow! The sound of gunshots went off. Blood splattered against the wall. Cam'ron looked down at his wounds. His eyes rolled to the back of his head as his body fell to the floor. Samir stood up, holding his injured arm. There was blood all over the sleeve of his shirt.

"Ah shit!" Samir yelled out in agony.

Chanel ran to his side sobbing. "Baby, I'm so sorry!"

"You don't have anything to be sorry for. I told you I would protect you, baby girl. It's over now."

Chanel ran to the phone and dialed 911. Within minutes, sirens sounded off in the distance, and police lights flashed through the windows. They stood by the door, as the officers made their way up the porch. They explained to the detectives what happened, and answered all of their questions. Paramedics took a look at Samir's gunshot wound and told him the bullet was a clean shot. They said it wasn't life threatening, but he still needed to get to a hospital to have it all cleaned out. Samir refused to go that night. He decided he'd get to a hospital when they reached home. He didn't want to spend the night away from Chanel.

The place looked like something from the ID channel. Caution tape surrounded the cabin, while people walked around doing their jobs. Samir and Chanel were just thankful they no longer had to deal with Cam'ron. It saddened Chanel that things had to take such a turn, but she was relieved that it was all over. They could finally move on with their lives in peace.

"Baby, let's get our stuff packed. We are out of here," Samir said, once everyone had cleared out. They went in their bedroom, and got their things.

"Need help packing?" a voice said from behind them.

When Samir and Chanel turned around, Keshawn and Renee were standing in the doorway.

"Man, I am so sorry! This is all my fault," Keshawn said, feeling bad.

"What are you talking about?" Samir asked.

"It was me, man. I'm the one who told him where you were. He pretended he was a friend of yours. I swear I didn't know, man."

"As soon as I realized it was him, I tried to call to warn you, but no one answered," Renee added.

"It's okay, don't stress over it. Y'all are not to blame. It would have happened sooner or later, anyway. I'm just glad it's over."

Keshawn and Renee helped them load their things into the car. Then, they all headed home with a fresh start.

Chapter 30

Two months later, everything had fallen into place. With Cam'ron out of the picture, life couldn't have been any greater. Their family was everything Chanel wanted it to be. Time spent with the kids seemed more meaningful.

Chanel felt as if she could finally exhale. No longer carrying the burden of threats from her ex, she could now be with Samir, without worrying that something would happen to him. It also felt good for her son Jaylin to have a real man in his life he could look up to.

The only concerns the couple now had were simple seating arrangements, as they sat together on the couch going over their wedding plans.

"Baby, I honestly don't care what you choose. As long as you're happy, I'm happy."

"But I want you to be a part of the plans."

"I'm paying for everything. Ain't that involvement enough?" Samir said jokingly.

"That's only because you won't let no one else help pay for anything. My mom offered to help, but you refuse to let her."

"Of course I'm not taking anything from sweet Ma Rose. And you know, I don't mind. I'm just ready to see my beautiful bride walking down the aisle," Samir said leaning over to kiss his wife-to-be.

"Just one more month, and I'll be Mrs. Chanel Hicks."

"Then, we can work on having another baby."

"There you go again. Are you really ready for a third child?"

"Of course, why wouldn't I be?"

"Uh-huh. Speaking of kids, I'm gonna check on the boys."

The doorbell rang as soon as Chanel stood to her feet. "Baby, go ahead and check on the boys. I'll get the door," Samir assured her.

The bell chimed through the house again. Samir rushed to the door in his big gray sweatpants, white cut-off sleeve tee, and Nike slide-in shoes.

When he opened the door and saw who was standing on his doorstep, he felt like he had the wind knocked out of him. His face went pale and he couldn't find words to speak. He was in pure shock and disbelief. Instead of welcoming the person with open arms, he stood in the doorway frozen solid.

Finally, he shook himself out of the trance. He closed his eyes, and then opened them again to make sure he wasn't just seeing things. But when he opened his eyes, she was still standing there before him. She still looked just as beautiful as the first time he laid eyes on her. Her hair was still long and curly, her body fuller and curvier than before, but just as sexy nonetheless. He just stood there and stared at those familiar, mesmerizing eyes .

"Asia!" he was finally able to say.

"Yes, it's me in the flesh!"

"No, can't be, but how?"

"Well, aren't you going to let me in?" Asia asked, a bit overjoyed.

"Of course, come in," Samir said, not taking his eyes off of her for fear that he was actually looking at a ghost.

Asia took a seat on the couch, as Chanel walked into the room.

Chanel looked at the beautiful woman, immediately wondering why she was in her living room seated so comfortably.

"Um, Samir, who is this?" Chanel asked.

Samir, who was still in shock, looked up at Chanel, eyes widened like a crazed man. "You see her too?"

"Huh?" Chanel asked, confused.

Asia got up from the couch and stood between Samir and Chanel. "I should explain. From the look on your face," she said, giving her attention to Samir, "you must have assumed I was dead."

"Asia?" Chanel asked in surprise.

"So, he's told you about me," Asia responded.

Samir was still too stunned to make sense of where he was, let alone what was going on.

Asia waved her hand in front of Samir's face. "Are you okay?" she asked.

"I don't understand. He told me you had died of a gunshot wound." Chanel sounded perplexed.

"As I said before, I have some explaining to do. When I was shot, I did die twice on the operating table, but then when I came back the second time, the doctors were able to get my body stabilized. The news reports had already announced that I was dead so my mother decided to let people believe it. She and my father had me transferred to a hospital on Long Island and once there, they kept me in a private room to make sure word didn't get out that I was actually alive. As soon as I was stable enough to survive a plane ride they moved me to a hospital in Texas. I was still in pretty bad shape when they moved me to Texas. I was transported on a stretcher in a helicopter and was barely conscious of what was going on. They took advantage of my condition and they gave me no other choice. We've been living down there ever since."

Streams and streams of tears ran down Asia's face. Chanel handed her a tissue, as she continued, "When I finally was aware of what had happened and was able to speak, I begged my parents to tell me where you were, but they wouldn't. They tried to force me to forget about you and my son, but I couldn't. There wasn't a day that went by that I didn't think about you two."

The tears continued to fall down Asia's face. Samir grabbed her hands, after finally making sense of everything. "There wasn't a day that I didn't think of you as well."

Chanel noticed his hands on top of Asia's. Discomfort took over, as she sat in silence, and attempted to let them catch up on lost time.

"I did not abandon you and our baby. I argued every day with my parents about where you were. I hate they made you think I was dead, even though at one point I honestly thought I wasn't going to make it. I'm so sorry for all the lies and the hurt me and my family put you through. Please forgive me." Asia sniffled.

"Asia, it's not your fault," Samir replied, as his eyes swelled and tears poured out of them. "I'm just so thankful you are alive, that you are safe, and that you are really here. It feels like a dream come true."

The more they talked, the more uncomfortable Chanel felt. She felt as if she was invisible, and no longer mattered in Samir's life. Though it was hard to watch she tried to remain neutral, and understanding of this unusual situation.

Chanel cleared her throat. "Um, so, Asia, how did you find Samir?"

"Yeah, how did you find me?" Samir asked, curiously.

"Well, as I said before, my parents continued to argue about the situation. They thought it would be best if I moved on, and stayed away from you. My parents did their best to brainwash me into thinking it was best if I did stay away. That it was best for you to think I was dead, and that you were too dangerous for me to be with. I finally built enough strength to leave, and I searched high and low for you. I went back to New York, talked to everyone I could think of, and that's when I connected with your lawyer."

"Damn, Paul! That's right! He called when we were on our cabin trip, and I never called back. He must have been calling to tell me he found you. Damn!"

"Well, either way, he led me to you, and so, here I am."

"Wow, this is so unbelievable!" Samir said.

"Yes. I am so happy to see you. You haven't changed a bit. Still just as handsome as the last time I saw you." Asia and Samir's eyes locked with one another's.

"So, Asia, now that you are here, where are you staying?"

"Oh, well, I have a room at the Marriott Hotel."

"How long will you be here?" asked Chanel.

"I don't know. That's something me and Samir will need to discuss, especially since I want to be involved in our son's life. I've missed him so much."

"Well, that's something we will definitely need to talk about. It has been almost four years now, and we want to make sure he is comfortable."

"I understand. I didn't come to interrupt anything. I know all of this will take time to sink in, but I can't wait to see him. Where is he?"

"Right now, he is taking a nap, but you can see him," Samir said.

Chanel walked off into the kitchen, while Samir led Asia to the boys' bedroom. Both Rasheed and Jaylin were asleep.

"Oh, my gosh, he's so handsome. And he's grown so much since the last time I saw him." Asia stared at her son as the tears fell down her face. "I just want to hold him."

"How about we take him to the park tomorrow? That way he can spend time with you. He'll warm up to you easier while he is playing."

"Sounds like fun. I can't wait." Asia looked Samir in his eyes. There was so much she wanted to say but couldn't. Time apart had stolen her most precious moments that a mother should be able to experience. She had missed out on her son's first words, his first steps, his first haircut, and so many other moments. And to top it all off, now the love of her life had moved on.

Looking into his eyes, she couldn't help but notice his handsome appearance and long, braided hair. So much had changed since she last saw him, yet when she looked into his eyes it was like things hadn't changed at all. She could tell by just talking to him that he was much more mature. The man she had waited for him to be, the man he had promised to be once D-Money was out of the picture, now stood in front of her. But now that man belonged to someone else. The realization of it all hit her like a ton of bricks, and tore her heart to shreds.

"Is everything okay?" Samir asked, placing his hand on Asia's shoulder.

"I don't know. I guess I am having a hard time accepting everything. You were supposed to be . . ." She hesitated to finish her sentence. "Never mind. Anyway, I should get going."

Samir didn't know what to feel about this entire situation. It was bittersweet for him. "Come on, I'll walk you to the door," he said.

When they got outside, Samir stopped Asia. "I can't believe you are really here."

Asia looked at him, and smiled, and then she leaned in and planted a quick kiss on his lips. "Believe it," she replied. Then, she got in her car, and drove off.

The house was quiet when Samir came back inside and went to bed. Chanel walked into the bedroom. Samir was so deep in thought he didn't see her come in. When he felt her come into the bed his whole body jerked and he almost fell out of the bed.

"Damn, girl, you scared me!" He laughed out of embarrassment that he almost fell.

"I bet," Chanel said, with an attitude.

"Wait a minute. What's wrong?"

"I don't understand how the hell your ex or fiancée, whatever she is, is all of a sudden is back from the dead!"

"Chanel, really? Obviously she survived. I was told she was dead. After all, her parents picked up and left without telling me, or anyone, anything. The most important thing is she is alive! Rasheed finally gets to meet his mom."

"Yeah, Rasheed gets to meet his mom. But my question is, what will her being alive mean for you?"

"I don't know!" Samir yelled.

"You don't know?"

"I'm saying, this is a lot to take in right now, and I don't need all these questions. She wants the chance to get to know our son, and she has that right."

"So now he is your and Asia's son? Now it's 'fuck Chanel,' right?"

"Chanel, you know damn well none of what you are sayin' is true! You are not being fair. I thought you of all people would understand!"

"I am trying to be understanding, but this changes everything now. I'm not saying I'm not happy she is alive, because I am. All I'm saying is do you want to be with her, since now you know she is not dead? It's not like you two broke up because y'all didn't want to be together anymore. You two were set to get married before her parents faked her death. What's going to happen now? Are you two just going to pick up where you left off? Does she get her happy ending and I don't get mine? Do you love her more than you love me, Samir?"

"I can't believe you. With everything that I've gone through. Everything that she's gone through. You wanna sit here and be mad and jealous? You can't be serious. I'm going to fucking bed."

Words could not describe how hurt Chanel felt. She hated herself for feeling jealous, instead of being supportive of him. She knew he had a hard time dealing with Asia's death, and now that he knew she was alive, he must have felt like a heavy burden was lifted off his shoulders.

There was no doubt in Chanel's mind that Samir and Asia still loved each other. She didn't want to overthink things, but given their actions, and the way things were left in the past, it led her to believe there was no way they couldn't want each other.

Later that night, Chanel stayed in the same spot on the couch pondering over the possibility that she could lose Samir. After much thought, she stood up, and walked into their bedroom. She threw on her nightclothes, and then hopped into bed. Samir pretended to be asleep, not even turning to pull her close to him as he did every night.

Honestly, he felt bad for hurting Chanel's feelings, but Asia was still fresh on his mind. Drifting off to sleep, he dreamed of her beauty.

The thickness of her thighs, her perky, round breasts, and her long, curly hair made him want her. He dreamt of running his hands up her thighs, until his fingers touched her thick, juicy center. Ripping off the denim shorts that she wore, then tasting her sweet nectar just like he used to. He remembered all the times they made love. The way she used to run her tongue from his neck to his earlobe. A moan escaped from his mouth from just the thought of her touching him.

Samir jumped up out of his sleep. He had dozed off without realizing it. His back faced Chanel, and he turned around to make sure she was asleep; then he went back to sleep.

Chanel's eyes popped open. Teardrops hit the pillow as she cried in silence. The sound of her fiancé moan in his sleep scared her significantly. *He's probably dreaming about her.* There was no way she could imagine living without Samir. The fear of losing him to Asia haunted her for the rest of the night.

The sun beamed down on the park playground. Asia and Samir sat on the bench, and watched Rasheed run around happily. He had warmed up to Asia very well, and even let her push him on the swings. With him calling Chanel Mom, it would be hard to explain to him that Asia was his biological mother, but for now, it was more important that he get to know her.

"Wow, I can't believe how big he is. I feel like I've missed out on everything."

"Yeah, but the main thing is that you are here now, and you are okay. When I found out your parents had picked up and moved, it was the hardest time of my life. I thought you were dead, and that your parents had your funeral somewhere else so I couldn't be there. I tried getting information to find out where you were buried so I could at least visit your gravesite, but I never was able to find anything. I don't know, all of this is just crazy."

"I know. I'm just glad you were able to move on, and provide Rasheed such a great life. He is so happy, and Chanel seems like a really great woman."

"Yes, she really is. You were great too. I feel so bad about all this, because I honestly didn't know you were still alive."

"You don't have to keep apologizing. I understand. I'm honestly happy for you. I just don't know how I'll ever forgive my parents for ruining my life."

"Yeah, just imagine how our lives would be right now."

Asia laughed. "It seems so weird to see you being a manly man. Not that you weren't before. I can just tell you have matured a lot. I remember you with your pants hangin' halfway off your ass, with a gun tucked inside."

"Ha-ha! Yeah, I was something. I still tote my heat, but not like a thug; only to protect my family. The tragedy that night made me see things differently. I don't want to ever go through anything like that again," Samir said, although he had just experienced something similar with Chanel's ex. He thought it was best not to tell Asia about that situation.

"So, how did you and Chanel meet?" Asia asked.

Samir propped his arm across the back of the bench. "Well, actually, I met her here. I was playing with Rasheed, and she came over, and introduced herself. That was over a year ago, and we've been together ever since."

"I see she had a ring on her finger. You plan on marrying her?"

"Yes, we are supposed to be getting married in a month."

"You sure you ready?"

"Of course. She is a really good woman, and I love her. I know this hasn't been easy on her, but she's very supportive."

Asia nodded her head in approval. "That's really good."

"Listen, Asia, I know I keep apologizing, but I really am sorry. I know this is hard on you too. I am here for you, and I mean that. I will always love you. I never stopped loving you. You are my first love, and that's something that will never change." Samir moved over closer to Asia, and hugged her.

Chapter 31

Over the next few weeks, Samir and Rasheed spent a lot of time with Asia. Asia decided to move to Atlanta. Samir helped her get into a nice condo, so that she could be close to their son. The joy of having Asia there by his side meant the world to him.

Asia watched as Samir and her son played in the room they had set up for him in her condo. She stood in the doorway smiling. It was the life they were supposed to have, yet she felt robbed. This was the life they had planned. The life they had dreamed of. In her eyes, Samir belonged to her, and watching him playing with their son in his room was exactly where he was supposed to be.

Rasheed looked up from playing with Samir, and pointed toward Asia. "She Mommy too?" he asked.

"Yes, son, she is Mommy too. You are lucky, because you have two mommies who love you very much."

Asia didn't like the sound of that, but she had to grin and bear it. She smiled, and bent down to sit on the floor next to Rasheed. "Mommy missed you so much," Asia said, giving him a kiss.

"He looks so much like you. Every time I would look into his eyes, I was instantly reminded of you."

Asia smiled. "Yeah, he does look like me, thank God," she joked.

"What you mean by that?" Samir laughed.

"I'm kidding. I see a lot of him in you. He definitely gets his handsome looks from you. We are going to have a lot of trouble when the girls come knocking at the door."

"Yes, just like his dad," Samir said playfully.

"You definitely had a lot of chickenheads fallin' at your feet."

At that moment, Samir's phone rang. It was Chanel, so he walked out of the room to answer it.

"Samir, where are you?" she asked, sounding upset.

"I'm at Asia's. I had to help her put Rasheed's bed together, and get the stuff in his room situated. Are you okay?"

"Now you want to ask me if I'm okay? I'm really getting tired of this! I know you are happy

Asia is here now. I know everything is like a miracle to you right now, which is why I have tried to be so patient and understanding. But, this is ridiculous. It's almost like y'all are a family!"

"We are a family! What the hell do you mean? Are you really about to start something right now? This is hard on everybody, not just you."

"Really? I have been here for you and Rasheed."

"And, I have been here for you and Jay. What the hell is your point?"

"The point is, we are supposed to be planning our wedding. I need you too, and I have to be honest when I say I am feeling neglected. Jay is asking for you. There is so much he doesn't understand. I think Asia wants you back, and you need to be able to let her know that this is strictly about Rasheed, unless you are feeling the same way as her."

"What the fuck? You can't be serious. Asia is just trying to make up for lost time. Don't worry, no one is trying to take your fuckin' spot, so chill with that! Man, I will see you when I get home. I'm not dealing with this nonsense right now."

Samir hung up on Chanel. He was furious. He couldn't believe how Chanel was acting. All he wanted to do was make everyone happy. The love he had for Chanel was undeniable, but he also loved Asia.

Asia snuck in behind him, and tapped him on the shoulder. "Is everything okay?"

"Yeah, everything is fine. Where's Rasheed?"

"He is knocked out. Fell asleep coloring with me. Do you want anything? I can fix you something to drink."

"A shot of Henney would be great."

Asia laughed. "I'm sorry, but I don't have that."

"In that case, I'll just settle for some water."

Asia came back out of the kitchen with Samir's water. She watched as he gulped it down. Asia bit her bottom lip as she watched him in awe. From his strong, rock-hard arms to his sexy smooth skin. His smell was intoxicating. Why couldn't he be single? Her eyes locked on his wet lips, and when he pulled the glass down, it reminded her of how he used to taste her sweetness. Just the thought of him between her legs made her moist. When he looked into her eyes, she knew she had to have him. There wasn't a man alive she had come in contact with who she craved more than Samir.

Asia tried to think of something to talk about to get her mind off him sexually. "So, how did you manage to get over the trauma of what happened in New York?"

"It's been hard, especially in the beginning, but I knew Rasheed was depending on me. It was because of him that I was able to learn to move on. It still hurts to this day. Some days I'd wake up in sweats, or hollering your name."

Asia looked up at him. "Hollering my name?" she asked.

"Yeah, I would sometimes have nightmares of the night you got shot, and I'd pop up out of my sleep screaming for you. It's truly miraculous, but I am so thankful you are here. I beat myself up every day for what happened to you. I hate that you had to suffer in pain, and then go without us in your life. But, like I said, I'm glad you are here now."

"I had a lot of bad dreams too. It was hard getting through the tragedy. I can only imagine what you were going through, but God brought us back together for a reason." Asia stepped up to Samir, gazing into his eyes. "We are not together by chance." Tugging at his shirt, she pulled him to her and kissed him. She pushed her tongue through his mouth, and wrapped her hands around his neck.

For a second, Samir fell into her trance, but he instantly pushed her back. She looked at him with a puzzled expression.

"What's wrong?" Asia asked, confused by his sudden rejection.

"You know what's wrong, Asia. That wasn't cool."

"Samir, you can't possibly marry this girl. You were mine! I didn't ask for any of this! It was supposed to be us, remember? It's our family! I'm here now!" Asia sniffled through tears.

It broke Samir's heart to see Asia so hurt, but after the kiss, he knew the feelings he had for her had changed. There was no way he could say that to her. Although he loved Asia and would die for her, the feelings he had for her were on a friendship level, and out of respect for her being his son's mother.

Reaching for Asia's hand, Samir looked her genuinely in her eyes. "Asia, you mean the world to me. It's not a day that goes by that I don't feel bad about the decisions I made. There is not a day that goes by that I don't feel like all this is my fault. From the bottom of my heart, I am sorry. I'll be here for you regardless, because you are a wonderful friend, and you are the mother of my child. I got you, hands down, but I'm in love with Chanel. She is my wife-to-be. There is no question in my mind that if things were different it would have been you, but that's the point: things are different. As hard as it may be, you have to realize we are not teenagers anymore, and so much has happened since you have been gone. Please understand, and respect that."

Asia gave a slight smile. "I totally understand. I guess it's hard to let go of the past. It's even harder to believe you found love in someone else, but it's obvious that you have, and I do respect that. Please forgive me."

"No, you have nothing to be forgiven for. We were both going back into the past, and for that I owe Chanel a huge apology. I know she is mad at me right now."

"Well, you can let Rasheed stay here with me tonight. That way I can spend more time with him, and then you guys can talk."

"That'll work. I appreciate it."

"Of course, I am his mother." She laughed.

"True. Well, I guess I'll head home. If you need me call me. I'll be back to get him tomorrow."

"Okay. See you later."

As Asia walked Samir to the door, he turned to hug her, and then walked down the driveway to his car. He threw his hand up to her as he drove off going home.

Chapter 32

When Samir got home, he looked around the house for Chanel. He felt so bad for the way he had treated her. Asia's return was very hard on her, and he had not been attentive or understand toward her feelings the way he should have. Chanel was in their bedroom packing her clothes into a suitcase. She didn't even look his way as he entered the room.

"Chanel, what are you doing?" he asked.

"I'm leaving," she answered bluntly.

"Excuse me?"

"Oh, now you notice me. Now when it's too late, and our relationship is over, you notice me?"

"Chanel, quit being dramatic. You are not leaving."

"Watch me."

"I don't have to watch you, because I'm not letting you go. We have worked too hard, and have come too far. We have been through hell and back, and we are not throwing it all away."

"Well, if you think I am going to sit here, and watch you reconnect with your son's mother, and leave me out of the equation, you've got another think coming. I'm not waiting around for you to cheat on me, or leave me for her. I'll do us both a favor, and save us a lot of future heartache."

"Chanel, I don't love her in that way. I love her as a friend, and as the mother of my child. I am in love with you. It's true, things did get out of hand, and I didn't do right by you like I should have, and I am so sorry. I'm so sorry it took me some time to get it, but I know now. Asia was my past and you are my now, my future, my everything, and I love you."

Samir got down on his knees. "Baby, I love you, and I'm sorry. I will never put you in an uncomfortable situation again. I messed up by neglecting you and focusing more on Asia since she came back into our lives. I was wrong for that and I am truly, very sorry. I want you, and only you. Please forgive me. Pweeese!" Samir pouted, jokingly.

Chanel couldn't help but laugh, while Samir stuck his lip out waiting for her response. "Okay, I forgive you, but you better not let that shit happen again."

He pulled her over to him while still on his knees. She wrapped her hands around his head. "It's funny how life turns out," Samir said, while looking up at his beautiful fiancée.

"Yes, and it's about to get even more interesting."

"Huh?"

Samir stood to his feet, while Chanel walked to her purse, and pulled out her papers from the doctor. She handed them to Samir.

"You're pregnant?"

"Yes, I am. You would have known that if you weren't so busy with Asia."

Samir's face lit up. "Baby, is this for real? Are you serious?"

"Serious as a heart attack."

"Yes! Now, I can have my beautiful baby girl."

"Ain't no guarantee it's gonna be a girl. All that matters is that he or she is healthy."

"Yeah, yeah, that too!"

"So, I guess Asia will be around for a while, huh?"

"Baby, what did I tell you? I will never put you in a situation like that again. No more visits alone at her house, but you have to trust me. She is my friend, and given the circumstances, I have to be there for her. But know, I will never do anything else to compromise our relationship. And, if ever you don't feel right about something, just tell me. That's what our relationship has been based on: communication."

"You're right, and from now on, I'll be more trusting."

"That's my girl. Now, we need to discuss this wedding."

"Are you nervous?"

"A little bit, but I'm marrying the love of my life, so that makes it a lot easier."

Chanel smiled. "Thank God I'm not too far along in my pregnancy. I wouldn't want to have to go down the aisle looking like a whale."

"You would still be beautiful in my eyes."

"Aww, thank you, baby."

Like always, Samir kissed Chanel's forehead. "Where is Jay?" he asked.

"He is still at my mother's house. I better call her, and let her know I don't need to stay there now."

"So, you told your mom I was being a bad boy?"

"No, I didn't go into details. Don't worry; you are still on her good side."

"I better be."

"Is Rasheed sleeping already?" she asked.

"He didn't come home with me. He is staying with his mother tonight."

"Are you sure it's time for that?"

"I think he will be fine. I told her I'd be back to pick him up tomorrow."

"Oh, okay," Chanel replied, trying not to appear uneasy.

"Baby, it's okay. Rasheed will be fine, and you will always be his mommy. You know that."

"I know, but hearing you say it makes me feel a lot better."

"We are going to work through this. It's not going to be as bad as you think. But, there is a positive to all of this. We have the house to ourselves. No crying, no running, no kids asking a million questions, just me and you."

"And what's that supposed to mean? You still in the dog house, remember?"

"I thought you forgave me."

"I do, but I'ma forgive you while you sleeping on the couch."

"You're joking right?"

Chanel went to the closet, and got extra covers and pillows. Samir followed her into the living room. She put the stuff on the couch, and walked back into the bedroom. He stood in disbelief with his mouth wide open.

"Guess the joke's on you. Good night. Love you though."

"Chanel, you can't be serious. I'm not sleeping on this couch. Why would you waste a perfect night making me sleep on the couch, when you could be cuddling up to me?"

"There will be other times, if you behave," Chanel yelled from the bedroom.

Samir shook his head, and looked down at the rumpled covers on the couch. "Damn, man," Samir mouthed to himself.

He jumped onto the couch, and flipped through the channels. He peeped in the direction of the bedroom. Chanel hit the switch to turn off the light. He wanted to go in the bedroom, and get in the bed so badly. The longer he stayed on the couch, the hornier he became.

Nothing on TV caught his attention. He felt like Larenz Tate's character, Darius, from *Love Jones*. The scene when Nina, Nia Long's character, wouldn't let him upstairs with her.

An hour later, Samir had fallen asleep on the couch. As much as Chanel wanted to punish him, she wanted him in bed with her more. She pushed him on his shoulder. When he opened his eyes she grabbed his hand, and pulled him off the couch.

He got up, and followed her into the bedroom.

"I think you have learned your lesson now," she said.

"Uh-huh, you just don't want to be in here alone. I should punish you, and make you go to bed without me," Samir teased.

"Shut up, and come here."

Samir opened her silk robe, and bent down to kiss her small belly. The thoughts of all he survived crossed his mind. He should have been dead and gone, but he was still standing. The whole time he thought Asia was dead, she had survived the storm as well. When it felt like all odds were against him, and he was put into another tough situation with Chanel's ex, he pushed through it and his relationship with Chanel became even stronger. And even though Samir had to go through hell to get where he was now, he was thankful for the man he had become.

Epilogue

The music played through the speakers, as Samir wiped the sweat beads from his forehead. Keshawn and Renee made their way slowly down the aisle to "Here and Now" by Luther Vandross.

As much as he'd been looking forward to this moment, Samir was now becoming nervous.

"You all right, man?" Keshawn whispered to Samir, noticing his faint behavior.

"Of course, I'm great," Samir lied.

"You sure? Don't faint before your bride gets here."

"I'm okay. A little nervous, but I'm fine."

"Okay, if you say so."

More music played, as Rasheed came down the aisle holding the pillow with the ring. The sight of his son made him smile. Rasheed stood in place like a little man. Samir noticed Asia seated in the front. She gave him the thumbs-up, and he quickly tried to loosen up. Sharon's three-year-old daughter was the cutest flower girl he had ever seen. It made him want a little baby girl that much more.

When she reached the front of the church, the DJ switched the song to Tamia and Eric Benét's song "Spend My Life with You." The doormen opened the double doors. The moment Samir had been waiting for had finally come. Samir could feel the tears forming in his eyes, as Chanel made her way down the aisle toward him, holding Jaylin's hand. Little Jaylin was grinning from ear to ear.

In the middle of the wedding, Rasheed took off toward Chanel and Jaylin, grabbing Jaylin's other hand. Chanel looked down at the both of them, and smiled. The pastor asked, "Who gives this woman to this man?"

Samir and Chanel looked at the boys. "We do! We do! We do!" the boys screamed, jumping up and down. Everyone laughed.

Chanel's mom grabbed the boys' hands. She brought them back to the seat with her.

The rest of the wedding went smoothly, as it transformed into a gorgeous reception. A beautiful chandelier hung from the ceiling, and the tables were decorated in white and gold. The crowd cheered, as the wedding party came in and took their seats. The caterers went to work, making sure everyone had food starting with the bride and groom.

Keshawn stood to his feet, and got everyone's attention. The crowd of people quieted down so that he could speak.

"Good evening, everybody. I just want to take the time out to congratulate my neighbor and good friend on a happy, everlasting marriage. I never would have thought when I walked across the road to introduce myself to Samir I would end up being his best man." The crowd, including Samir, laughed. "I'm thankful to have him as a friend, and am honored to be his best man. Samir," he said and turned to face Samir directly, "I have been there during some tough times, and I've seen you survive the deadliest storms, but being able to survive against an argument with your wife is a whole different hurricane," he teased. Samir looked at Chanel, and laughed. Renee smacked Keshawn on the arm. "Anyway, congratulations, man, and I wish you nothing but joy and happiness!"

Everyone clapped. Samir reached over to shake Keshawn's hand. "Thanks, man, I appreciate that," Samir said, as they all lifted their flutes of champagne into the air. Asia stood up to say a few words. Samir looked in her direction.

"Hello, everyone. I won't be long, but I just wanted to take the time to say congratulations to you both. From the bottom of my heart, I am truly happy for you. And to Chanel, I can't thank you enough for being there for Rasheed. You are a great mom, a great woman, and I couldn't have prayed for anyone better to be there for both Samir and Rasheed. You are truly heaven sent. Thank you so very much, and I wish you both nothing but the best."

Chanel mouthed, "Thank you," to her. Samir raised his glass in her direction.

The party continued to the dance floor. The DJ turned on "Electric Slide" and people hit the floor. Samir turned around facing Chanel. He burst out laughing.

"What's so funny?" Chanel asked, both still moving along to the music.

"Who would have thought my life would end up this way?"

"How else did you expect it to end?"

"Not as great as this."

The DJ changed the music to a slow song. Samir grabbed his wife's hand, and she melted into his arms.

Asia stood by the bar watching the happy couple dance like they were the only two in the room. She really was happy for Samir. She realized the night that they kissed in her apartment that she no longer loved him the way she had in the past. Her love for him had transformed over the years. He would always have a special place in her heart, but that passionate love they once shared was long gone. She knew that they would always be the best of friends but that was as far as the relationship could ever go. She was grateful to him for having shown her what being in love felt like, so that when it happened to her again, she would instantly recognize it. Asia was looking forward to meeting her future husband and getting her happily ever after.

"Hello, beautiful." A man approached Asia at the bar. Asia looked up, and smiled. "I'm Jason, and you are?"

Asia looked the man up and down. Just from his sexy appearance with his smooth, dark skin, bald head, and nice build, Asia was instantly attracted to him. His six foot two inch stature made him even more attractive, coupled with his deep, sexy voice.

"I'm Asia. Who are you here representing?" she asked.

"I was invited by Chanel. I'm a doctor at the hospital she works at."

"Oh, okay. Y'all haven't been physically involved, have you?" Asia quizzed.

"No, of course not. Chanel is a great woman and all, but we don't mix business with pleasure. She's a great friend, almost like a sister to me, so you don't have to worry about that. What kind of man do you think I am?" he joked.

"I'm just checking. You can never be too sure these days."

"So, are you here with anyone?"

Asia smirked. "Um, no. I'm not here with anyone and I am not seeing anyone if that's what you are trying to figure out."

"Well, that's good news for me," he said as he extended his hand. "May I have this dance?"

"Yes, you may," Asia said, as she placed her hand in his, and he led her to the dance floor. His clean-shaved head glistened under the light. As he drew Asia close to him, she inhaled the scent of his cologne, and he smelled amazing. She didn't know what the future would hold with this handsome eye candy, but for now, she going to enjoy the moment and dance the night away.

The End

About the Author

Kinshasha Serbin, wife and mother, grew up in Henderson, North Carolina, and was born on August 15, 1988.

Kinshasha is the author of the debut urban suspense novel *I Am My Father's Son*. This author fell in love with writing urban fiction because she wanted people in the urban community to have stories they can relate to and learn from.

Growing up in a small community and having to tackle many struggles of her own, Kinshasha wanted to be able to entertain her readers in addition to shedding light on urban topics and situations.

Kinshasha Serbin is currently working on part two of her urban fiction series, *I Am My Father's Son*.